W9-AZX-405

JENNIFER BROWN

TORN AWAY

Little, Brown and Company
New York   Boston

ALSO BY JENNIFER BROWN

Hate List
Bitter End
Perfect Escape
Thousand Words
Say Something: A Hate List Novella

This book is a work of fiction. Names, characters, places, and incidents are the product of the author's imagination or are used fictitiously. Any resemblance to actual events, locales, or persons, living or dead, is coincidental.

Copyright © 2014 by Jennifer Brown
Excerpt from *Hate List* copyright © 2009 by Jennifer Brown

All rights reserved. In accordance with the U.S. Copyright Act of 1976, the scanning, uploading, and electronic sharing of any part of this book without the permission of the publisher is unlawful piracy and theft of the author's intellectual property. If you would like to use material from the book (other than for review purposes), prior written permission must be obtained by contacting the publisher at permissions@hbgusa.com. Thank you for your support of the author's rights.

Little, Brown and Company

Hachette Book Group
1290 Avenue of the Americas, New York, NY 10104
Visit us at lb-teens.com

Little, Brown and Company is a division of Hachette Book Group, Inc.
The Little, Brown name and logo are trademarks of Hachette Book Group, Inc.

The publisher is not responsible for websites (or their content)
that are not owned by the publisher.

First Paperback Edition: November 2015
First published in hardcover in May 2014 by Little, Brown and Company

Library of Congress Cataloging-in-Publication Data

Brown, Jennifer, 1972–
Torn away / Jennifer Brown. — First edition.
    pages cm
    Summary: In the aftermath of a tornado that has devastated her hometown of Elizabeth, Missouri, sixteen-year-old Jersey Cameron struggles to overcome her grief as she is sent to live with her only surviving relatives.
    ISBN 978-0-316-24553-1 (hc) — ISBN 978-0-316-24551-7 (electronic book) — ISBN 978-0-316-24554-8 (pb) [1. Tornadoes—Fiction.   2. Grief—Fiction.   3. Families—Fiction.   4. Missouri—Fiction.]   I. Title.
PZ7.B814224To 2014
[Fic]—dc23

                                                                    2013021598

10 9 8 7 6 5 4 3 2 1

RRD-C

Printed in the United States of America

For Scott and Pranston,
You are my home

Marin wanted to teach me the East Coast Swing. It was pretty much her only goal in life. She was constantly pulling on my arms or standing in front of the TV, her hands on her square little hips, sparkle nail polish glinting and ratty rose-colored tutu quivering.

"Come on, Jersey, it's fun. You'll like it. Jersey!" Stomp. "Are you listening to me? Jerseeey!"

She'd learned swing in Miss Janice's dance class. Technically, it wasn't a routine they were there to learn, but one evening Janice, in an old-school mood, had popped in a swing CD and taught them how to do it. Marin thought it was the best dance ever.

She was forever counting off, her pudgy five-year-old arms around an imaginary dance partner, her brown curls bouncing to a beat only she could hear as she hummed what she remembered of the song they'd danced to in class.

But she really wanted me to be her dance partner. She probably imagined me grabbing her wrists, pulling her through my legs, tossing her into the air, and then catching her. She probably envisioned the two of us in matching costumes, wowing an audience.

"Not now, Marin," I told her time and again, too busy watching TV or doing homework or texting my best friends, Jane and Dani, about what pests little sisters can be. Especially little sisters who think the whole world is about the East Coast Swing.

Marin lived in leotards. She had sequined ones and velvety ones and some that looked like tuxedoes and plain ones in every color of the rainbow. She wore them until they were so small her butt cheeks hung out and her tutus sported holes in the netting that she could fit a fist through. Still, Mom had to throw them away when Marin wasn't looking, and had to buy new ones to make up for the favorites that were lost.

We'd begun to wonder if Marin would insist on wearing leotards when she started kindergarten in the fall and what exactly would happen when the teacher said she couldn't. We feared meltdowns, epic morning battles, ultimatums.

Because Marin wore those dance leotards everywhere. Around the house, to the store, to bed.

And, of course, to dance class.

She was wearing one on the day of the tornado. It was tangerine-colored with black velvet panels on the sides, a line of rhinestones dotting the neckline. I knew this because it was what she'd been wearing when she asked me to do the East Coast Swing with her before she went to class that day.

"I can teach you," she'd said hopefully, hopping on her toes next to the couch, where I was sprawled back doing nothing but staring at a car commercial. As if I'd ever have money for a car.

"No," I said. "Get out of the way. I can't see the TV."

She'd glanced over her shoulder at the TV, and I could see where something sticky had adhered a bit of black lint to her cheek. Wisps of curls around her face looked like they'd once been sticky as well. Probably a Popsicle. It was the end of May and already warm enough for Popsicles. School would be out in less than a week, and I would officially be a senior. She leaned in closer and prodded my shoulder with her fat little fingers—also sticky.

"It's a commercial. Get up. I'll show you."

"No, Marin." I'd groaned, getting annoyed, brushing my shirt off where her fingers had touched, and when she'd commenced to jumping up and down in front of me, repeating *Pleasepleaseplease*, I yelled at her. "No! I don't want to! Go away!"

She stopped jumping and pouted, sticking out her bottom lip the way little kids do when they're getting ready to cry. She didn't say anything. Didn't cry. Didn't throw a fit. Just blinked at me, that lower lip trembling, and then walked away, the bling on her leotard catching the light from the TV. I heard her go into Mom's room. I heard them talking. And when they left for dance class, I felt relieved that she was finally out of my hair.

I loved Marin.

I loved my little sister.

But after that day, I would hear myself over and over again: *Go away!* I would shout at her in my dreams. I would see that trembling lip. I would see the slow blink of her big, pixie-like eyes. I would see her walk away, up on her toes the way she always did, the glint of the rhinestones from her leotard blinding me.

CHAPTER
ONE

The day of the tornado began gray and dreary— one of those days where you don't want to do anything but lounge around and sleep while it mists and drizzles and spits. All of the classrooms looked dark and shadowy and gross and there was no energy in the building whatsoever. And all of the teachers were practically begging someone, anyone, to answer one of their questions, but when they turned their backs to write on the whiteboard, they were stifling yawns of their own because they felt it, too.

Spring is like that around Elizabeth, Missouri. One day it's really beautiful and sunny and the birds outside your window wake you up, they're tweeting so loud. And the next day it's chilly and windy and you can hear gusts lashing up against the side of your house and buzzing against the blinds of the laundry room window that has never been very airtight. And then the next day it does nothing but rain and drum up earthworms onto the sidewalks, only to shrivel them with the next day's sun and wind.

Welcome to the Midwest, Mom used to say. *Where the weather keeps you guessing and you're almost always sure to hate it.* We made complaining about the weather a full-time job in Elizabeth. It was the one thing we could count on to blame for our migraines and our blue funks and the reason we overslept and our bad-hair days. The unpredictable weather could derail even the best day.

When the final bell rang that day, Miss Sopor, my language arts teacher, hollered out, "Quiz tomorrow on *Bless the Beasts*, people! Got some thunderstorms coming in tonight. Perfect reading weather. Hint, hint!"

And sure enough, when we walked out to the bus, the clouds were pressing in on us, thickening up and making it seem much more like evening than 3:15 in the afternoon.

"Sopor's quizzes are stupid," Dani said, her hip brushing up against mine as we slid down the bus line. "I've never studied for one and I always get As."

"'Quiz tomorrow! *Bless the Beasts*, people! Hint, hint!'" I mimicked, because I did a pretty good impression of Miss Sopor, and we both laughed. "I already read most of it anyway," I said. I peered over my shoulder. Kolby, my neighbor, was several steps behind me, carrying his skateboard as usual. I waved to him and he waved back. "Where's Jane?" I asked Dani.

"Had to stay after for orchestra rehearsal. Better her than me. I've been ready to go home since lunch. I can't imagine having to hang out in this prison for another three hours. But you know Jane and her violin. She's happy about it."

"She's going to die with that violin permanently attached to her hand," I added.

Jane was ultradevoted to her instrument, and Dani and I mercilessly teased her about it. But we both knew that without Jane our trio would never be complete. She was musical and scrappy and her hair managed to make frizz look cool. We'd all been friends since the seventh-grade musical. Jane was in the orchestra, Dani was the lead, and I happily knocked around in the pitch-black lighting booth with my clipboard and headset.

It was sort of a metaphor for our lives together, when I thought about it. Dani was the beauty—front and center, lapping up the spotlight and the applause. I was the support crew—uncomfortably hiding my pudge and shyness beneath a loose T-shirt. And without Jane, neither of us had any reason to be onstage at all.

We got on the bus and bumped our way home. In keeping with the rest of the day, everyone seemed sleepy and subdued. The sky continued to darken, and the wind picked up, blowing some of the newly budding flowers almost flat against the ground. Dani and I sat in weary silence, Dani texting some guy from her economics class and me watching the neighborhoods roll by. The windows were open, and the warm breeze felt good against my face.

On Thursday nights, I had exactly one hour between the time I got off the bus and the time Mom got home with Marin. Just enough time to claim a snack and the TV, but not nearly enough to decompress to a level where I could handle Marin's excessive energy. Something about preschool amped her up—made her loud and squeaky so she practically vibrated around the room. It was my least favorite part of the afternoon, that space between when Mom and Marin bulldozed through the front door and when they left for Marin's dance class, leaving me to start dinner.

That day, Marin tumbled into the living room, already wearing her orange-and-black leotard with the rhinestone collar, her face sticky from a Popsicle or whatever it was they gave her at school. She hopped over to the couch and immediately began bugging me about the East Coast Swing.

Mom, still in her work skirt and low, scuffed heels, bustled around us, mumbling things about the living room being "a damn cave" as she snapped on lights, making me blink and squint.

"No! I don't want to! Go away!" I yelled at Marin, and she went into Mom's room, where I could hear her chattering incessantly and rifling through things while Mom tried to change clothes. I ignored them, finally satisfied that it was quiet and I could watch TV in peace.

"Jersey?" Mom called from her room, and I pretended I didn't hear her because I didn't want to get up. A few seconds later, she came into the living room, pulling her earring out, her panty hose draped over one arm, her toes looking red and taxed against the carpet. "Jersey."

"Huh?"

"Didn't you hear me calling you?"

"No."

A look of annoyance flitted over her face as she reached to pull the earring out of her other ear. "Did you put the towels in the wash?"

"No, I forgot," I said. "I'll get them in a minute."

This time the annoyance crossed her face, full force. "They need to get done. I want them in the dryer before I get back."

"Okay," I mumbled.

"And start dinner," she continued, heading back toward her room.

"I will."

"And take the dishes out of the dishwasher," she called from her bedroom.

"I will! God!" I called back.

I was ten when Mom married Ronnie, but until then it had always been just Mom and me. My alcoholic dad had walked out on us when I was barely a year old. According to my mom, he was constantly in and out of jail for crimes that usually started with the word "drunk," he was hardly a parent to begin with, and most of the time she felt like she was raising two kids, not one. Still, she stuck it out because she thought they were in love. But one night he left and never came back. She'd tried to find him, she said, but it was as if he'd disappeared from the face of the earth. Every time I asked about him, she told me that if he was still alive, he didn't want to be found. At least not by us.

I hadn't seen him since I was a toddler. I couldn't remember what he looked like.

And because Mom's parents were control freaks who wrote her off when she got pregnant with me, I had never seen them, either. I didn't even know where they lived. I only knew they didn't live in Elizabeth.

Ten years of being the Mom-and-me duo meant a lot of chores fell on my shoulders. Mom needed help, and I didn't mind giving it most of the time, because she worked really hard, and though I might not always have had the best stuff or the most expensive vacations, I had the things I needed. And I loved my mom.

But after Mom married Ronnie and had Marin, the chores for two turned into chores for four, and that got old. Sometimes it seemed like Mom was constantly reminding me of the stuff I needed to get done.

Mom and Marin continued rushing around, Marin prancing in and out of the living room, singing, humming, and I pressed the back of my head harder into the throw pillow and wished they would get going already and leave me alone.

Eventually, Mom came into the living room, calling for Marin to go to the bathroom and shoving her feet into the black flats she'd left next to the front door. She'd changed into jeans and a T-shirt and was digging through her purse.

"Okay, we're going to dance class," she said absently. "Be back in an hour or so."

"'Kay," I said. Bored. Uninterested. Ready for them to leave.

Marin raced into the living room, her own purse draped over her arm, looking like a miniature version of Mom. In truth, it was Mom's old purse, an ugly black thing Mom had given to Marin after she got tired of it. Marin adored it, carried it everywhere, stuffing it with her most prized possessions.

"No, leave that here," Mom said, pushing open the screen door with her shoulder.

"But I want to take it," Marin argued.

"No, you'll forget it, like last time, and I don't want to have to make another return trip to Miss Janice's. Leave it here."

"Nooo!" Marin cried, getting her Meltdown Voice on.

Mom gave her the no-nonsense look I recognized all too well. "You're going to be late, and then you'll miss the hello dance," she warned.

Marin, head down and shoulders droopy, placed the purse on the floor next to the door and followed Mom out onto the porch, her glittery little shoes looking dull and lifeless under the cloudy sky.

"Don't forget the laundry," Mom said on her way out.

"I know," I singsonged back sarcastically, rolling my eyes.

I thought I knew so much—knew there was laundry to be done, knew when Mom and Marin would come home, knew how the rest of the evening was going to go.

But I didn't know anything.

I had no idea.

CHAPTER TWO

After Mom and Marin left, I got up and put the towels in the washing machine. It had gotten so dark I had to turn on the overhead light to see what I was doing. The cloud cover almost made it feel like nighttime.

I poured soap over the towels, thinking once again how it seemed like everything had changed when Mom married Ronnie. I'd gone from being the most important thing in her life to being *one of* the most important things in her life. Sounds like the same thing, but it isn't. Sharing the spotlight gets kind of crowded sometimes, especially when you were used to having so much space in it before.

When Mom got pregnant, I was excited. Being an only child could get lonely, and I'd always envied my friends who had siblings. I didn't think ten years was that much difference, really. I thought Marin would look up to me and I could teach her all kinds of things and be like her hero or something. But what I hadn't banked on was that there would be a lot of years where she would be a baby. *The* baby. The center of everything.

And even though I knew I was that once, too, it still sucked when it was her turn. Which made me feel like a jerk. What kind of horrible person resented her little sister for something she couldn't even control?

After I got the laundry started, I went into the kitchen and pulled out the hamburger meat and a skillet. I crumbled the burger into the skillet and turned on the stove, then wandered back toward the living room to watch some more TV while I waited for the meat to start cooking. On the way, I grabbed my backpack off the kitchen table, dug my reading homework out of it—*hint, hint, ladies and gentlemen!*—and carried it to the couch with me.

But as I turned on the lamp next to the couch and sat down, the TV station switched to the news, a meteorologist standing in front of a giant map with a radar image on it, a bright red patch moving across the screen in jumps and fits.

I picked up my book and started reading, waiting for him to finish talking and get back to the show. Seemed like every time a raindrop or snowflake fell anywhere near Elizabeth, the weather forecasters acted like the end of the world was coming.

I read, tuning in and out of what he was saying, catching bits and pieces.

…system that is producing tornadoes in Clay County is moving east at approximately…seems to be picking up speed…had two reported touchdowns…headed toward… will hit Elizabeth at five sixteen…

I heard the meat start to sizzle in the kitchen and put down my book. Rain or shine, we still had to eat.

As soon as I picked up the spatula, the sirens started.

I paused, my hand in the air, and listened. One of the sirens was in a field behind my old elementary school, two blocks away from our house, so it was loud. When I was a kid, the tornado sirens used to freak me out. They used to freak all of us out, and the teachers were always having to tell us to calm down. Kids would be crying, holding their palms over their ears and asking for their moms, and the teachers would be standing at the front of the room with their hands up in the air, shouting to be heard over us and the sirens, reminding us that they were only monthly tests and there was no emergency. By fifth grade, we were all cool about it—*Oh, it's the tornado sirens, no big deal*—and by middle school we barely even noticed the sirens at all.

I leaned back and glanced into the living room, where the meteorologist was still standing in front of the Doppler photo, still pointing and talking, a sheaf of papers in his right hand. I sighed, looking back at the half-cooked meat. I didn't want to turn it off, only to have it be another false alarm and have dinner ruined and Mom pissed. But technically, we were under a tornado warning. And even though there was a warning about every third week in Elizabeth, we were supposed to take it seriously each time and go downstairs.

Hardly anyone ever did, though. Midwest weather was crazy, after all, and half the time too crazy to really predict. We'd all learned to ignore the warnings. Most of them never turned out to be anything anyway.

I moved over to the kitchen sink and peered out the window. I could see wind pushing the swings on our neighbors' swing set. The rings danced merrily, and the slide quivered. Kolby, who'd lived next door to me since we were toddlers, was standing outside on his back porch, hands in his pockets, gazing up into the sky, his hair whipping around so that I could see his scalp with each gust. Kolby always did this when the weather turned bad. A lot of people did, actually. They wanted the chance to see a funnel cloud for themselves, should one ever appear. I reached up and knocked on the window. He didn't hear me. I knocked again, louder, and he turned, pulled a hand out of his pocket, and waved. I waved back.

He was peering out over Church Street, where plenty of cars were creeping along with their headlights on. Rush hour was starting and everyone was coming home, like normal. It wasn't even raining.

I went back to the stove, still holding the spatula, and decided to wait until it started to rain or do something more serious than just look nasty.

But I had no more than touched the meat with the spatula when the power went out, bathing me in darkness and that blatting of the emergency sirens, which went on and on, so loud I only barely heard the buzz of the blinds in the laundry room as the wind pressed against the house harder and harder.

"Great," I said aloud. "I guess we'll have McDonald's for dinner, then."

I put the spatula down and turned off the stove, then grabbed my backpack, stuffing my book inside, and headed for the basement, aka Ronnie's Room.

The basement wasn't a terrible place to kill time, especially

15

since Ronnie had put a pool table, a couch, and a mini-fridge down there. Every so often he'd have some friends over and they'd all disappear downstairs, and we could hear pool balls cracking up against one another and smell the cigarette smoke as it drifted up through the living room carpet. He didn't love us hanging out in his space, but tonight I had no choice.

I rummaged around on Ronnie's worktable and found a flashlight, then clicked it on; it worked. Giving a quick glance to the one small window—it was still dark and windy—I flopped down on the couch and opened my book.

My phone buzzed and I pulled it out of my pocket.

"Hey, Dani, I guess it's a good time to catch up on some reading for tomorrow's quiz," I said in my Miss Sopor impression.

"Are you downstairs?" Dani's voice was worried, thin.

"Yep. Waste of time, but since the power's out, I have nothing better to do, I guess."

"My mom said a tornado touched down on M Highway. She said it's headed right toward us. She wanted me to make sure you knew."

M Highway was closer than I wanted it to be, and that news startled me a little, but it was still the country out there. It seemed like tornadoes were touching down on those country highways all the time.

"Yeah, I heard the sirens. I'm good," I said, though I realized that my voice might have sounded a bit thin, too.

"Is Jane still at school?" Dani asked.

"I haven't heard from her," I said. "I can text her."

"I already did. She didn't answer."

"They were probably playing and she didn't hear her phone." *Plus*, I added inside my head, *the orchestra room is in the basement anyway. She's fine.* "I'll try her. Kolby is standing outside right now."

Dani made a noise into the phone. "I'm not surprised. He's nuts. He's not gonna be happy until he gets carried away in a tornado."

"It's not even raining out there."

"Still, he's crazy. One touched down on M Highway."

"I know."

"Call me if you talk to Jane?"

"Okay."

I hung up and sent Jane a quick text. The sirens stopped for a minute and I would have thought maybe the storm was passing, but it had gotten even darker outside, and then they started up again.

I chewed my lip, held my phone in my lap for a few seconds, then called Mom.

"Jersey?" she shouted into the phone. The noise around her was even louder. Emergency horns, police sirens, and the loud chatter and crying of little girls. "Jersey?"

"Dani's mom said a tornado was on M Highway," I said.

"I can't hear her," I heard my mom say, and another woman's voice close by said something about more touchdowns. "Jersey?" Mom repeated.

"I'm here!" I shouted. "Hello! Can you hear me?"

"Jersey? I can't hear you. If you can hear me, go to the basement, okay?" she yelled.

"I am," I said, but I knew she couldn't hear what I was saying, and fear really began to creep into my stomach. She sounded afraid. Mom never sounded afraid. Ever. She never wavered; she was always strong. Even when I fell off the monkey bars in second grade and landed straight on my neck and had to go in an ambulance to the hospital. Mom had simply sat next to me in the ambulance, talking in a low, steady voice, one that calmed me. "Mom? Hello? You there?"

"Everybody this way!" she shouted, her voice sounding farther away from the phone, like maybe she was holding it at her side and had forgotten that it was on. There was a bustling noise, and the crying and talking got louder and more jumbled and then was overtaken by a rumbling sound.

"Mom?" I said.

But she didn't answer. I could hear her shouting, "Get your heads down! Get your heads down!" and lots of screaming and crying. I thought I might have heard glass breaking.

And then I heard nothing but the drone of the sirens outside my window.

CHAPTER
THREE

"Mom? Mom!" I kept yelling into the phone, even though I knew the connection had been lost. I tried to call again, but the line wouldn't connect. I realized that my hands were shaking, and my fingers didn't want to work around the phone's keypad anymore. I dropped it twice and then tried to call Ronnie, but that call wouldn't go through, either.

The sirens screeched one last time and then abruptly stopped, and I could hear wild clicking against the window—hail—and something else. Something louder. Thumps and thuds and scrapes against the house, like larger items were slamming up against it. Metallic clangs and broken sounds.

For a moment I sat there, frozen on the couch. I thought I heard what sounded like a train rumbling down our street, and I remembered one time in fourth grade when our teacher read us a book that described the sound of a tornado as being something like the sound of a locomotive. I hadn't believed it at the time—it didn't make sense that a tornado could sound like anything but blowing wind. But there it was, the sound of a train passing. I held my breath in frightened anticipation.

The moment stretched around me—the noise getting louder and then muting as my ears began popping—and I gripped my cell phone like I was holding on to the side of a cliff. I tried to be still so I could listen. Maybe I was mistaken. Maybe it was my imagination and there was no train sound out there. I was hearing what I was scared to hear.

But then something really huge hit the house. I heard the tinkling of glass breaking upstairs, on the other end of the house, over where Marin's bedroom was. A loud metallic grating noise seared the air outside as something was pushed down the street. I only had seconds to think about Kolby, to wonder if he was still out there, when the basement window suddenly shattered, ushering in an enormous roar of noise.

I screamed, my voice getting lost in the din. I instinctively covered my head and then scrambled under the pool table, pulling my backpack and cell phone with me.

Noise blasted in and I rolled up in a ball, cradling my head with my arms. I squeezed my eyes shut. There were great, loud creaks and bangs. Glass shattering and shattering and shattering. Thunks as things spun and flew and hit walls. Groans and wooden popping sounds as walls gave, bricks tumbled. Crunching thuds as heavy building materials hit the floors.

I heard these things happening, but it was unclear where exactly they were happening. Was it in the basement? Upstairs? Down the street? Space and time were distorted, and even the most basic things like direction didn't make sense.

Wind whipped the hem of my shirt and pulled at my hair, and I felt out in the open, as if the tornado had somehow gotten into the basement.

Small items blasted across the floor and battered me. I opened my eyes and saw one of Ronnie's work boots thud against my side. Papers whipped around me, bending over my arms. A wall calendar screamed past. An empty milk crate, which had spilled its contents, tumbled up against my shins. An ashtray knocked me in the back of the head, making me cry out and inch my fingers over to where it had hit, feeling the warmth and wetness I was sure was blood. The pool table spun half a circle and came to rest again.

It felt like a never-ending stream of chaos. Like my whole world was being shaken and tossed and torn apart, and like it would never stop. Like I would be stuck in this terror forever.

I was confused, and my arms, legs, back, and head stung. I coiled into myself, gripping my head and crying and crying, half-sobbing, half-shrieking. I don't know how long I stayed that way before I realized it was over.

CHAPTER FOUR

When I opened my eyes, at first I stayed in my safety position. I could hear rain now, pelting the ground, only the ground seemed very close. It was still dark, still windy, but had already lightened up some since the tornado had passed.

At last, I forced myself to let go of my head and felt around for my cell phone. It was lodged between my backpack and my stomach and I pulled it out, my fingers white and shaky as I clung to it. I tried to call Mom.

No connection.

I tried Ronnie.

Same.

911.

Nothing.

I tried Jane. Dani. Everyone I could think of.

I was getting no bars. No cell service.

I lay there for a few more minutes, trying to catch my

breath and quell my panicked sobbing. My arms and legs felt tingly from adrenaline and fear. I listened. I could hear talking and loud cries and car alarms bleating. A stuck police siren. A plea for help. And off in the distance, just maybe, the growling chug of the funnel cloud moving on.

Growing up, we were taught over and over again what steps to take in case of an approaching tornado. Listen for sirens, go to your basement or cellar, or a closet in the center of your house, duck and cover, wait it out. We had drills twice a year, every year, in school. We talked about it in class. We talked about it at home. The newscasters reminded us. We went to the basement. We practiced, practiced, practiced.

But we'd never—not once—discussed what to do *after.*

I think we never thought there would be an after like this one.

It seemed like forever before the rain and wind stopped. It was still gray around me, but the sky had lightened up enough that I could see fine without the flashlight, which I'd dropped in my scramble to the pool table.

Kolby. I would go get Kolby. See if he could call my mom from his phone. Slowly, I uncurled myself and, after a moment of hesitation, slid out from under the table and sat up.

At the opposite end of the basement, where Ronnie's workbench normally sat, there was no ceiling. The floor I had been standing on while rummaging for a flashlight just fifteen minutes before was now buried in a dusty pile of rubble—what used to be our kitchen, except the table was gone and the walls were gone and the plates had all fallen out of their cabinets, which were also gone, and now lay in a heap on the concrete basement floor.

What was worse—I could see sky where the kitchen used to be. Wires and broken pipes jutted out here and there. Water gushed from somewhere.

"Oh my God," I said, pulling myself up to standing, unsure whether my wobbly legs would keep me that way. "Oh my God."

I took a few steps toward the rubble. The closer I got, the more sky I could see. The kitchen walls, they were gone. Completely and totally gone.

I could have walked right up the rubble pile to the outside if I'd wanted to, but the sight of my broken kitchen was so foreign, the bare and jutting wires so frightening, I couldn't make myself approach it. The basement stairs were still standing, and for some reason walking up them and through the basement door into the house seemed like the right thing to do, so I made my way over to them, a part of me hoping that maybe if I went up the stairs, the rest of the house wouldn't be as bad as the kitchen looked.

The couch had been pulled to the rubble and turned up on its side. There were clothes strewn everywhere.

I glanced down at my hands, my fingers streaked with dried blood, my right hand wrapped around my useless cell phone. I stuffed the phone into my pocket and reached around to the back of my head again. It was sticky and my hair felt kind of matted, but it didn't really hurt or anything, and it wasn't gushing blood, so I ignored it, trying to keep things in perspective. It was just a cut. It could wait until Mom got home. Everything would be fine once she got here.

I crept forward, edging around things that didn't belong there. A hunk of Venetian blinds. A DVD. A carpet of wet papers. A dog leash. A swing from Kolby's little sister's swing set, the ends of the chain twisted and broken, as if chewed up by a giant monster.

Slowly I crept up the stairs and pushed on the door, which would only open a little before it was stopped by something wedged against it. I tried leaning into the door and pushing harder, but it wouldn't budge, so I sucked in my stomach and squeezed through the opening.

I stepped into the room, my dried-bloody hand flying up to my mouth. Had I not known I was standing in my living room, I never would have guessed this was my house. The roof was completely missing. The whole thing. No holes or tears—gone. Some of the outside walls were also missing, and the remaining walls were in perilously bad condition. One was leaning outward, the window blown and the frame hanging by a corner. Farther away, where the living room and the kitchen normally met, the house just...ended. I knew, from what I'd seen downstairs, that much of it had toppled in on itself. But I hadn't been prepared for how gone it was. Even the stove was missing. Not moved, but completely absent. Nowhere in sight.

I couldn't make it to my room. I couldn't even really tell where my room was. And for a few minutes I stood dumbly in the basement doorway, my hand over my mouth, my eyes wide, my heart beating so fast I thought I might throw up, trying to take everything in. I'd seen photos of houses destroyed by tornadoes before, but never had I seen anything like it in real life. The destruction was complete, and terrible.

Outside. I needed to go outside and see if anyone else's house had gotten hit. I needed to find help. To find Mom. To find someone who could take me to her, so I could break it to her how bad the house was damaged, and let her know I was okay.

I made my way to the front door, which was, oddly, still there, still on its hinges, though it was hanging on to a partial wall.

It took me several minutes of clawing at scraps of wood and climbing over debris to get to the door, treading carefully in my bare feet, wishing I'd been wearing shoes when the tornado hit, or at least had brought a pair down to the basement with me. I cut my hand on glass twice, more blood seeping out and mixing with the dried blood and grime already there. I wiped it on my jeans and kept going, trying to force down the frantic feeling welling inside me as I heard more crying and voices outside.

As I took a final step toward the door, my foot sank into something soft and cold. It was Marin's purse, the one Mom had made her leave at home. I pulled it out of the rubble, then held it up and studied it. Other than being dirty and dusty and a little bit wet, it looked fine. I set it on top of a bent kitchen chair next to me for safekeeping—Marin would want her purse when she got back.

Finally, I wrenched the door open and immediately went

breathless, as if I'd had the wind knocked out of me. I saw little lights dance before my eyes, and my lips felt tingly. For a shaky moment I thought I might pass out.

It hadn't been just our house.

It had been everyone's houses.

There was no street. Just piles upon piles of scraps and glass and broken furniture and wood and trash. I leaned back against the remaining wall of my house, but it groaned under my weight and I stood up again, quickly. I couldn't get my breath.

I wanted my mom. Or Ronnie. Somebody to hold me up.

Several neighbors were standing in the street, in various poses of upset. Mr. Klingbeil stood with his hands on his hips, staring at what used to be his house and shaking his head. Mrs. Fay was locked in an embrace with Mrs. Chamberlain. They were both weeping loudly. Some of the little kids were crouching in the street, their faces looking curious and half-excited as they picked up branches and toys and bricks, but also very somber, like even they understood that this was bad, bad, bad. A couple of people were bent at the waist, mucking through the rubble of their houses, picking up little busted pieces of this and that and discarding them again.

I could see movement where our road normally connected with Church Street. A trickle of people were trudging along, looking shocked and lost. Off in the distance I could hear the wailing of sirens—emergency vehicles—but nothing nearby. How could they get to us, I wondered. There was no street to drive on. It was impossible to find it under all the rubble.

One man fell and a woman near him dropped to his side, pushing on his shoulder and yelling out, "Help! Anyone! Please!" but the people kept walking around them, looking dazed and wounded. Finally, a man stopped and after a few minutes helped her get the fallen man to his feet. Together, they trudged along, the man between them, his arms slung around their necks.

"Holy shit," I heard. Kolby was pulling himself through his basement window, which appeared to be the only opening to the basement at all. Unlike my house, which still had that one wall standing, Kolby's house had been completely razed to the ground. "Holy shit!" And then he yelled it. "Holy shit!" His little sister scrambled out the window behind him, silently taking in the scene as I'd done, her feet bare, her legs and feet smudged with dirt.

"You okay, Jersey?" he shouted, and I could feel my head nodding, but I still wasn't entirely sure I wasn't going to pass out, so the movement felt very slow and fluid.

He turned and dropped to his knees, sticking his head back through the basement window, and then came out again, holding his mom under her arms and tugging her. She tumbled outside and sat where she landed, her hands going to her cheeks. "Oh, dear Lord," I heard her say, and then she began praying. "Thank you, Jesus, for keeping us alive. Thank you, dear Jesus, for saving us."

Kolby started in my direction. "You should get away from that wall," he said, climbing across boards to get to me. He stepped on a baby rattle, cracking it. I stared at it, wondering where it might have come from and what had happened to the baby it belonged to. "Jersey? Hey, Jersey? You okay?"

I nodded again, but the image of a baby flying through the air, caught in the eye of a monster tornado, was about all I could take, and I felt myself starting to go down.

"Whoa! Whoa!" Kolby said, and he lunged up to the porch to grab my shoulders and keep me upright. "Any help over here?" he called out.

"I'm okay," I mumbled. "I just need to sit down."

"You're bleeding," he said, maneuvering so he was next to me, his arm around both of my shoulders. He walked me off the porch and toward where our front yard used to be. Kolby and I had played more games of Wiffle ball on that front yard than I could count. Now that seemed like forever ago.

"I'm okay," I mumbled again, but when Kolby eased me toward a cinder block on the ground, I was glad to be sitting.

"You're bleeding," he repeated. "Where are you hurt?"

I reached up to the back of my head again. It seemed dry now. "An ashtray hit me," I said. "But I think it's just a cut."

I heard his mother calling out to someone else, asking if anyone was hurt. Kolby squatted in front of me so that his face was only inches from mine. "Where is everybody?" he asked, and when I didn't answer, he said, "Your mom and Ronnie? Marin?"

I closed my eyes. It was easier to concentrate when I wasn't looking at the wasted neighborhood. "Mom and Marin are at dance class. I don't know where Ronnie is. I don't know if he was on his way home from work or..." I trailed off, watched as Mr. Fay pointed out to Mrs. Fay a two-by-four that had been driven into the side of their house and was sticking out like a dart. Mrs. Fay snapped a photo of it with her phone. "The whole street is gone."

He stood up and peered down toward Church Street, with its trickle of refugees heading away from the destruction.

"I know," he said. "It's just...holy cow."

"How far do you think it went?" I asked.

He shook his head but didn't answer.

"Kolby? How far do you think it went?"

"I don't know," he said, his voice sounding flat and croaky. "Looks like far."

"Do you think...?" I started, but I trailed off, afraid to finish my question, afraid that the answer would be no.

Do you think Mom will be able to get to me?

CHAPTER FIVE

The next few hours went by in a blur. Some of the men were going house to house, cocking their heads and listening for cries for help under the rubble. Every time they heard even the tiniest noise—the mew of a cat or the wooden click of a board settling or anything that might have sounded like a whimper—they fell on it, down on their knees, ripping things apart with their hands, their faces dripping with sweat and determination. A yell went up every time a hole to a basement was found, an expectant and grateful face peering up out of it.

And then they found Mrs. Dempsey.

Too fragile to make it to her basement, the old lady had cowered in her bathtub to ride out the storm. She'd even brought some pillows in with her. They found her there, pillows still surrounding her but a central air unit crushing the top half of her body.

They pulled the air conditioner off her, and Mrs. Fay found a shower curtain and they draped it over Mrs. Dempsey's body.

After that, the mood got very somber and people started wondering aloud when the emergency vehicles were going to come help us. We could still hear them braying and warbling in the distance, but the sounds weren't getting any closer. We thought we even heard the staccato bark of someone talking through a PA system or megaphone, but none of us could make out the words. It was all very muffled and so very far away. Why were they so far away?

The rescue efforts got slower. People started saying they were thirsty, or tired, and spent more time sitting or picking through their own things halfheartedly. I had no doubt that after all that digging, the men were thirsty, but I had a theory that the new focus on preventing dehydration was a way of not admitting that they were really afraid of finding another dead body—only the next time it might be a toddler or a teenager or someone they'd had lunch with just last week.

I stayed on my cinder block, watching them. Every so often I would try my cell phone again. Wait for it to ring, which it never did. Peer down the street for Mom's car, which never turned the corner. Kolby's shadow fell over me.

"We're going for a walk. You wanna come?" he asked, touching me lightly on the shoulder.

I shook my head, not looking up.

He waited a moment. "You sure? We want to see how bad the damage is, and see where everybody's going."

I saw his shadow gesture toward Church Street, but again I shook my head.

"Will you be okay by yourself?" he asked, shuffling the toe

of his shoe awkwardly against the cinder block I sat on. "I can stay."

"No," I said. "Go ahead. I'm fine. It's just if I'm not here when Mom gets back, she's gonna freak out." But even I wasn't sure how honest that statement was. Part of me knew I was staying because I was afraid to see how far the damage went. I didn't want to know why a steady stream of people continued to trickle down Church Street.

After he left, I tried not to let my mind wander, tried not to think about the small things I'd lost in the tornado, especially not with Mrs. Dempsey covered by a shower curtain a couple houses down, but I couldn't help myself. My clothes, my earrings, my music. Granted, I didn't have trendy clothes or expensive earrings, but if it had all blown away…I had nothing. Even a few cheap somethings is better than nothing.

How much of Mom's stuff was gone? How much of all of our stuff was gone? And how long would it be before we got it back?

I looked down at my feet and noticed that one was resting on a photo. I picked it up, pulled it out of the grime, and studied it. I wondered where our photos had gone, if our past would end up under a stranger's foot, would be tossed in the garbage.

The thought left me cold. It seemed impossible to still have a past if your memories were resting beneath blackened banana peels in a landfill.

I stared at that photo for a long, long time. A family, dressed in matching T-shirts and jeans, stood by a tree. The little boy up front mugged for the camera. He was smiling so hard around gaps of missing teeth, his eyes were pushed shut. His mom's hands were on his shoulders protectively. An older sister with long, straight hair smiled sweetly with her dad's arm around her waist. A whole, happy family. I wondered if the tornado had hit them, too. If it had done to their house what it had done to ours. I wondered where their street was. Where that tree was.

A jolt went through me and I stood up. The trees.

For the first time, I noticed that they were gone. Not just a few broken or blown over here or there, which happened pretty regularly during spring storms in Elizabeth. They were *gone*. Big holes where some had been. Snapped-off trunks. Stripped branches. Our once-tree-lined street had been robbed of all things green. I turned in circles, craning my neck to see around and above the mounds of boards and broken houses. I couldn't see any trees.

I dropped the photo back onto the mountain of junk and plopped down again.

The afternoon stretched on, and then evening began to set in. My stomach started to twist with hunger and I idly thought about the hamburger I'd left in the pan on the stove when the storm hit. I wondered what we'd do for dinner, and the thought prompted me to try my cell phone again. Still no service. Still no Mom.

Kolby and his mom and sister came back, their figures shadowy under the graying sky of evening combined with what looked like another approaching thunderstorm. Slowly, people who'd stayed behind crawled out of the rubble to greet them, dropping whatever bricks or boards or old appliances they were holding, curiosity winning out on their faces. I got up and walked toward them, too.

"Gone," Kolby was saying when I reached them. He was out of breath, his eyes bright and cheeks gritty. "Gone," he repeated. He shook his head. His sister clutched the hem of her mom's shirt.

"We walked at least a mile," his mom said, her voice loud and take-charge. The emergency sirens had finally stopped, leaving us in a blanket of confused silence. "Everywhere it looks like this. And there's people..." She paused, her jowls trembling. "Dear Jesus, please be with those people," she whispered.

"Are the ambulances...?" Mrs. Fay asked, but tapered off when Kolby shook his head.

"No way they can get to us. The streets are covered. Like this one. The houses are gone. And it looks like it goes on forever. I can't even see Bending Oaks. It's gone, too. A whole school."

Bending Oaks was the junior high Kolby and I went to. It was a good three miles away, but it sat atop a hill, so it was visible from almost anywhere in Elizabeth. I had a hard time wrapping my head around what the hill would look like without the big building silhouetted in the sun.

When I tuned in again, Kolby was saying, "...a two-by-four through his leg. He was trying to drag himself out of his house, and his neighbor found a wheelbarrow. But they said the hospital's been hit, too, so nobody knows where to go. Nobody's ever seen anything like this."

I thought back to all the people I'd seen walking along Church Street. About the man who had collapsed. They'd been trying to make their way to help, but what if there was no help? How far would they have to go before they found it?

"Dear Jesus, please be with us in our time of sorrow and need..." Kolby's mother had begun again, her eyes shut tight, her palms facing upward. Kolby glanced at her, seemed to consider saying more, but thought better of it and hung his head. A couple people gathered around his mom and muttered "Amen" every so often, listening as her prayer tumbled through our devastated portion of the street.

The hospital was at least five miles in the opposite direction. If it had been hit, and Bending Oaks had been hit, that meant this tornado had reached in and swept away a huge chunk of Elizabeth.

It also meant that Marin's dance studio had been right in the tornado's path.

Nobody knew what to do. We stood gathered around Kolby and his mom and sister for a long time, and more neighbors joined us, one by one.

Someone's son had been sucked right out of his bedroom while he rummaged for a weather radio. Someone hadn't heard from her husband, who was driving home from work. Someone wondered if his wife, a nurse working a rotation in the PICU, was okay. Someone had heard pounding and yells coming from beneath a car and was sure there were still neighbors trapped inside their homes. And speaking of homes…nobody had one anymore. Where would we go? What would we do? That became our mantra: *What are we going to do?*

Then the sky opened up and raindrops tumbled onto our arms and our cheeks and pattered against the boards we stood on, releasing an earthy smell. And we had no trees to huddle under. We had no umbrellas. Our only shower curtain was covering poor Mrs. Dempsey. So we stood in the rain, squinting against it, our shoulders hunched, for as long as we could, adding to our mantra: *It's raining now, and we have nowhere to go, what are we going to do?*

A couple of the men were able to wrench open a car door, and a few people climbed inside. The windows fogged and it was like they were gone. Saved.

And then the wind picked up and began to drive the rain sideways into our ears, and our hair began to drip, and it felt good, but it also felt cold, and we couldn't help wondering what was next for us, especially after Kolby's mom began praying, "Dear God, please let there not be another tornado on the way," and it wasn't clear if she was actually praying for this or just stating the same fear that had begun to trickle into all of our minds.

Some of the neighbors worked together to prop a piece of wallboard up against the side of what was left of their house, and they huddled under it, their clothes soggy, their feet sinking into the now-saturated debris. Tears began to flow along with the rain as the reality of what had happened to us truly began to sink in.

Kolby's mom and sister joined them, and soon it was Kolby and me standing in the street alone, blinking at each other through raindrops clinging to our eyelashes.

"There was this guy," he said, now that it was just the two of us. He blinked off into the distance, took a breath, and turned his gaze back to me. "It was like... like he'd been hit by a bomb. He was in half, Jersey. I didn't even see where his legs had gone. I think they were buried."

"Oh my God. What about Tracy?"

"She didn't see it. Mom kept walking with her. But I can't stop seeing it, you know? I don't think I ever will."

I touched his shoulder lightly, then, embarrassed, pulled my hand away.

"I puked," he said. "And I feel like such a pussy for puking. It's..." He shook his head. "Forget it."

The rain drove into us. I didn't know what to say to him about the half-man or about his puking. I didn't know what he wanted from me. Our relationship had always been about playing pickup games of baseball or tag or building forts and riding bikes. We didn't talk about puking, or crying, or being scared.

And I was. I was so, so scared.

"I'm going inside," I said, like I'd said to him a million times before. Like I was tired of playing hide-and-seek or wanted to watch TV or eat dinner or something else totally ordinary.

"Inside where?"

I gestured to what was left of my house. "Basement. In case..." *In case of another tornado.* "In case my mom comes home."

He shook his head. "You shouldn't go back in there. It's not stable. Look how it's leaning. And the ceiling's been ripped out."

"It'll be okay. It's better on the inside." Which was a total lie, but the more the thunder roared above us, the more Kolby's haunted eyes transferred that image of the half-man into my soul, the more his mom prayed into the wind, the more frightened I became. *Please, God, don't make me have to go through another tornado. Not again. Not alone.*

My heart started pounding and I started breathing heavy and I knew I needed to get back into the basement, back to where I'd been safe, right away. "I'll come out when the rain stops."

Kolby grabbed my arm and I gently pulled away from him. I smiled. Or at least tried to. It felt like a smile, anyway.

"I'll be fine, Kolby. You should be with your mom and Tracy right now."

A bolt of lightning crashed and we both jumped.

"You want me to go with you?" he asked, though I could tell by the way he stared anxiously at the house that he wanted the answer to be no. I could tell he felt torn between protecting me and protecting his mom and sister.

I didn't want him there. Kolby was a great friend, and a part of me wanted to latch on to him and hope he could keep me safe. But for some reason, the devastation behind that leaning half-wall of my house felt too personal, too embarrassing. It was my family's life, all bunched up and bundled and twisted into heaps, and I didn't want him to see it, even though I knew that most of our stuff was probably lying on the street right now, getting turned into mush by the rain, and that most of his stuff was, too.

"It's okay. I'll be fine," I said. "When my mom comes, tell her I'm inside, okay?"

"Okay," he said reluctantly. "But if you need anything..." He trailed off, probably thinking exactly what I was thinking, which was *What? If I need anything, what? What can you do? You lost everything, too.*

I nodded and turned back toward my house on shaking legs.

There was more thunder, and my heart pounded as I climbed the steps and slipped in through the front door.

My brain expected to find the scene on the other side of the door exactly like it had always been. Brown carpet, vacuum lines still scratched through it from Monday's chores. The TV on. The wall of mirrors behind the dining room table—a throwback from when the house was built in the 1970s—reflecting our mismatched garage-sale table and chairs. The white linoleum with the pale blue flowers stretching into the kitchen, the light of the dishwasher blinking to indicate that the dishes inside were clean. The hum of the refrigerator and the air conditioner.

Instead, it was raining. Inside my house. The wet plaster of the fallen walls smelled chalky. The only sound was the rumbling of the sky.

I tried to make out something familiar. And finally I did. The television stand was missing. But the television sat there in its place, as if someone had picked up the TV and taken the stand, then set the TV back down. Of course, what use was a TV when there was no outlet to plug it into?

Marin's purse was still on the chair where I'd left it. I opened it and looked inside, leaning my head over it to try to keep the relentless rain out.

It was filled with three packs of gum and a tube of iridescent pink lipstick that Mom had handed down to her. Marin's treasures.

I looped the purse over my arm and headed along the path I'd cleared earlier, trying hard not to step on anything sharp or dangerous, picking my feet up high with each step and placing them down carefully. There was so much broken glass.

When I finally made it to the bottom step, I was out of the rain's reach, so I stood there and stared, squeezing water out of my hair and wiping my cheeks dry with my hands, trying to figure out what to do next.

Trying to figure out how I would survive until Mom and Ronnie came home.

CHAPTER SIX

There were a dozen bottles of water in Ronnie's mini-fridge, along with a few beers, some cheese in a jar, and a package of hot dogs. I'd had to dig through broken boards and rubble with my hands to get to the refrigerator. By the time I unearthed it, I was so thirsty, I downed one of the waters while I sat on a clear spot on the floor in front of it, my fingers torn up and sore.

My stomach growled heartily as I spotted the cheese, but I was afraid to eat it, unsure what we would do about food once Mom and Ronnie and Marin came home. I wanted to make sure there was enough for all of us. I wondered when we would get help on our street, and if the helpers would have food. I wondered if our real refrigerator was still upstairs somewhere, and if it still had food in it, and tried to bat away a panicked thought that the refrigerator upstairs could at any minute cave in the floor it was sitting on and bury me. I scooted back from the area where the kitchen had spilled into the basement, into the opposite corner. That section of floor had felt solid.

I sat on the concrete and sipped my water, listening to the thunderstorm, watching as the rain picked up and tapered off, only to do it again, bathing the basement in shadows that got deeper and deeper as night fell full force.

I didn't hear anything else outside. No voices, no sirens, no cars. Just the tapping of the raindrops, the clap of the thunder.

Eventually, I got up and made my way over to the flipped couch; it was wet on the back side, but the cushions underneath were dry. I pulled them out and carried them to the pool table, which I'd pushed closer to my safe corner. I placed the couch cushions under the table and rounded up my backpack, Marin's purse, the flashlight, and my cell phone. I rummaged through an old dresser that Mom had stuck in the farthest corner of the basement, and found a blanket we used for picnics and on the Fourth of July to watch fireworks at the park, some beach towels, and a deck of playing cards with the date of Mom and Ronnie's Vegas honeymoon embossed on the box. I took them all, lumping the towels together like a pillow and covering myself with the blanket. I stuffed the playing cards into Marin's purse, along with the gum and the lipstick, and then clicked on the flashlight and stretched out across the cushions on my stomach, feeling safer, as if I could wait for everyone down here until morning if need be. I didn't want to, but I'd be okay if I had to.

The book I'd been reading before the tornado hit—which seemed like forever ago already—was a little damp, and one of the pages had been torn. But for the most part it was all still there, and I decided to finish it to pass the time. I wondered if Miss Sopor's house had been destroyed, too, and if the high school was still standing.

Surely it was. It had to be. Jane might have been inside it.

I imagined everyone going back to school, with stories to tell about how they'd weathered the storm. About how their houses were damaged or their cars were messed up. *What about Jersey Cameron and Kolby Combs?* I imagined them saying. *They aren't here. I heard they lost everything.* I didn't want them doing that. I didn't want everyone talking about how Jersey Cameron, the mousy drama club girl, had nothing now. I groaned and rolled to my back, staring up at the bottom of the pool table, the book slack in my hands. With my free hand, I dug my cell phone out of my pocket and tried to call Mom again. Still nothing. *Where are you, Mom? When will you get to me?*

I pulled up my messaging and thumbed a text to Dani— Am in basement. Ok but everything destroyed. You?—and then typed out a similar text to Jane—Made it thru tornado. U ok? I stared at my phone's screen, hoping that the messages would go through, but after a few seconds an error message popped up instead.

My stomach rumbled again and I turned over and opened Marin's purse. A waft of cinnamon and mint puffed out in my face, along with the familiar scent of my mom's makeup and my sister's shampoo. I dug around until I found a full pack of gum, unwrapped a piece, and stuck it into my mouth to quiet my hunger. I chewed, listening to the rain continue, and turned the foil wrapper in my fingers.

I thought about my sister. Marin hated storms. She was probably freaking out right now, especially if she was trapped in a dark closet with her dance classmates, smushed together, the skin of their arms sweating up against one another. Mom would be trying to calm her, rubbing her sticky curls and talking to her. Maybe singing to her. Trying to think of a way out.

I hoped they were okay. I hoped they were in the police station or a grocery store or someplace safe, trying to call me, trying to figure out how to navigate the car to the house. To save me.

I pulled a pen out of my backpack and bent over the little square of foil. I drew a stick figure on tiptoes, arms out and legs bent, curved lines surrounding the figure to indicate motion. I gave the stick figure big eyes with long eyelashes and a smiling mouth, then added a princess crown to the top of its head just for fun.

Marin does the East Coast Swing, I wrote under the picture, then held up the foil and gazed at it, a smile curving my lips. Marin would love it when she saw it.

I folded the picture over itself into tinier and tinier squares, then tucked it in the zippered pocket inside the purse.

By the time morning came, the rain had stopped, leaving in its wake a sharp light that gave everything a vivid edge. I unwound myself from my blanket and slid out from under the table, blinking, the events of the day before rushing in on me.

It wasn't a dream, I thought with disappointment. *The tornado really did happen.*

I pulled my phone out of my pocket and checked the time. It was 11 AM, and I had no messages. I tried to call Mom's phone again and wasn't surprised when my attempt was greeted with an automated message saying my call couldn't go through.

It was hot. Already. My hair stuck to my neck, and I could feel a bead of sweat slowly making its way down the small of my back. My legs were goose bumpy where the blanket had wrapped around them and trapped in body heat all night. The wreckage on the open side of the basement had become saturated and was now baking in the May sun. It was already starting to stink.

I was hungry.

I was thirsty.

And, worst of all, I had to go to the bathroom.

My eyes landed on a paint bucket Ronnie used to store rags. How embarrassing. I would hold it.

To keep my mind off my bladder, I went to the refrigerator and ate two cold hot dogs, which were starting to not be so cold anymore. I wondered how long they would still be good. After I finished them, I took out a bottle of water, shutting the door as quickly as possible to conserve as much cold air as I could. I leaned back against the refrigerator and listened to the noises outside.

I heard disjointed words like "in there" and "destroyed" and "keep pressure on it" and "ambulance" and "overwhelmed." Somewhere in the distance I heard the buzzing of a chain saw.

I listened for Mom's voice. For Ronnie's. Marin's. I listened for my name, for cries of hope.

I didn't hear any of that.

When the pain in my bladder got to be too much, I finally mustered up my courage and walked over to the bucket, feeling silly and embarrassed, hoping nobody suddenly came down to "rescue" me at that moment.

Next to the bucket, I spotted an old pair of Ronnie's work boots. They were filthy and ugly, clumps of dead grass and blots of dried paint crusted on them. But old shoes were better than no shoes.

One by one, I tipped them upside down and pounded them against the floor in case there were bugs in them, then crammed a rag into the toe of each and slipped them on, lacing them tight around my ankles.

I felt like Frankenstein stomping across the basement floor, and I tripped over the toes a couple of times. My feet were hot, making me feel sweatier than I already was, and I wished I had an air conditioner to sit in front of, or a cold shower to stand under. But instead I had the humid Missouri air pressing in on me, keeping my sweat tight against my skin.

With the light flooding in, it was easier to see where I was going this time, and I was able to spot some of our things buried under toppled furniture and shingles. I made my way upstairs and stood in what used to be our living room, pulling out items I thought Mom would be interested in keeping. Her bathrobe, dripping and smelly and warm, streaked with mud, which I draped across an overturned table. DVDs, still in their cases, which I stacked neatly on the floor. Bedsheets, which had twined their way around furniture legs and twisted into ropes. I wondered what those must have looked like as the tornado passed over. Did they reach up to the sky, great white flags of surrender?

I cleaned up as much as I could—which wasn't much—and then headed outside, searching for Kolby. I found him sitting on a patch of grass eerily close to where I'd seen him standing outside my kitchen window the day before. He was holding a cloth against his arm. I headed over.

"You made it through the night," he said when he saw me coming.

"What happened?" I motioned to his arm as I sat down next to him.

He shrugged. "Cut it on a window."

I could see blood seeping through the makeshift bandage, which appeared to be a damp purple bandanna. "Is it bad?"

He stared off into the sky, pressing the cloth down harder. "It probably could use some stitches, but how am I gonna manage that?"

I reached over and picked up a corner of the bandanna and gasped. A deep five-inch gash sliced through his skin and was weeping blood. "That's really bad. You need..." But I didn't know how to finish the sentence. He needed a doctor to look at it, yes, but how were we going to get him to one?

"I'll be okay," he said. "I just need to find something that I can use to tie this to my arm."

I scanned what would have been our backyards, trying to make sense of what I was seeing, trying to pick out individual items that might be useful. It was hard to see anything but massive piles of trash.

"There," I said, and pulled myself up, clunking over some bricks to where Kolby's mom's clothesline used to stand. The pole was still there, but the line was snapped and wrapped around the base of it. I unwound it and brought it back to Kolby, then sank down next to him and began wrapping it around the cloth on his arm, trying to get it tight enough to stay, but not too tight.

"How long have you been up?" I asked.

"Most of the night, really," he said, wincing every time I tugged on the line. "We remembered that Mrs. Donnelly had an old cellar. It took us a couple hours to pull everything off the doors. But I don't think anyone really slept at all. My mom's down there now. She was up most of the night praying over people. I should have come and gotten you."

I shook my head. "I made a bed under the pool table. I was okay."

I got to the end of the twine and knotted it, tucking the loose ends under. Kolby smoothed the bandage over his forearm. Already, blood was blooming on the outside of it. I could see darker-purple spots growing under the rope.

"Some trucks made it through this morning," he said, looking out at nothing. I followed his gaze. He turned to meet my eyes. "It's bad, Jersey. They said a lot of people died."

I held his gaze for a few seconds, then looked back over the field of fallen houses. A couple of children had appeared and were climbing on top of a car. The car's nose had been punched in, the windshield caved.

"I can't believe we're all just...homeless now," I said. "Where are we supposed to go?"

Kolby picked up a splintered board and tossed it to the side, unearthing an iron. He picked up the iron and studied it idly. "We're going to Milton to stay with my aunt. I think some people are going over to Prairie Valley to stay in motels. People are going...wherever they can." He pulled himself up with a grunt and started back toward the rubble of the house. When he reached the edge, he picked up a section of siding and tossed it away. "I'm trying to find my mom's purse so we at least have some money. Who knows if it's still here? Could be ten miles away, for all I know."

I got up and followed him, clomping over things in Ronnie's boots, bending to pick up a brick here, a board there, a hill of sopping clothes or a ruined book somewhere else.

"Careful," Kolby kept murmuring. "I don't know how stable everything is."

"I'll be okay," I repeated over and over again, sweat rolling down my lower back and dripping off my forehead.

We searched until we were both filthy and thirsty. One of the trucks that came through had deposited a couple of cases of bottled water on the street, and we took a break to get a drink.

"I don't think we're gonna find it," Kolby said at last.

"We might," I said. "Marin's purse was still by the door."

He took a long sip of water and didn't respond. I watched Mr. Fay toss little bits and pieces of things into a hip-high pile.

"Where do you think they are?" I said at last, giving voice to the thought that had been running a loop in my head ever since Kolby had told me that trucks had made it through.

Kolby looked down at his feet. He knew who I was talking about without me even saying it. "I don't know. Where were they when it hit?"

"Mom and Marin were at dance. I don't know where Ronnie was. But..." I trailed off, unable to say what had been weighing on my mind. If they could have gotten through, they would have. Mom would have come to get me. She'd have been scared out of her mind for me.

If they weren't here, it was because something was keeping them from coming.

"We can go there," Kolby said. "It's not that far."

My hand shook, the water inside the bottle rippling with the motion. "It's a couple miles, at least."

He motioned toward our houses. "It's not like there's anything good on TV right now," he said, and though he was joking, neither one of us laughed. Nothing about any of this was funny. "Let me tell Tracy, so my mom won't worry when she wakes up," he said.

And before I could say anything in protest, he loped off toward Mrs. Donnelly's cellar.

Part of me was definitely ready to do this. To go out and find my mom and Marin and Ronnie. If they couldn't get to me, I'd get to them.

But part of me was scared.

What if I didn't find them?

What if they weren't there to be found?

CHAPTER SEVEN

More and more vehicles were creeping down Church Street by the time we got to it, some of them stopping to pick up people who were still walking toward town, still hoping to find help. Some passengers offered bottles of water and first-aid kits. Others rolled by with cameras, taking photos and gabbing about the devastation as if it were there for their entertainment.

By comparison, all the people who were walking looked filthy and grim. Some wore stony, distant expressions, as if they had no idea where they were or where they were going. Some were carrying children. Some were covered in dried blood. Some were telling stories, and all of the stories were similar—the house fell apart, the wind tugged at us, we got hit with something, our houses are gone, our cars are gone, our streets are gone, our lives, as we knew them, are gone.

"About a half mile that direction will get you out of the

storm's path," one woman told Kolby, pointing to the east. "It ran north and south, so if you go east, before long you'll come to regular pavement."

So we walked east on Kentucky, taking in the devastation there as we headed toward normalcy.

"You smell that?" Kolby said, wrinkling his nose. "Stinks."

I thought about the hamburger I'd crumbled up in the skillet right before the storm hit. Who knew where it had been flung, but wherever it was, it was rotting in the sun now, along with dinners and the refrigerator guts of hundreds of other houses.

"Smells like the washing machine when I forget to take the wet clothes out," I said.

"It's only gonna get worse, you know," he said. "That smell. All that wet stuff and the heat."

"Food rotting," I added.

"And people," Kolby said, and he said it so matter-of-factly, I stopped walking and stared at him.

"What?" he asked, turning to face me and shrugging. "There are dead people under some of this stuff. And dead animals, too. It's reality."

I started walking again. "Yeah, but you don't have to say it like that. Like it's no big deal."

"I don't like it, either," he mumbled, following me.

We came up over a hill and could see where the destruction stopped, not too many yards ahead of us. It was strange, seeing how the houses went from totally razed to beat up and broken to lightly damaged to completely fine. Literally, where one house was gone, the neighbor three houses down would only need to replace some shingles.

It was at that end of the street where most of the people were congregating. Chain saws buzzed and whole crowds sifted through rubble, people calling out to one another, offering help and drinks, the effort much more concerted than on our street. Someone had set up a few tents and folding tables covered with food and drinks and tools and supplies. Two of the tents shaded an assortment of lawn chairs, and some women sat there with babies. Little kids squatted on the ground and munched on grapes, watching as Kolby and I scuffed by.

"You all right?" a woman hollered to us from one of the chairs. "You need help?"

"We're fine," I yelled back, smiling as if we were simply out on a midday stroll.

"You need something to eat?" she called. "There's plenty. None of us has power, so we've got to eat it while it's still good."

My stomach growled, and Kolby and I looked at each other. We diverted to the tent, where I immediately grabbed a banana and Kolby palmed a sandwich, taking a huge bite out of it and closing his eyes while he chewed.

"You're hurt," the woman said, softer now as she approached us. "We've got bandages. Is it bad?"

"It's okay," Kolby said, but I overrode him.

"It's pretty bad. How big are your bandages?"

The woman rifled through the first-aid kits, then disappeared into her house. Kolby and I snacked while we waited, shoving crackers and cheese cubes into our mouths greedily. She came back out with a roll of gauze and some tape.

"It's kind of old, but it's going to be better than that," she said, handing me the gauze.

We made our way over to the chairs and Kolby peeled off the bandanna and clothesline from his arm. I winced when I looked at the cut, the skin around the edges swollen and angry red.

"You're gonna want to keep that clean," the woman said, making a pained face. "It looks pretty bad. What did you cut it on?"

"Glass," Kolby answered.

"Good, at least it wasn't rusted metal. You're probably gonna need a tetanus shot anyway. Although I don't know where you'd go to get one right now," she said. "I suppose the Elizabeth Clinic was spared yesterday, but it's probably packed. And nobody has power."

"I'm sure it'll be fine," Kolby said as I wrapped the gauze around his arm and secured it with a strip of tape. "How far did the tornado go, do you know?" he asked.

"My husband drove around this morning," the woman said. "About seven miles or so. Hit some of the schools, the library, the hospital, the police station, fire station. Hit everything. You two need a ride somewhere? I'm sure Jerry'll take you."

"We're going to Janice's Dance Studio," I said. "That's where my mom was. She hasn't come home yet, and I'm trying to find her."

The woman's face paled. "On Sixth?" I nodded. "Oh, honey, he won't be able to get you in there. Sixth got hit bad."

"Oh. Okay," I said, trying to ignore the lump that had suddenly formed in my throat. "We'll walk."

The woman offered a smile that didn't quite hold up the corners of her mouth. "I hear they're setting up tents at some of the churches," she said. She looked at Kolby and lowered her voice, as if I weren't standing right there. "They'll be starting to compile lists. There's a Lutheran church right around the corner on Munsee Avenue."

Kolby nodded and grabbed my elbow, pulling me back into the street.

"What kinds of lists?" I asked when we got a little way down the road.

He took a long time to answer. "Of missing people," he finally said. "And...you know..."

My heart went cold. "I know what?"

He stopped, still holding my elbow, his knuckles grazing my side. Ordinarily, I would be mortified at a boy touching my side, afraid that he'd feel the wobbly skin there. But I was too intent on hearing him say it aloud—that they would be compiling lists of the missing and the dead—to worry about something so stupid as whether or not I was stick-skinny. "Come on, Jersey, it doesn't matter," he said. "We'll go to Janice's and see what's up before we worry about what kind of lists they've got at the churches. Just because she said it doesn't make it true."

When we turned onto Sixth Street, we navigated in the

direction we'd come from, making our way back into the heart of the destruction. Under normal circumstances, I knew this part of town like the back of my hand, but the farther west we went, the harder it was to recognize anything. The woman had been right—Sixth Street had been hit bad, most of the buildings ripped right off their foundations, no leaning walls here. There were no signs, no street markers, no landmarks at all. Other than a handful of people determinedly digging through debris where Fenderman's Grocery used to be, there weren't even any people.

"I think it was here," I said, stopping and facing a mostly bare rectangle of concrete. Around the concrete was mud; even the grass had been stripped. It was almost as if the tornado had tried to dig down into the ground with its twisting fingers and scoop Janice's off the earth.

Kolby walked over to the concrete and bent to pick up something. It was a small ballet shoe. Too small to have been Marin's, but still the sight of it brought tears to my eyes.

"They aren't here," I said. Kolby dropped the shoe. I tried to remember where the cloak closet was—it had been a while since I'd come to the studio with Mom and Marin, and I was turned around by everything being gone. I stumbled across the concrete to the far corner. Where walls had once been anchored into the floor, now just a few splintered boards stuck up from the ground. There were a couple of empty gym bags caught on a ripped-off piece of stud, but otherwise there was nothing.

"They aren't here," I repeated.

"I know," Kolby said. "Sorry."

I sank to the ground on my knees. When I'd called Mom, had she been right here? Had this been where she'd been shouting to get down, where she'd been ordering me to the basement, where she'd been unable to hear me? I pressed my palms onto the gritty floor. A handprint stamped itself into the drying grime.

"I don't know what to do," I said, but Kolby didn't answer, which made me unsure whether I'd said it out loud. "Kolby, what do I do?"

Kolby used his foot to scrape some shattered glass out of the way, then came over to where I knelt on the ground. "I don't know," he said.

I turned my eyes up to him. "What if they're dead?" I asked. "What if they all died?" The question felt like a punch to my stomach.

Kolby knelt next to me. He didn't try to tell me they weren't dead. I guessed that was because he knew this looked as bad as I thought it did. They might be dead, or they might be injured or in comas or God knew what else. Telling me they were anything other than that would be a lie, and we both knew it. If they were alive and fine, they would have come home. Mom would have come for me.

The food I'd wolfed down in the tents roiled in my stomach as Kolby's silence sank in. I scrambled clumsily up to my feet and thunked as far away from him as I could before bending at the waist and vomiting on a bare spot of dirt. I heard shuffling sounds as he stood up. "I'm sorry," I said between retches. "I'm sorry."

"It's okay," he said, and when I finished and came back to him, he clumsily patted my back between my shoulder blades. "Let's go to the church," he said. "Maybe they'll know something."

We scuffed away from Janice's and toward the Lutheran church. The woman we'd talked to was right—they had set up a tent full of supplies. Kolby and I grabbed water bottles from a bucket of ice as soon as we reached the tent. I opened mine and began sipping it while Kolby downed his. The tent was stuffed with people who looked just as homeless and dazed as we were.

"Can I help you?" a woman in sandals, a tan vest, and a safari hat said, hurrying to greet us.

"Do you have lists?" I blurted out, getting to the worst before I tried to talk myself out of wanting to know.

"What kind of lists are you looking for, honey?" she said, putting her hand on my shoulder and pulling me toward a table, where she eased me into a folding chair.

"I can't find my mom or my sister," I said. "They were at Janice's Dance Studio?" The last came out as a question, as if part of me was hoping that the woman would tell me I was wrong—that my mom and sister had never been at the studio, that they'd ridden out the storm safe and sound in someone's basement instead.

The woman's face fell a little, but she recovered very quickly. She leaned to the side and picked up a clipboard. "You want to add them to the list of those who are missing?" she asked.

"Is there…another list…?" I asked. "Of people who didn't make it through?"

She shook her head. "It's too early, and I'm afraid we haven't been getting many updates about that," she said. "The power's out all over Elizabeth, which is making communication a challenge. But we're compiling a list of the missing, so families who aren't in contact with one another can at least see that someone else in the family is looking for them."

"Is her name on there?" Kolby asked, pointing to the list. "Jersey Cameron?" He looked at me eagerly. "Maybe they're looking for you, too."

The woman scanned the list, running her finger down the names, her lips moving. At last she looked up and gave a rueful head shake. "No, honey, I'm sorry, it's not. But we'll add your mom and sister to this list—"

"And my stepdad," I interrupted miserably. I felt my chin shake. "Everyone."

"Okay, we'll put their names down on the list, and that way when they get their bearings and come looking for you, they'll know you're fine," she said.

I gave her my information, along with Mom's, Ronnie's, and Marin's, but my voice got thick and tears welled in my eyes as I talked.

The woman put down her pen and stared at me sympathetically. "Honey, do you have somewhere to go? Someone you can try to get ahold of? We've got some cots we're setting up in the sanctuary and the basement, and we can work with you to get in touch with any family you might have outside of Elizabeth. Or Child Protective Services."

60

Fear wracked my body. I couldn't go sleep on a cot in a church basement and wait for a social worker to show up and send me off to foster care. I didn't know what I was going to do, but I knew I wasn't going to do that. I eyed Kolby, who had gone over to another table, where a woman was pouring peroxide over his cut.

"I'm staying with his family," I said. "Until we find mine." I tried to smile, though it felt counterfeit on my face. Kolby was going to be leaving town to stay with his aunt, he'd said. He wasn't going to take care of me. His mom wasn't going to take care of me. They hadn't offered, and even if they had, I wouldn't go. What if Mom came back after I left?

"Okay," the woman said. "But our doors are always open. We've had donations of clothes coming in all morning. You might go through those boxes over there and pick out a few things. Also, feel free to take any food and supplies you may need. We expect we'll be getting lots more donations by tomorrow. Plenty of folks have already been coming in with truckloads of stuff."

"Thank you," I said, but I didn't take anything. My stomach was still sour with nerves and exhaustion, and the last thing I cared about was my clothes. I still had water in the mini-fridge in the basement. I wanted to get out of there before I ended up having to stay.

The woman who was tending to Kolby's arm slathered some cream on it and rewrapped it, telling him about the cots and the clothes and the food as well.

"You going to stay?" he asked when we were alone again.

"No. I'm going back. I don't want them to freak out if they somehow make it home and I'm gone."

My words felt hollow to me. Like something I didn't really believe in.

But Kolby must have known how much I needed to say them. He didn't question me, just started walking back the way we had come.

We got a ride back to our street from Jerry, the husband of the woman at the tent on Kentucky. He filled us in on details, what the radio newscasters were saying about the tornado. At least one hundred people dead. So many more injured.

But Kolby only answered him in grunts and thoughtful humming noises. He didn't add anything of his own. And I didn't respond, either. I watched out the window as the destruction rolled into view and thought, *Home. This is my home.*

And wondered if three of those one hundred dead belonged to me.

And how soon I would find out for sure.

CHAPTER
EIGHT

It rained again that night.

I sat outside on what used to be my front porch and watched the rain fall. Let it soak into the skin of my forearms and drip off my earlobes. I took off Ronnie's boots and wriggled my toes in it, the closest I could get to feeling somewhat washed.

Kolby's mom tried and tried to get me to join them in Mrs. Donnelly's cellar.

"Honey, your mama will find you there," she promised. "You can leave her a note." I stared at the raindrops, which landed in heavy splats on the toes of Ronnie's boots, washing away the dirt and dust that had gathered there during our walk. "Sweetheart, you need to take care of yourself. The last thing you want is to get sick now. Come into the cellar and dry off. Get yourself something to eat. We've got canned pickles and peaches down there. Mr. Fay brought over some crackers as well." I blinked slowly and shook my head. "Honey, nobody's gonna be staying here much longer. You're gonna have to go someplace, too. It's unsafe. It's unhealthy." A drop of water slid down my nose. Finally, Kolby's mom said a quick prayer that I was too numb to listen to and picked her way back to Mrs. Donnelly's cellar, her big hips shaking with every step.

I watched the rain. I watched people disappear into the cellar and into their relatives' cars and into the night. A few of the neighbors had already fled to nearby motels. Kolby would be leaving for Milton first thing in the morning. Soon I would be the only one still here. If Mom didn't show up, I would eventually lose my options. Someone would find me, would force me to go to the cots in the church, would force me to go to Child Protective Services, to a foster home. I wasn't about to voluntarily give up my freedom before then. In so many ways, control over where I slept and ate was all I had left, and maybe not for much longer. I was going to hang on to it as long as I could.

After a while, goose bumps rose up on my arms, and when thunder boomed off in the distance, I began to shiver, even though I didn't feel cold. I didn't want to go inside. I didn't want to be afraid. I wanted to be like I always had been—the kind of girl who didn't pay attention to the weather, the kind of girl who sometimes went outside and danced around in the rain, who stuck her bare feet under the downspout to wash grass clippings off. The kind of girl whose mom stood on the front porch, soda in hand, smiling and watching as her daughter let the crying sky drench her until her shirt and shorts were stuck to her like a second skin.

Instead, I was shaking, my heart pounding, my eyes drifting worriedly to the sky, trying to remember what it had looked like before the tornado touched down and if it had been similar to what it looked like now. Wishing I'd paid more attention.

By the second crash of thunder, I couldn't take it anymore. I ducked back into the house, not even bothering to stop and sift through our belongings this time—heading for the basement and the safety of the pool table, carrying Ronnie's boots in my hands.

Once downstairs, I dropped the boots and climbed under the pool table and wrapped myself in one of the towels I'd found in the bureau, pulling my knees to my chest, my teeth chattering. I sat next to the couch cushion, bent forward at the shoulders so my head would clear the bottom of the table, wondering what I would do next. My body was tired from all the walking, but my mind was racing. What little food I had would spoil soon, and the water bottles would only last so long. I was filthy. The living room floor could cave in on me at any time. Rain was beginning to pool on the basement floor, inching toward me. Soon I would have no choice but to leave.

I wished, more than anything, for a TV. Or a radio. Anything to break the silence. Anything to cover the noise of the relentless rain pattering and the weird sound it made on our house now that our house was no longer standing. I longed for voices, or music, or laughter, or chanting—anything to break up the monotony. Anything to remind me that I was still here, still alive.

What I wouldn't have given to listen to Marin's chatter, to have her stand in front of my face begging me to dance with her. Life with Marin was never quiet. Life without her seemed so still it was maddening.

I snaked my hand out from under the towel and unzipped her purse. I pulled out Mom's lipstick and opened it. I closed my eyes and smelled it, letting the scent of Mom wash over me, cradle me. I missed her so much.

"Please, Mom," I said aloud, "be out there somewhere. Be alive. Come find me."

I closed the lipstick and dropped it back into the purse, then grabbed a stick of gum and popped it into my mouth. Thunder rolled and I jumped, thinking about Marin and how much she hated thunderstorms. When one came through Elizabeth, Marin would wander the house on her tiptoes holding her hands over her ears, her eyes big and wet and worried. She constantly asked, "Is it over? Huh? Huh, Jersey? Is it fine?"

Once, a few weeks before, when Mom was gone on an errand, I couldn't take it anymore. Marin's eyes had gone from wet to spilling over and her voice had gotten smaller and smaller. "Is it fine, Jersey? Is the noise fine?" She was nearing Full Meltdown Mode, and I knew I had to do something to distract her.

I had learned during fifth-grade summer camp that I was apparently some sort of card genius. I'd taken a gaming elective and had paired up with a counselor named Jon—"with no 'h,'" he was constantly telling people, to the point where everyone called him Noaychjon, all one word, like that was his name—who spent the entire four weeks teaching me new card games and then trying in vain to beat me at them. He couldn't do it. Nobody could. I guess everybody is naturally gifted at something. If my gift couldn't be music or sports or theater or chemistry or something worthwhile, I supposed being gifted at cards wasn't all that bad a sentence. It had been a long time since I'd played, but I still remembered all the games, and that afternoon I'd decided Marin was finally old enough to play with.

"Is the noise fine, Jersey? Is it over?"

"C'mere, Mar," I'd said, pulling a worn deck of cards that Noaychjon had given me as a good-bye present when summer camp was over out of my top dresser drawer. "I'll teach you how to play Sixty-Six."

She'd followed me into my room, warily taking her hands down from her ears, and had climbed up onto my bed. I sat cross-legged across from her and shuffled the cards.

"Okay, so you know how the princes and princesses always get married in those movies you like?"

Marin nodded, already sucked in.

"That's pretty much what this game is about. You want the kings and queens to get married."

The storm had moved through, Marin and I playing Sixty-Six and then Go Fish. When we started playing solitaire, I told her that technically, solitaire was a game for one person, not two. She'd argued that we were playing our own kind of solitaire, the kind that two people play, so I'd dubbed the game Couples Solitaire and had gone with it. The wind beating the rain against our house went unnoticed by my sister. The hail that dropped for a few seconds was totally ignored. Even the thunder didn't register with anything more than a concerned upward glance as she held a fan of cards in her pudgy hand.

That was all it ever took with Marin. Just some time together. Just some attention. I could make her day by saying hello to her. I could have made her so happy if I'd just once gotten off the couch and danced with her.

I flicked on the flashlight and smoothed out the foil gum wrapper. I drew a picture of a stick figure with its hands over its ears, a window behind the figure streaked with dashes of rain.

Marin hates thunderstorms, I wrote.

I drew a vertical line down the center of the foil and drew a hand holding some playing cards. I colored in the tiny fingernails. Marin always had polished fingernails.

Marin likes thunderstorms sometimes, I wrote underneath.

I studied my artwork appreciatively and then folded the foil into a tiny square and stuck it in the zippered pocket, along with the other I'd drawn.

The thunder crashed again, a flash of lightning blooming brightness into the basement, and I jumped.

I grabbed the deck of cards I'd found alongside the towels in the dresser drawer. I opened the box and pulled out the cards, idly wondering if my deck from Noaychjon was buried under rubble upstairs or if it was blown away. If the dresser was gone entirely. Or if it sat there, pristine and untouched amid the debris the way Marin's purse had been.

I counted the cards, pulling out the jokers, and when I was satisfied that I had a full deck, I shuffled them and laid them out in a line.

For you, Marin, I thought, beginning my first game of solitaire. *And for Couples Solitaire.*

I played hand after hand, winning some, losing others, cheating a couple times so I wouldn't have to redeal. I played until my eyes were tired and my fingers were lazy and the flashlight beam began to dull, making me squint to see the numbers.

I slapped the cards on the floor, all the while wondering what the next day would hold for me. Kolby would be gone. My cell phone would probably still be useless, if it even had battery left. I would be hungry and thirsty and dirty. I would spend some time digging through broken stuff that used to be our belongings, our treasures. I would worry and wonder and wait for Mom.

Eventually, the storm picked up, the rain hammering against the ground and the wind raking it farther and farther into the basement. I tired of my game and gathered the cards together, stuffing them into the box, then putting the box back in Marin's purse. As the lightning flashes came closer and closer together, I wound myself up in my blanket and stretched out over the couch cushions, falling asleep almost immediately, trying to push my worries about the next day out of my head.

Hoping for a miracle.

CHAPTER NINE

I awoke to a voice.

"Dear Jesus," it said, and I opened my eyes to the underside of the pool table, unsure where I was. I had been dreaming about school—I'd been at the lunch table with Dani and Jane, but none of us could find any food and I was so thirsty—and for a few seconds I had forgotten about the tornado. But then the voice, anguished, got closer. "Jersey?"

I was fully awake then. At first I thought it was Kolby, coming down to say good-bye. But the voice was older, gruffer.

"Ronnie?" I croaked, sitting up and letting the blanket fall off me. It was done raining but was still gray outside, and I wasn't sure if that was because it was cloudy or because it was early.

"Jesus," Ronnie repeated, his breath expelling the word in a gush. "Oh, God."

I slid out from under the pool table and rushed to him,

wrapping my arms around his waist, which I'd never done before. Marin was constantly climbing all over her dad, but I'd always sensed a barrier there—he wasn't my father, so hugging him felt weird and awkward. Too close.

Now part of me needed to hold on to him, if for no other reason than to prove to myself that he was really standing there. It wasn't my imagination. Ronnie was real and he was standing in the basement. The tornado hadn't gotten him.

I buried my face in his chest and sobbed with relief. Ronnie rested his hands tentatively on the backs of my shoulders and at first he made shushing noises, like he used to do when Marin was a cranky infant, but after a while I was pretty sure he was crying, too.

Finally, I pulled away, rubbing my blurry eyes. Ronnie turned, his hands on his hips, and surveyed the basement, taking deep, sniffling breaths through his nose.

"Gone," he said. "Everything."

"Where were you?" I had so many things I wanted to ask and say, and I wasn't sure where to begin. "Have you heard from Mom? Is your phone working? Where are they? What are we gonna do?"

He scuffed over toward his workbench—or where his workbench used to be, as it was now covered with most of the kitchen—and kicked something metal. His curses echoed over the clanging, then he kicked something else.

I stepped forward tentatively. What had once been puddles of rainwater on the floor was now one big pool, and Ronnie was standing right in the middle of it.

"Goddamn, everything is gone!" he shouted, and crashed through a pile of broken dishes with the heel of his boot. "All of it!"

"Ronnie," I said. "Have you heard from Mom? Is she okay?"

He turned, and it was only then that I noticed how horrible he looked. Probably at least as bad as I did. Grungy, sweaty, stubble coating his chin, his hair greasy. His face was red and his nose was running right down over his top lip. His eyes were bloodshot like he hadn't had any sleep in days. Or like he'd done a lot of crying. He stared at me as if he didn't recognize me.

"No," he finally said.

"No, you haven't heard from her, or no, she's not okay? Where've you been?"

"Ah, God," he said, turning his face down to the floor and taking a few breaths. Then he looked up at me again. "You've been here alone this whole time?"

"Here and Miss Janice's," I said. "But I'm okay. I had Kolby."

This was not Ronnie the way Ronnie usually was. That Ronnie was steady, even-tempered, quiet. This Ronnie was vacant and frantic and seemed ready to bust open.

"Is there anything worth saving?" he asked. "Have you looked through?"

"Some. But no, not really." I didn't tell him about Marin's purse. He'd probably think it was unimportant, anyway. "I haven't been to the other side. With the bedrooms."

72

He rubbed one hand over his chin. "I can't...I can't..." he repeated to himself a couple times. "Do you want to look for anything? Clothes or anything?"

I thought about all the rain we'd had. How it had smelled out there yesterday afternoon, with the May sun baking a mildewy stench into everything. I couldn't imagine that anything I had would be worth saving. But still I nodded.

I followed Ronnie outside, bringing along my backpack, inside of which I'd stuffed Marin's purse.

Together, we walked around the leaning front wall of the house, to the side where our bedrooms used to be. To my surprise, two interior walls remained standing. One in Marin's room, and one in mine. Of course, the outside walls were gone, so most of our stuff was tossed and spun and pulled out and torn.

I scaled the mountain of mess to get into my room, and Ronnie walked around the interior wall to where his and Mom's room would have been. I heard some muffled exclamations, and clanks and thuds as if he was pushing or kicking or throwing things out of his way.

I pulled on some boards and tossed them, the way I'd done with Kolby the day before. I found a couple of old CDs, some clothes that had been stuffed in the back of my dresser, and—thank God—my cell phone charger. I found some old ribbons from elementary-school field competitions, but those didn't seem important to me anymore—or at least not important enough to keep. In fact, not much of anything in my room seemed all that important anymore. Not after everything that had happened.

But as I stepped over my bookshelf, which had tipped and spilled books everywhere, something shiny caught my eye. I bent to pick it up.

It was a porcelain kitten—a black-and-white one with great staring blue eyes and a big, curvy 6 across its chest. I wiped the grit off it and held it up. It was in perfect condition, which seemed impossible.

I'd had sixteen of them—one for every birthday. Each kitten was different. Each one fragile and shiny, and each holding a large number across its chest. They came in the mail, always a few days before my birthday, always in a plain manila envelope, always wrapped in the comics section of the newspaper, and with no return address.

Marin never got a single one.

Mom's mouth turned down at the corners every time one showed up, her face deepening into a bitter frown. I assumed they were from my father. Guilt gifts, I'd come to think of them. His way of pretending he hadn't abandoned me after all.

But secretly I loved those kittens, and hung on to a warm hope that maybe the kittens meant my father did care a little bit. Like maybe they were a secret message that he still wanted to be connected. That maybe he'd only meant to leave her, not me. Sometimes the kittens felt like the only connection I had to half of myself.

"I want a kitten," Marin had screeched when I'd gotten the last one. "I want a real kitten. A gray-and-white one with blue eyes. Can I get a kitten, Mommy?" My mom had rolled her eyes as, for the next two months, Marin had begged and begged for a kitten of her own.

"Ronnie's allergic," Mom had always said. "We can't afford a kitten. And they puke in the house. Who's gonna clean up the hairballs and the litter box? Not me, and certainly not you girls."

I could understand why Marin wanted a kitten of her own. I had a whole collection of them.

Carefully, I set the kitten down with the CDs, then used both hands to right the bookshelf it had once been sitting on, hoping to find the others. Instead, all I found was broken porcelain. Shiny pieces of trash. Six was the only survivor.

I heard the wooden clonk of boards being flung on top of boards over where Ronnie was, and decided I'd looked enough. I was tired and thirsty and I wanted out of there. I stumbled over a sneaker, which set me on a frantic search for its twin. I found it a few feet away, under a plastic-coated wire shelf that was normally housed in the hall bathroom. I cradled the shoes in my arms, excited for them to dry out so I could take off Ronnie's boots. Then I gathered up the clothes and the phone charger, pushed the kitten into my pocket, and headed to Ronnie.

"I'm ready," I said as I rounded the wall. "I didn't find much...."

But I trailed off when I saw my stepdad, who was squatting next to the bed—which, oddly, didn't appear to have moved an inch—his face pressed into the mattress, his hands holding something on top of it. He was crying, his whole body shaking.

I took a step forward and saw what he was holding—a framed wedding photo of him and Mom.

"Ronnie?" I said, but my heart had shriveled and fallen down into my toes. I knew. Right then I knew that my only miracle had been waking up to the word "Jesus" this morning. I knew there would be no other good news.

I knew that Mom and Marin were gone.

CHAPTER TEN

On the day of the tornado, Ronnie had been delayed at work by an irate customer who wouldn't leave until she'd had her say, no matter how ominous the sky looked. Normally, this wouldn't have bothered Ronnie too much, because he understood that when you managed a hardware chain store, you didn't ever get out at the time you were supposed to get out. You got angry customers, or guys late in returning the rental flatbeds, or indecisive women who sauntered into the store five minutes before closing and stared at the mailbox display for half an hour.

But with the sky looking so ominous, he was anxious to get the customer out of the store so he could get home. There was a storm coming, and the weather radio had been saying the possibility of tornadoes was high.

Ronnie was like everyone else in Elizabeth—he didn't get too worked up about storms. But this one felt different somehow.

Ronnie said he couldn't explain it. He felt uneasy, and like he needed to get home to me and Mom and Marin before the bad weather hit.

But he'd gotten delayed. And by the time he'd hit the highway, it was too late.

"I could see it from the road," he told me, the two of us sitting in shadows in our motel room. Neither of us had bothered to turn on the light. Neither of us would bother to turn it on for the whole next day, either. I think we were each afraid to see the other, afraid that our brokenness would become contagious if we shined light on it. "I've seen videos of tornadoes before, but, Jersey, I've never seen anything like this. It was huge. Had all these little tornadoes circling it, too. The thing was so big it looked like it could swallow the whole world."

It did, I thought. *It swallowed my whole world.* But I didn't say anything aloud. I sat on my bed, staring at the wallpaper across the room, unsure whether the design was pineapples or diamonds, and listened.

"I tried to beat it home, I really did," he said. "But it kind of veered off toward me and I had to stop the truck. Everybody was stopping their cars in the middle of the highway and running as fast as they could to the underpass. So that's where I went, too." He shifted forward, resting his elbows on his knees so that his words fell directly to the floor. "It never went over us. But I could feel it. The wind, I mean. It was so loud. And it had...I don't know...a smell to it. Like...electricity or something."

Immediately I was taken back to my spot under the pool

table, the wind roaring around me, tugging at my clothes, my hair. Like it was alive.

"I keep thinking about your mom," he said. "And Marin." And once again he was choked with sobs, as he had been off and on since I'd come up behind him in the wreckage of his bedroom. "They must have been so scared."

Rescuers had found them yesterday, not too far from where Kolby and I had been standing. Apparently, when the storm had started rolling in, Janice had decided that their building was too full of windows to be safe, and since it had no basement, everyone had rushed across the street to Fenderman's Grocery. Ronnie said he thought maybe they were hoping to get into the milk cooler.

But they didn't make it in time.

Janice and three others survived. Three of the moms had crawled out of the downed building, crying weakly for help. Janice had not yet regained consciousness. None of the little girls in Marin's class made it. Not one.

According to Ronnie, rescuers rushed to Fenderman's Grocery right away, picking through the massive bulk under the curtain of rain, until the one remaining emergency siren—the one too far on the other end of town for us to hear on our end—cranked up another tornado warning and they'd been forced to take cover. In the morning, after the sun came out and only hours before Kolby and I were trekking toward Sixth Street, a crowd of helpers—including my stepdad—fell on Fenderman's again. They found eleven employees—alive and well—wedged inside one of the walk-ins. And in the aisles heading toward the walk-ins they'd found everyone else. Including Mom and Marin, who were buried under a massive shelf of canned goods.

Marin's hands were over her ears, Ronnie said. Mom had been lying over her, trying to protect her.

I thought about all the times I'd told Marin that the storm was fine. That it was only noise. That it couldn't hurt her as long as she was inside.

I wondered if she'd remembered I'd told her those things. I wondered if she'd died feeling like I'd lied to her.

Is the noise fine, Jersey? Is it over?

Yes, Marin, you'll be fine. It's just noise.

Dance the East Coast Swing with me, Jersey! Miss Janice taught us. It's fun!

No! Go away! You're blocking the TV!

But the noise…

It's fine! Just go!

Three moms had made it out. But none of them were my mom. It seemed impossible that the same wind that had left my fragile porcelain kitten untouched could have destroyed the flesh and bone of my mother.

"Where are they now?" I asked Ronnie, closing my eyes. The stupid wallpaper design had imprinted itself into my eyelids—purple blobs against the black.

"At the morgue," he said. "I went to the hospital, but it was chaos in there. So many people. And a lot of people still missing. So I went home and you weren't there. I had no idea where you were and I thought maybe you'd gone with your mom and sister to dance class, so I went back to Fenderman's to try and find you. I didn't know what else to do."

"I was looking for them, too," I said, a big tear rolling down my cheek. In my mind flashed a thousand images. Images of my mom and me, all the fun things we did, all the times she made me feel special and loved and happy. Images of Marin, who was so sweet and innocent and who I resented for being the baby, even though I knew it wasn't her fault. She looked up to me and wanted me to accept her as a person. She wanted me to say she was cool. She wanted me to look up to her, too.

I realized that the worst part of someone you love dying suddenly isn't the saying good-bye part. It's the part where you wonder if they knew how much you loved them. It's the part where you hope you said and did enough good stuff to make up for the bad stuff. It's the part where there are no second chances, no going back, no more opportunities to tell them how you feel about them.

At some point I drifted off, and though I woke a few times to the coarse sobs of my stepdad in the bed next to mine, I slept better than I had in two days. I'd showered and changed into the clothes I'd picked up at home. I'd used the toilet and had eaten a hamburger that Ronnie had fetched for me. And it felt like forever since I had been in a bed.

But when I woke in the morning, I was no longer confused about where I was. I was no longer waking up to those blissful thirty seconds or so of forgetting about the tornado. I was aware of it from the very moment I opened my eyes. It was all I could think about.

On the third day, Ronnie was gone when I awoke. He'd left a note, along with a box of doughnuts, saying he was at the house and would be stopping by the hospital later.

There was a part of me that wished he'd asked me if I wanted to go, too, but then I decided I didn't want to go back to the house. Ever. There were too many memories there. Memories of things I knew I would never get back. I would never again listen to Mom singing along to the radio while washing dishes or hear Marin laugh over some dumb slapstick stunt on one of her favorite cartoons. I would never again put towels in that dryer or crumble hamburger in a skillet to have dinner ready after dance. Those things were gone, and I didn't want to find them.

But the hospital. Ronnie was also going to the hospital. Why hadn't he asked if I wanted to go, too? Would they let me see Mom and Marin? Would I be able to look if they did? I ached so hard to lay eyes on them, even if the thought of identifying dead bodies freaked me out, made my limbs go tingly with fear.

When my phone was fully charged, I texted Kolby.

U make it to Milton?

He answered right away. Yes. Where are you? You safe?

At motel in Prairie Valley with Ronnie.

Ur mom?

I gripped the phone against my chest, unsure if my fingers could type out the words. In the end I settled on only one: No.

There was a long silence before my phone vibrated with his response. God. I'm sorry.

Thanks. Me too, I typed back.

What are you gonna do? he asked.

It was my turn to pause. I still couldn't wrap my head around what life would be like with just Ronnie and me. It seemed like it would be so silent and depressing and impossible. I don't know, I typed.

Keep me posted ok? Let me know if you need anything.

Yep, I answered, and I knew I could. The tornado had ripped so much away from me, but I still had Kolby. I was grateful to at least have that much, to at least have someone to lean on.

Ronnie didn't come home until it was dusk outside, and I spent the entire day in bed, alternately watching news footage about the tornado and drifting off in fitful naps where I dreamed about my friends, all bloodied and battered and wondering why I hadn't died along with them.

The tornado's path was much easier to get a grip on by watching aerial coverage. They said it was nearly eight miles long and two miles wide. They said the downtown area—the area of Fenderman's Grocery and Mace Tools and Janice's Dance Studio—was hit the worst and was where most of the victims were found. They estimated more than 120 dead, and lots of people were still missing. With every minute that someone wasn't found, the prognosis looked worse and worse. If those who were still trapped didn't die from their injuries, they could die from dehydration instead.

Every few minutes victims would appear before the camera, recounting what they'd gone through. Some of them still looked shell-shocked. Others didn't appear to be taking it so seriously. Almost all of them had lost nearly everything they had.

Despite myself, I scanned the crowds behind the people on camera, hoping for a glimpse of my mom or my sister. I knew that Ronnie had seen them at Fenderman's, had pulled them out of the rubble himself, but still a part of me wanted to believe that they might have survived. That Ronnie had been in shock and he was wrong about what he'd seen. Maybe he'd found two other people who just happened to resemble Mom and Marin. Doppelgängers. Happened all the time.

I also scanned the faces for signs of Jane and Dani, especially when the news showed footage of the high school, which had been ripped nearly in two. The newscasters said the tornado appeared to have skipped right down the middle of the field house. People had left flowers and teddy bears and notes on the front lawn. But nobody said whether anyone in the high school had lived or died.

God, what would I do if Jane and Dani had died, too?

I pushed the thought away and tried instead to focus on an old sitcom rerun, but within a few minutes my mind wandered to the tragedy that was our town, and I flipped the news on again.

When Ronnie came back, he didn't say a word to me. He barged through the door, letting it slam shut behind him, and walked straight to the bathroom.

"You see them?" I asked as he passed me by, but he didn't answer. He disappeared into the bathroom and seconds later I heard the shower hiss to life.

"You see them?" I asked again when he came back out of the shower, wearing a pair of shorts I didn't recognize, but he only fell face-first onto his bed, pulled the blankets up around his ears, and within minutes was snoring.

I blinked at the TV, wondering whether I should turn it off. I hadn't eaten since the doughnuts he'd left for breakfast, and my stomach was growling.

"Ronnie?" I asked a couple of times, my voice sounding very loud in the small room, even though it felt like I was whispering. He was exhausted. Physically and emotionally. I understood, or at least I tried to. Because if I let myself think about how physically and emotionally tired I was, if I let myself feel it, I might pass out, too. I would sleep for days.

I gathered the change he'd left on the night table and got some chips out of a vending machine for dinner, then fell asleep, too.

The next day, Ronnie didn't get out of bed at all. He moaned and turned over when I said his name, then pulled the dingy blanket up to cover his head. I was running out of change, so I dug his wallet out of the pants he'd left puddled on the bathroom floor, and used his credit card to order a pizza. I saved him half, but he never got up to eat it.

For most of the afternoon, I watched TV coverage, but it was getting spottier as news crews found new tragedies to focus on. I decided to try Jane and Dani. I went down to the motel lobby and sank into the ratty couch so I could talk without having to worry about waking up Ronnie.

I dialed Jane's cell, but it rang and rang. Either the call didn't go through, or she wasn't answering. I refused to think of the third option—that it might be buried with her under our broken high school.

I hung up, then called Dani. She answered on the second ring.

"Oh my God, Jersey!" she cried. "Are you okay? Where are you?"

My stomach fluttered with relief, and immediately tears squeezed out onto my cheeks. "You're okay," I breathed, which I knew didn't answer either of her questions, but those were the only words that would come out.

"Yeah, I'm fine. It pretty much missed our house. Broke all the windows in my brother's car, though. Where are you?"

"At a motel with Ronnie. Did you see the school?"

"Yeah. It's trashed. They said there won't be any more school this year. Obviously. So it's summer break now. What a crappy way to start summer break. You hear anything from Jane?"

"No. You?"

"No. A lot of people still can't get cell service. I tried to call you, by the way, but it wouldn't go through. But everybody I've heard from seems to be pretty much the same. Freaked out. Lost all their stuff. I'm glad you guys made it through okay."

I paused, blinking rapidly. I opened my mouth, but my throat felt closed tight. *We didn't. We didn't make it through okay at all.*

"What about Kolby?"

I took a deep breath, steadied myself. "He's fine. He went to Milton. But, Dani...I have to tell you something." I paused again, unsure of how to say it. I'd never had to give anyone bad news before—not like this—and I wasn't sure how you eased into it. Instead, I blurted it out, my mouth working faster than my brain. "My mom died. And so did Marin."

There was such utter silence on the other end of the line, I could hear myself breathing into the speaker. When Dani spoke again, her voice was barely more than a whisper. "Are you serious?"

I nodded, unable to speak, even though I knew she couldn't hear me nodding, and I felt stupid, but there was nothing I could do to stop it. The words wouldn't come out.

"Oh my God, Jersey. I don't know what to say." There was a long, wrenching silence. "I'm so sorry."

"So yeah, we're in Prairie Valley right now," I said, swallowing, trying to get control of myself and get as far away from the word "died" as possible. "I don't know when we'll be back home. Our house is pretty much gone."

"I know. We drove around a little last night. My mom wanted to take pictures so she could send them to my grandma in Indiana. I guess all those houses have to be rebuilt. Is Ronnie going to rebuild yours?"

"I don't know. He isn't talking."

Dani's voice went soft. "Yeah, I guess he's pretty messed up right now. I can't believe they died. Do you know when the funerals will be?"

"No. Ronnie isn't talking. About anything. He's not even getting out of bed." I considered telling her that I'd been stealing money out of his pants so I could eat, and that I was wearing the same underwear I'd been wearing when the tornado hit, and that I was starting to get scared that he would never get out of bed and that I would starve to death or something stupid because I was too numb to think of how I could save myself. But I didn't want to worry her any more than I already had, so I let the silence sit between us again.

"Listen," she finally said. "I'd have to ask my mom, but if you need to come stay with us, at least until the funerals are over, I'm sure it would be okay with her. We don't have any power and our roof is leaking in, like, ten places, but they're going to fix it today and they're saying we might get power back by the end of the week, maybe."

Part of me wanted to jump at the chance. I wanted to tell Dani to come get me right now, wanted to hop into her car and let her mom soothe everything the way my mom would have done if she had just stayed home, if she had just skipped Marin's dance class. I would borrow Dani's clothes and be happy to wear something that smelled like fabric softener rather than sweat and rainwater, even though she was easily two sizes smaller than I was. I would eat peanut butter and jelly sandwiches, thick on the peanut butter, and drink endless sodas, even if they were warm and I had to eat by candlelight.

But I couldn't do it. I kept thinking about how much Mom loved Ronnie and how disappointed she would be in me if I left him, stinking up the bedsheets and mopping his unwashed face with the pillow, starving himself to death because he wouldn't get up to eat. Even if I'd never had a deep connection with Ronnie, Mom had loved him like mad, and I couldn't leave him, because Mom wouldn't want me to.

"Okay, thanks, I'll tell Ronnie."

"Just call me."

"I will. I should go. If you hear from Jane, let me know, okay?"

"Of course. I'm sure she's fine. You shouldn't worry."

"Yeah," I said, but how did we know? Not everyone came out of the tornado fine. I didn't come out fine at all.

"And, Jers?"

"Huh?"

"Let me know when the funerals are? I want to come."

I squeezed my eyes tighter; a tear slipped out and down one cheek. Burying my mother and my sister seemed like something I just couldn't do. I wasn't strong enough. I wanted my mom. I needed her. How depressingly ironic that the one person I needed to give me strength to face my mom's death was the one who'd died.

"I will." I hung up and sat with the phone in my lap for a few minutes, staring at the water that dripped off the bottom of the window air conditioner into a plastic tub on the floor.

"You okay?" the desk clerk asked, leaning over the counter to peer at me. She twisted her watch around on her wrist anxiously.

I nodded. "Fine." A lie. I got up and started to walk toward the door.

"It's real terrible what happened over there in Elizabeth," she said.

"Yeah."

"I'm real sorry about it."

"Thanks." I hurried out of the office as quickly as I could. I didn't want to hear anyone else tell me they were sorry. What did *I'm sorry* mean, exactly, when someone had died? Wouldn't it be much more accurate to say *I'm grateful* when someone close to you was hit by tragedy? *I'm grateful*, as in, *I'm grateful that this didn't happen to me*. At least that would be honest.

I stood outside and looked up at the sky. The day was sunny and warm again, and here, twenty miles away from home, it almost seemed like a normal day. Except on a normal day I would be in chem class right now, excited about theater club practice and the lighting cues I still had to learn. On a normal day I would be seeing Mom tonight, would be telling Marin that I was too busy, too busy, always too busy.

I gazed down the line of motel room doors. Behind one of those, Ronnie was drowning in his own grief. Behind one of them, he was alone and I was alone, only feet apart, unable to talk about the things we needed to say.

I couldn't go in there. Not yet.

Instead, I turned and walked down the sidewalk, Ronnie's credit card in my pocket.

I wandered past a strip mall, which was filled with real estate offices and computer repair shops and dry cleaners, and headed toward a big chain pharmacy a short distance away. My clothes and shoes felt coarse and gross against my skin. I gazed at all the perfect buildings, the perfect people. Why had they been spared?

I stopped at the pharmacy and filled a cart with packages of ugly underwear and socks that I normally wouldn't be caught dead in, T-shirts and flip-flops emblazoned with the logo and mascot of a high school I'd never attended, and packs of chips and cookies and cups of Easy Mac. I stood for a long time in front of the cold section, letting the refrigeration fall over me in waves, closing my eyes and soaking it up until my arms were goose bump-y and tight. After I'd bought as much as I could carry, I walked back to the motel, shopping bags looped over my arms, wondering how I was going to lure Ronnie out of bed.

What would Mom want me to do?

If Ronnie and I had been closer, maybe I would know. But Mom had always been the buffer between us, had always been the one trying to bridge a relationship where there really wasn't one.

"You can call him Dad, you know," she'd said one night not long after they got married. "He's technically your dad now."

"My dad lives in Caster City," I'd said, my bulbous ten-year-old belly sticking out under the bottom of my shirt.

"That man," my mom had said, her eyes fiery and narrow, "was never a dad. A dad doesn't just abandon his child. Ronnie would never be that kind of dad."

I knew she was right, of course. And it wasn't like I had any deep connection with my so-called dad in Caster City. Even by the time I was ten, I couldn't remember what my real father looked like. I didn't have one single memory of the two of us together. But I always kept Ronnie at a distance anyway. Maybe being abandoned by my real dad was *why* I'd always kept Ronnie at arm's distance. How many dads was I going to give the chance to hurt me?

I stood outside the room for a few seconds, key card in hand, while I took a deep, readying breath.

But when I pushed open the door, Ronnie's unmade bed was empty. The bathroom door was open, the light out—he wasn't in there, either. Relieved, I shut the door and hustled to the bathroom myself, anxious to put on some clean underwear and then eat a quiet dinner by the TV.

It wasn't until somewhere around 3 AM, when I woke to find the TV still on and Ronnie's bed still empty, that I began to wonder where he might have gone.

CHAPTER ELEVEN

Ronnie didn't return until late the next day. I squinted, sitting cross-legged on my bed playing cards, and held my hand up to shield my face from the strip of sunlight that flooded the room when he opened the door.

"Where were you?" I asked.

He let the door close behind him and turned to open the curtains. The heat of the afternoon sun blazed through the window onto my bed.

"You need to get your stuff together," he said.

I gathered the cards and dropped them into their box. He paused for a second at the foot of my bed, as if he was going to say something, the lines deep in his face and shaded by the several days' beard he had grown. There were bags under his eyes and he had a smell about him that I recognized as stale alcohol. But he only stared at the bedspread uncomfortably and then moved on toward the bathroom. I heard him unwrap a plastic cup and turn on the faucet.

"Why?" I said. "Where are we going?"

The water ran for a while longer and then he reappeared, the edges of his hair damp as if he'd splashed water on his face.

He let out a sigh. "Listen, Jersey, I don't know how to say this," he said, but then he didn't say any more. He sank down on his bed, sitting with his back to me.

"Say what?" I finally prompted, turning and letting my legs dangle over the edge of the bed. "What's going on? Is it the funerals? Are they today?"

"I don't know about the funerals. Stop asking me about the goddamn funerals." He smacked the bed, a muffled *whump*. He took another breath, wiped his face. "I can't . . . I can't even think about it," he said more softly. "I can't think about anything. The funerals. The house. You. Every day I wake up and there's all these things to do, and I can't even get my head around them."

I wanted to get up and go to him, sit next to him, wrap my arms around him and tell him how much I missed them, too. I knew it was what my mom would want, for me to comfort him and for him to comfort me, for us to be there for each other. But I stayed put, staring at his back, at his hunched shoulders and blackened elbows and the ragged hole in his T-shirt, that same invisible barrier keeping me at a distance.

"We've got to have the funerals sometime, though," I said. "We can't just let them . . . rot . . . in the morgue."

"I know what needs to be done," he said. "But it isn't that easy. I've lost everything important to me."

I slipped my big toe along the bumpy inside of my flip-flop. *Almost*, I amended for him. *I've lost* almost *everything important to me*. But I knew he'd said what he meant. He'd lost Mom and Marin—the important things. He was as stuck with me as I was with him.

"I did, too," I said instead.

He finally turned to face me. "I got hold of your grandparents. Billie and Harold Cameron."

I frowned in confusion.

"The ones down in Caster City," he added.

"I know," I said. "I know who they are." They were my father's parents, the only grandparents I had, and Ronnie knew that all too well.

Mom's parents had disowned her. In all my life, I'd never heard her talk about them unless one of us asked a specific question. But she'd talked about Billie and Harold Cameron. I don't remember ever seeing them, and I never once got a birthday card or a Christmas gift from them, but I knew who they were in a vague sort of way. I knew that Mom disliked them. She thought they were cold as reptiles, and they'd probably gotten that way by being screwed over by their own kids so many times. I knew that she'd blamed them, in part, for my father leaving us, but that she'd kind of felt sorry for them, too, because all they ever did was clean up their kids' messes and they never had any enjoyment of their own. She said they seemed depressed and jaded. Like life, and everyone in it, was out to get them.

"You told them about Mom? Why?"

He finally raised his tired, bloodshot eyes to meet mine, which made my shoulders shrink and my stomach slip. "Jersey,

I'm sorry," he said, and that was pretty much all he needed to say. I got it from just those three words.

"But why?"

He spread his hands apart, and I got some satisfaction from seeing them shake, from seeing his chin quiver and the string of saliva that connected his top tooth to his bottom lip. "I can't do it. I can't raise you alone. I never meant to..."

Call me your daughter, my mind supplied, and that right there was the reason I could never embrace Ronnie as my dad. It had nothing to do with being abandoned by my drunk father down in Caster City. It was a barrier that neither of us could acknowledge but that we both knew was there. Ronnie never intended to call me his daughter. I was simply part of the package deal he got when he married my mom.

"So they're coming up here to help you? Is that it?"

He shook his head miserably. "They're gonna take you down there."

"What? I don't want to go down there. I want to stay here. I was planning to help you rebuild. I don't need some vacation from the storm."

"It's not a visit. They're taking you to Caster City to live with them."

"Uh, no they're not," I said, standing suddenly. "No way."

"You don't have a choice."

"But why? I can help you. We can help each other. You're overwhelmed right now. We both are. But it'll get better. Besides, my friends are all up here. I can't just leave them. I need them."

"You need a mother, and I can't give you that," he said.

"Billie Cameron isn't my mother! Mom was my mother! She's gone and I'll never have another mother, and sending me off to live with strangers isn't going to change that."

"It's the only option you've got," he said.

I moved toward him, reaching for him. "No, it's not. It's not an option at all. I want to stay here. I want to stay with you. Please, Ronnie, don't make me go live with them. I don't even know them."

"I'm sorry," he said, and turned onto his side, his face smushed against the ugly bedspread. He said something else, but it was too muffled for me to make out.

I turned and looked around frantically—for what, I didn't know. I felt like I needed to do something that would show him what a bad idea this was. Something that would make him change his mind.

"Please, Ronnie, no. I don't want to go. Please," I begged, kneeling by the side of his bed, but he stayed with his face buried, spewing unintelligible noises into the polyfiber. "I'm not going!" I cried, trying to sound defiant but knowing that I had no real threat to make. I had no money, no stuff, no other family to turn to. "You can't make me do this."

Finally, Ronnie sat up and wiped his eyes. "I'm sorry," he said, calmer now. "I don't want this. But I don't want to take care of you right now. I know that sounds horrible and makes me a bad person, but I can't help it. It's how I feel. I don't know what to do with you. Except this."

"Mom would hate it." My jaw ached from being clenched so hard. "She would hate you for doing it."

"Your mother would understand."

"No, she wouldn't. She would never understand why you would send me to live with them."

"I'm sending you to someone who can take better care of you than I can. She would want that."

I stood. "She wouldn't."

"They'll be here in a few minutes, so you should get your things together," he answered.

Anxiety washed over me. A few minutes? There was no way I'd convince him this was a horrible idea in just a few minutes. Of course, he probably knew that, which was why he had waited to tell me. My mind raced, trying to think of an offer, a deal, anything I could do to change this. But I came up with nothing.

"Fine," I said, bending to gather what few items I had and stomping across the room to stuff them into my backpack. "Wait." I froze. "They're coming now? What about the funerals?"

He looked down at the floor, smashing his lips together. "I'm sorry, Jersey" was all he said. Again.

Fury engulfed me. He was *sorry*? I was going to miss the funerals because he was too selfish and cowardly to let me stay with him, and he was *sorry*? "You can't be serious. You can't actually be thinking it's okay to send me away before I get to say good-bye to my mother and my sister." At this, my voice cracked, and tears started anew. "How could you do that?"

"I don't know when the funerals are going to be. I can't even make myself go to the hospital or talk to the funeral home. I don't know where I'll get the money. We'll have a memorial...later. After I get things figured out."

"The right thing to do would be to let me help you figure

out those things, not send me away. I didn't get to say good-bye, Ronnie. I didn't get to tell them..." I pressed my lips together, unable to go on.

There was so much I hadn't gotten to tell them. So much I wanted to. So much I should have been able to.

But who was I kidding? Saying any of those things at their funerals wasn't the same as saying them to my mother and sister. They were already gone. I'd already missed my chance.

"I'm sure Billie and Harold will bring you up for it," he said.

"I can't believe you're doing this to me. I hate you," I said, and I meant it with every fiber of my body.

Ronnie slunk off to the bathroom and turned on the shower.

Desperate, I reached for my cell phone and dialed Dani.

"Hey," she said. "I was just thinking about you."

"Glad someone is," I said. "I need your help."

"What's going on?"

"He's sending me away," I cried.

"Who is? Sending you away where?"

I pressed my forehead against the wallpaper—pineapples, how weird—feeling like I couldn't breathe. "Ronnie. He's sending me to live with my grandparents in Caster City."

"No way. For how long?"

"I don't know. Forever, I think," I said. "He says he can't take care of me. Help me, Dani."

"He can't send you away forever," she said. "Can he? Is that, like, legal?"

"I don't think he cares. I mean, they're technically my family, so it probably is. But I don't want to go. You've got to help me. Let me stay with you. Ask your mom."

"She's not home. You want me to call her?"

"Yes," I said, but deep down I knew by the time she got ahold of her mom and called me back with an answer, it would be too late. They would have already come and taken me. I would be on my way to Caster City with people who were, according to my mom, cold as reptiles.

I hung up and continued to stuff things into my bag. I pulled out my Western Civ book and my math binder and threw them in the trash, keeping only *Bless the Beasts & Children* (*hint, hint, ladies and gentlemen!*) and a few pencils and pens. I rolled up the few clothes I had and crammed them inside the bag, cradling the porcelain kitten I'd brought from home. I pulled out Marin's purse, running my fingers lightly over the fake leather.

I sat with it on my lap and waited, bitterly watching the TV rerun more footage of the tornado destruction. What the news crews couldn't show was the real damage Elizabeth's monster tornado had left behind. How do you record the wreckage left in someone's heart? I pulled out a piece of gum and popped it into my mouth, then smoothed out the foil. I found a pen on the nightstand and drew a picture of a big stick figure holding a little stick figure.

Marin has a dad, I wrote beneath the picture, and then folded the foil into a tiny square and added it to the stash.

Marin has a dad.

Even in her death, she has a dad.

But I don't.

I never did.

CHAPTER TWELVE

As predicted, my grandparents arrived before Dani called back. She'd texted—Mom not picking up. Will keep trying—but it was too late to save me.

I refused to answer the knock on the door, forcing Ronnie to get up. He could send me away, but I wasn't going to make it easy for him.

We hadn't spoken since I'd told him I hated him. I didn't know if he was staying silent in an attempt to make me feel guilty, but if so, it wasn't working. If I'd been the one who'd died with Mom in the tornado, he would never have turned Marin out. He would never have sent her to live with strangers in a strange city.

He opened the door and a white-haired woman with a face as wrinkled and tan as a tree trunk stepped inside.

"She ready?" she said, talking about me rather than to me, as if I weren't sitting right there. Ronnie nodded and she turned toward me. "You got things?"

"Only a few," Ronnie interjected. "We lost everything in the storm."

"Yes, you told me on the phone," she said, no softness, no tenderness in her voice. As much as I'd gotten tired of hearing everyone tell me how sorry they were, this was worse. It was like she didn't care at all. Like she was here to pick up an unwanted couch. All business. "Harold's in the car," she said, raising her voice. "You eaten? He'd like to hit the diner on the way out."

"I'm not hungry," I muttered, forcing myself to stand up. I searched Ronnie with my eyes as I walked past him, hoping he would change his mind. I would forgive him if he let me stay. It would hurt, but I'd pretend he'd never called them. I'd try to understand. But he simply looked down at his feet and let me pass.

I followed Grandmother Billie, who didn't so much walk with me as walk determinedly ahead of me, her step as steady as a warden's. And I realized that was what this felt like— being led to a jail cell, my freedom stolen. Actually, this felt worse than prison. At least in prison, my friends could visit me. I'd already lost Mom and Marin—now I was losing Dani, Kolby, Jane, everyone I knew, everything that was familiar to me. What else could possibly be taken from me?

We approached an old, mostly rust and maroon car idling at the curb, Grandfather Harold sitting behind the wheel, squinting in the sun. He pushed a button on the dash with a fat finger, and the trunk popped open.

"You want to put your bags in?" Grandmother Billie asked, lifting the trunk lid all the way.

I shook my head, squeezing Marin's purse closer to my side. The thought of lowering the pocketbook she loved into the motor oil–scented trunk on top of a tangled snake of jumper cables felt too much like ripping out my lungs and jumping up and down on them. I opened the back door and slid inside the car, which also smelled like oil, mixed with something more organic. Grass? Skin? I couldn't tell.

Grandfather Harold lifted his chin once to acknowledge me, and my stomach clenched with fear as he put the car into drive, Grandmother Billie slamming the trunk and easing herself into the passenger seat in front of me. I didn't want to go. *Please, Ronnie*, I begged inside my head, *come out and get me. Make it like the movies, where at the last minute the girl is loved after all, and gets saved by the hero. Be the hero, Ronnie.* But our motel room door had slowly swung shut, closing the space between me and the last familiar thing in my life. He didn't even wave good-bye.

"She ain't hungry," my grandmother said, her blunt fingers working to find the seat belt as my grandfather pulled away from the curb and into traffic.

"Well, I don't s'pose she has to eat," he mumbled.

"She's just gonna sit there?"

"If that's what she wants to do. As long as she knows we ain't stopping halfway down to Joplin for anything. She don't eat, she don't eat."

"Well, we can't let her starve to death."

I chewed my lip and listened to them argue about me, as if I were invisible.

We navigated way too slowly toward the highway. If Grandfather Harold was going to insist on driving like this, we would never get to Caster City. Which would be fine with me.

I stared out the window and thought about the time Mom had taken Marin and me to Branson for an all-girls weekend. I'd watched the fields roll by, thinking that southern Missouri was so many worlds away from Elizabeth. As we passed Caster City and the landscape changed, the Ozark Mountains bursting around us, looking untouched and untamed, I had felt so far away from home.

I remembered that there had been a dead, flattened scorpion behind the curtains in our cabin and I'd freaked out, refusing to step down off the couch until Mom had checked the whole cabin over. But Marin had been fascinated by the bug.

"It's got poison?" she kept asking, and when Mom would answer, "I don't know, honey. Some scorpions are poisonous," Marin would crouch low, her butt hanging inches from the floor, her bare toes pushed into the nap of the carpet, cords of her hair dangling down past her knees, and would stare at it. A few seconds later, she would look up. "Is it the poison kind?" And Mom, checking under a couch cushion or in the linen closet, would absently repeat, "I don't know, honey."

At one point, Marin was crouched so low her nose was between her knees and I couldn't help myself. I tiptoed off the couch and snuck up behind her.

"It moved! It moved!" I shrieked, bumping her in the back with my knees and making her pitch forward.

Marin had shrieked, catching herself just short of falling

over, and had shot straight up and run out of the room, bawling her eyes out while I laughed.

"Really, Jersey, did you have to?" Mom said, exasperatedly chasing after my sister.

Marin had spent the whole rest of the weekend terrified, crying and running from every bug she saw.

Sitting in the backseat of my grandfather's car, heading toward the part of the state where I'd seen my first and only scorpion, I thought about how I'd done that to her. I'd taken away her fascination and replaced it with fear. She'd died scared of bugs, because that was how I'd shaped her.

Without thinking, I reached into her purse and pulled out another stick of gum, cramming it into my mouth with the first. I spread the foil out on my knee and drew a picture of a stick figure crouched over a little black blotch on the ground. *Marin loves scorpions*, I wrote. I liked that truth better. I folded up the foil and dropped it in with the others, then leaned my head against the window and closed my eyes so I wouldn't have to see the chain stores and strip malls fade away into the fields and farms that were to become my new reality.

Neither of my grandparents bothered to shake me awake. Instead, they relied on the slamming of their doors—*whoomp! whoomp!*—to alert me that we'd stopped. I lifted my head from the window, wiping my damp cheek on my shoulder, and blinked the parking lot into focus. My grandfather had come around the car and was standing next to my grandmother, both of them staring at the doors of a grungy-looking diner.

After a few seconds, my grandmother turned and bent to look in the car window. "You comin' in?" she said, her voice muffled by the closed window.

I didn't answer, didn't move. Wasn't sure how to do either one. So she simply nodded once and turned away. Together, they walked into the restaurant without me.

I shook my head and gave a disgusted little snort.

I didn't want to go inside. I wasn't hungry—my stomach was too tied in knots to even think about eating—and I really didn't want to have to try to make conversation over dinner with these two people. But it had been days since I'd had any sort of real meal, and I knew that now it was up to me to make sure I did things like eat and shower and sleep. Nobody else was going to care.

My grandparents were sitting at a table near the restrooms, side by side, their shoulders touching. *Who does that? *I thought. *What couple doesn't sit across from each other so they can talk?* But then I decided that I was just as happy it wouldn't be my shoulder grazing against one of theirs, and I slid into the chair across from my grandmother.

"We already ordered," she said by way of greeting, but the waitress had appeared, carrying two glasses of iced tea, which she plunked down in front of my grandparents. "Didn't think you were coming."

"That's okay, sweetie, I haven't put the order in yet. Need a menu?" the waitress asked. Something about the softness in her eyes reminded me of Mom, and I had to bite the inside of my cheek to hold myself back from crying out or flinging my arms around her waist. *Maybe in my movie, the waitress could be the hero who loves the girl after all. Save me!*

"No, that's okay," I managed. "I'll have a burger and fries. Some water."

"Sure," she said, and took off.

"Now, I don't know how your mom did things, but don't you go expecting to eat a lot of fancy dinners out," Grandfather Harold said, his voice deep and ragged, the kind of voice that would scare a little kid. Hell, the kind of voice that was already scaring me.

I didn't know how to respond. If they thought my life with Mom had been fancy after their son abandoned us, they were crazy.

"And don't be expecting any fancy dinners at home, either," Grandmother Billie said, frowning at the saltshaker, which she turned in circles between her hands. Almost like she was nervous. What did she have to be nervous about? "And you'll be cooking some of them yourself, so don't be expecting to be waited on. We run a house, not a hotel. Everyone pitches in."

"Okay," I said, my voice a squeak.

"Yes, ma'am," my grandfather corrected.

The waitress brought my water, and I picked it up and sipped it, grateful to have something to cool down my burning cheeks.

"Don't drink too much," Grandfather Harold said. Lecturing must have been his strength. "We don't plan to stop again until we get home. You got an emergency, you'll have to hold it."

I put the glass down, uncomfortable silence pressing over our table like a thick covering of fog.

The waitress brought our food. Once I started eating, I was surprised at how hungry I was, at how good hot food tasted. My grandparents dug into their matching chicken-fried steaks, shoveling gravy-drippy forkfuls into their mouths. A dollop of white gravy clung to my grandfather's bottom lip.

"We don't got that much space at our house," Grandmother Billie said after a few bites. "On account of everyone living there. We believe in taking care of family when they're in need, and unfortunately you're not the only one in need."

"Goddamn flophouse," my grandfather said, crumby spittle collecting in the corners of his mouth. He licked one side clean and I had to turn my eyes toward my plate to keep from feeling nauseous at the sight of his food-covered pink tongue slithering out between his dry lips.

"So we'll find a place for you, but it probably isn't gonna be the same kind of bedroom you had in your old house."

"'Course that bedroom's halfway to Marceline by now anyhow," my grandfather said. I wasn't sure if he was trying to make a joke or if he was just insensitive. He seemed to specialize in the latter.

"We could put her on the porch sofa for the time being," my grandmother said, turning to Grandfather Harold, her forkful of meat suspended and dripping over her lap. He didn't answer, but she didn't seem to be looking for an answer. "It gets cooler out there at night than in the house, anyways. And it's all covered," she added, "so you wouldn't need to worry about that. We'll figure out something else for you in the winter. Maybe set up a room in the basement."

"Yes, ma'am," I said, thinking that the last place I wanted to be "set up" in was a basement. The very thought of setting foot in a basement made my palms sweat.

"It's a shame what happened to your mom," Grandmother Billie said between bites. "But there's nothing to be done about it. Terrible things happen every day. To everybody, not just you."

Again I was reminded of Mom's theory that Billie and Harold were unhappy people because of the pain life had dealt them. I wondered what terrible things had happened in their lives, and if Mom was right, and they'd simply shut down to shut out the hurt. I wondered if I would end up cold as a reptile, unhappy, jaded, someday telling someone fresh in their grief that "terrible things happen every day."

We ate in silence for a while, each of us staring at our plates. I was full before I'd even gotten halfway through my burger, but still nibbled on my fries.

They tasted like the school's fries, which were the best thing in the cafeteria. Almost every day Dani and Jane and I would get a chocolate milk shake and a large order of fries to split. We'd sit the shake and the fries in the middle of the table and take turns dunking the fries into the ice cream.

People who saw us do it for the first time would always act all grossed out about it, but then they'd give it a try and next thing you knew they'd be eating fries with chocolate shakes at their tables, too. It was the sweet and salty, hot and cold together that made it perfect.

Sort of what made Dani, Jane, and me perfect together. We were all different. We complemented one another.

I missed them so much my ribs ached as I breathed. Jane didn't even know I'd left. That is, if she'd made it through the tornado okay. Would I ever find out? If Dani's mom didn't pick up her phone soon, I would be well on my way to my new life in Caster City. I tried not to think about what this meant: If I was living in Caster City, three hours away, I wouldn't be sharing fries and shakes with my two best friends anymore. I wouldn't be sitting cross-legged next to them on the edge of the stage during theater club meetings, and I wouldn't be spotlighting Dani's face as she belted out the lead lines anymore or listening to Jane practice a new piece on her violin. I wouldn't graduate with them.

I maybe wouldn't ever see them again.

It was so unfair.

"Of course, Clay will be there," Grandmother Billie said, adding to the conversation after such a long pause it took me a minute to understand what she was talking about.

Immediately, Dani and Jane were forgotten, as were my fries. "Will be where?" I asked.

"Ma'am," my grandfather reminded sternly.

"Will be where, ma'am?" I repeated.

She looked up at me, chewing, her forehead wrinkled in thought. "At the house. Like I was saying," she said.

Of course, that made sense. Clay would be at their house every now and then. He was their son, after all.

He was also my father. The father I hadn't seen in sixteen years.

"He's..." I hesitated, so many questions racing through my mind. *He's still alive? He's not in jail? He's the kind of guy who visits his mother?* "He's in Caster City?" I finally landed on.

"Of course he's in Caster City. That's where the whole family is. His sister, Terry ... his nephews ... us."

"He only ever lived up here because it's where your mother wanted to live," my grandfather remarked. My insides burned at the thought that I would, after sixteen years, finally see my father. "He was born in Waverly, about an hour thataway." He pointed out the window with his fork. "But we left that town years ago, moved on down to Caster City. Clay refused to come with us. Said love went where it needed to go. When she ruined his life, he come down to his family. Shoulda never stayed up here, to be honest."

My cell phone buzzed in my pocket. I peeked at the incoming text from Dani: Mom said she needs to talk to Ronnie. Sorry. I'll keep working on her.

I put the phone back in my pocket, my stomach twisting in knots. This was happening. I was going to Caster City with these people. I was going to see my father, after all this time. "So does he come over a lot?" My throat felt coated by French fry grease. I cleared it nervously. "Ma'am?"

"No," she said, still giving me that look, as if she expected me to know about my father's life, even though I'd never been a part of it. She set down her fork and took a sip of iced tea. "He lives there. With us. And his wife, Tonette, and their two daughters. You'll meet them all tonight."

CHAPTER THIRTEEN

Grandfather Harold was true to his word. After we left the diner, we didn't stop again until we got to Caster City. Not that I asked him to. I sat in the backseat and thought about what they'd said. I was going to meet my father today. For the first time ever, really.

It was evening when we crunched up the gravel driveway, but the days had been getting longer, so dusk was just starting to fall. I peered nervously through the windshield at the tiny house we were approaching. It was white, with falling-down shutters and a front stoop covered on three sides with wooden lattice, which had holes punctured throughout. I wondered if that was going to be my bedroom. I didn't see how I'd possibly live in such a place until winter.

Two boys who couldn't have been any older than eight burst through the front door as we settled into park. Neither of them had shirts on, and their faces were filthy. Their voices drifted through the car's open windows.

"Give it back!" one of them yelled, clobbering the other on the back of his head with a fist. "Ya turdface, ya smelly fart-wad!" They fell into mutual headlocks and spewed cusswords while rolling around on the damp ground, punching and gouging at each other.

My eyes widened in surprise. I held my breath waiting to hear Grandfather Harold's response. But if my grandparents had heard the boys, neither of them acknowledged it. At that moment, Marin seemed so very innocent to me. Like a little angel.

Grandmother Billie tugged at the hem of her shirt and the thighs of her pants, then leaned down and peered at me through her open door.

"This is it," she said. She shut her door and ambled up the walk.

Welcome home, Jersey, I thought. *This is it.*

As I opened the door and unfolded myself from the backseat, a woman stepped out on the front porch, holding a diaper-clad toddler on her hip. The baby's hair and face were as messy as those of the two boys on the ground.

"Nathan! Kyle! Cut that out!" she yelled. The baby pointed at the boys and babbled something loud and unintelligible. The woman shifted her attention to me. "You can come on up," she called.

But my body didn't want to move. My legs trembled and my arms shook under the weight of my backpack. I wasn't sure I could keep from throwing up the burger and fries that still churned in my stomach.

This was not my life. Cussing children and dirty babies whose gender I couldn't even identify and scowling grandfathers and a sofa on the porch for a bedroom and no friends, no school, no Kolby standing outside watching storm clouds roll in. And somewhere in there...my father. The man who'd abandoned me. He'd ruined Mom's relationship with her family, so that when he left, we were completely and totally alone. And without Mom, it was just me. Alone. In this place.

At that moment, I would have given anything to have Marin back, to have Marin ask me to dance with her. I would have East Coast Swung until my legs gave out. I would have hummed right along with her.

I turned my eyes upward and blinked hard, wishing I would wake up from this nightmare.

But it didn't happen.

"Come on, she don't bite," Grandfather Harold said, startling me back into reality. He tugged on one of the straps of my backpack, but I held it tight.

"I've got it," I said, and then when I felt his shadow shrivel me, added, "sir."

He paused, then grunted. "Suit yourself."

I followed him up the walk, which was cement crumbled to almost as much gravel as the driveway, past the boys, whose breathless exertion had finally drained the cusswords out of them. Instead, they lay mostly static on the ground, groaning in various wrestling holds.

"Hey," the woman said when I hit the porch, stepping back warily, as if Grandfather Harold were escorting a dangerous animal into the house. "You coulda come on up. Didn't you hear me?"

I met her gaze but didn't know what to say. Was this my father's wife? Was this the woman who'd replaced my mother? This woman in a threadbare and faded maternity top and unbrushed hair, with a bevy of foulmouthed children?

I turned my eyes to the wooden porch boards and followed my grandfather into the house, hearing the woman yell after I'd passed, "You boys, I told you to cut that out and get your butts inside the house!" The baby echoed a garbled version of the latter end of her sentence. At once I felt sorry for the kid, while at the same time grateful that this was not how I'd grown up. Except now it was going to be part of how I grew up.

Grandmother Billie was standing in the living room when we came inside. A couple of teenage girls scowled at me from the couch. The shades were drawn and the TV was on, giving the room a dark, impenetrable aura.

"She meet Terry?" my grandmother asked, talking about me in third person.

"We passed her on the way up," my grandfather answered, as if the terse, one-sided exchange could be considered an introduction.

I recalled the conversation from the diner. Grandmother Billie had mentioned my father's sister, Terry. So that woman out there was my aunt, not my stepmother. I wasn't sure whether this was good news or not. In a way, finding out that my stepmother was loud and foulmouthed would be better than continuing to wonder what she was like. There is relief in the known, even if the known is ugly.

"These here are Lexi and Meg," my grandmother said,

gesturing to the two girls on the couch, who'd gone back to watching their show and didn't even bother to look up at the mention of their names. Instantly, I was flooded with guilt. How many times had Marin felt like this, with me refusing to acknowledge her so I didn't miss some lame crap that some lame reality star was saying? "I guess they're your sisters." I pushed Marin's purse closer to my side with my elbow.

"Half," one of the girls intoned, giving me the most cursory nasty flick of her eyes.

"Well, yes, half sisters, I suppose," Grandmother Billie corrected. "Come on. I'll show you where you can sleep."

I followed her through a cluttered kitchen. Food-caked dishes clung to the sink, and the microwave door stood open. We walked out to an enclosed porch that looked over the backyard, letting a whoosh of fresh air into the stifling kitchen. Grandmother Billie held the screen door for me with one hip.

"We call this our family porch," she said. "But for right now it's yours. You can pull the shades on those screens for privacy, I suppose, but you can't lock the door to the house because it locks on the inside."

She tossed an armload of bedding onto a couch that looked a hundred years old, with big orange flowers on top of a backdrop that might once have been white but was so coated with the outdoors it appeared almost beige.

"You got any clothes?" she asked.

I shook my head. "I bought a few pairs of clean underwear at the pharmacy. I need to do some laundry."

"Well, you're a little thick to borrow from Lexi or Meg, but maybe Terry's got something you can squeeze into." She eyed me up and down, making me feel bloated and uncomfortable. "It seems to me that beggars shouldn't be choosers, anyway," she said, and I had to restrain myself from asking her what the heck she was talking about, since I hadn't said anything about not wanting to borrow Terry's clothes. She sized me up a bit more, then added, "You can get settled, and then when you're done, come on in and wash the dishes. Lexi's gonna be real happy she ain't got to double up on chores now you're here."

She left, and I sank down onto the couch, not sure what to do to "get settled." I didn't have anything to put away. I was afraid to leave everything I owned unattended, especially in this place. And the last thing I wanted to do was go back inside that kitchen and do dishes that I hadn't dirtied.

I gazed at the screen door leading out to the backyard, wondering what would happen if I walked through it and never stopped. Just headed out, walking, walking, walking. Be my own hero. Save myself.

To where, though? That was the problem. I could walk all I wanted. What I didn't have was a destination. I didn't have a home. This was it. This couch tucked away on a "family porch," whatever that was, out in the middle of nowhere, where little boys cussed like sailors and half sisters sneered at you.

Nothing like my old home, where Marin played on the swings outside and Mom sat on a lawn chair and painted her fingernails Easter colors while humming that old Spandau Ballet song she loved so much.

"Jersey, watch this!" Marin would call if I so much as came close to the back door when she was out there. She'd do something that she thought made her a daredevil—like tilt her head way back while swinging or stand up at the top of the slide or hang upside down from her knees on the trapeze bar.

"Monkey Marin," Mom would call out cheerfully, then turn to me. "Come on out, Jers. I've got robin's-egg blue." She'd hold up the bottle of fingernail polish and shake it.

"No, thanks," I'd say. "I've got homework."

But I didn't. Hardly ever was it really homework that was keeping me away. It was always something completely stupid.

I never once sat outside and watched Marin and listened to Mom hum and let her paint my nails. Not one time.

"This much is true," I whispered to myself, sitting on my grandparents' "family porch," remembering the lyrics at the end of the song. I wiped a trickle of tears off my cheek, then reached into Marin's purse.

I popped a piece of gum, unfolded the paper, and drew a picture of my sister hanging upside down from a bar, a thought bubble saying, "Watch, Jersey!" *Marin is a monkey*, I wrote. And then added: *Mom is robin's-egg blue.*

CHAPTER FOURTEEN

I heard a door slam inside the house, followed by muffled shouting—sounded like those two boys and my aunt Terry again—and hurriedly zipped Marin's purse shut. I wedged it between the back of the couch and the wall and then did the same with my backpack. I guessed that meant I was settled in.

I made my way to the kitchen sink and began washing the dishes, jumping each time someone made a sharp noise behind me—which happened every few minutes. I could hear the family convene in the living room. The volume on the television ratcheted up, my grandmother and Aunt Terry talking, occasionally barking a laugh or groaning or making loud "ooooh" sounds. These were the sounds of a home, but they weren't the sounds of my home. Nobody was asking how my day went, whether or not I had homework to do, how the spring musical was coming along, or whether I was ready for finals. There was no humming, no chirping cartoon voices in the background, no hiss of Ronnie popping open a beer. The sounds in this house didn't belong to me—they belonged to another family, one I wasn't a part of. In some ways it seemed like a lifetime ago that I'd last heard the sounds of my home. It seemed like I'd belonged to another family in a different life, a dream life, one that wasn't even real.

Nathan and Kyle ran in and out of the kitchen randomly with what seemed like endless energy.

"You've got pimples," one of them—I wasn't sure which was which—said to me, and they both burst into giggles. I ignored them, tried to feel sorry for them, which didn't work. I was too busy feeling sorry for myself.

By the time I was finished drying the dishes and opening and closing cabinets until I figured out where they all were supposed to go, I was exhausted. Instead of following the voices into the living room, I went back to my porch, looking forward to being alone and going to sleep.

So much of my life was about being alone now.

I pushed through the screen door, only to find the two girls, Lexi and Meg, sitting on the couch. I froze.

"You got any money?" the older one, the one Grandmother Billie had called Lexi, asked.

I shook my head. "I don't have anything at all," I said.

The other one, Meg, squinted her eyes at me. "You came in here with a purse and a backpack. We saw." She unwound her legs from the couch and stood up.

She was about nose-height to me, and skinny as a rail. She looked like she was maybe fourteen or so, a couple years younger than me.

"There isn't any money in those," I said, forcing my voice to come out steady, strong.

"We know you were a little rich girl," Lexi said, standing next to her sister. "Our dad told us about your mom's job and all."

I laughed. "My mom had a job, but we were far from rich. She didn't get any child sup..." I trailed off, tucking my lips in against each other. My life without Clay wasn't any of their business.

I studied their faces, looking for a resemblance. We shared blood, so in theory we should have looked alike in some way. My mom had always said I got my dad's facial structure, which was why I didn't look anything like Marin. Marin's features were a perfect combination of Mom and Ronnie. I always felt like when it came to me, they should be singing that old *Sesame Street* song: *"One of these things is not like the others."*

But I couldn't see myself in these girls, either. Their jaws were sharp where mine was soft. Their eyes were wide and blue, as opposed to my brown, narrow ones. They were skinny enough to squeeze through prison bars, where I was round and curvy. They each had a smattering of freckles across their upturned noses, which somehow made them cuter than they already were, where my face was lined around the edges with what my mom called sweat pimples. *Don't worry about them, sweetie*, she'd say whenever I'd get frustrated and call myself ugly. *Everybody gets sweat pimples. They'll go away.*

Meg tilted her head to the side. "Just so you know, we don't want you here," she said.

"And our mom and dad don't want you here, either," Lexi added. "You're only here because Granny says you've got to help family, even if they've never acted like family before. But we don't really think it's fair to have to be all sisterly just because that's what Granny believes."

I ground my teeth, concentrating on trying to look steely. "Well, I don't exactly want to be here, either," I said. "But I didn't really have a choice in the matter."

"Granny says you're a sad case because you're an orphan," Meg added, the last word sucker-punching me.

I'm not an orphan, genius, I wanted to say. *You're only an orphan if both of your parents are dead, and my dad is still alive.* But I wasn't so sure if that was true. Could someone be an emotional orphan? If so, I was an orphan all the way.

"Our dad told us about your crazy mom," Lexi said, but Meg bumped her ribs.

"We're not supposed to talk about her mom," she hissed.

My breathing went steady and deep, my fists clenching at my sides. I had my moments of being mad at Mom, sure, but something about hearing these two talk about her enraged me. *You don't know my mom*, I wanted to say. *You never will know my mom. She had more class than all of you combined.* "Well, my mom's gone now," I said. "She has nothing to do with anything anymore." Inwardly, I cursed at how shaky my voice sounded. There were so many other things I wanted to say at that moment. I wanted to remind them that Clay was still my father, as much as I didn't want him to be, and that made them my family, whether they liked it or not. Whether any of us liked it or not.

We stared each other down for what felt like forever. Inside the house, the TV blared, the children ran and cussed and knocked into things. Inside the house, the dishes were done. Inside the house, nobody cared how Lexi and Meg welcomed me.

Finally, Lexi said, "Come on, Meggie. We'll get money out of her later."

The two of them burst through the porch door and into the backyard, all the while stage-whispering names over their shoulders—a weak attempt to keep me from hearing them. *Whale. Moron. Orphan.*

I sagged onto the couch, my hands shaking so hard I had to sit on my fingers to calm them.

Not that I'd been expecting to be best friends with my half sisters, but there was no way I could live with them. If I called Ronnie and told him they'd called Mom names and said horrible things about her, he would care, right? I mean, he might not have cared about me anymore, but he loved my mom. Surely he would take me back to defend Mom.

I pulled my cell phone out of my pocket. I had another text from Dani. Still no news. Also still no Jane. Worried! I typed a message back: I hope she's ok. Call me as soon as you hear from her! I sent the message, then typed a second one: This place is awful. Half sisters from hell. Save me! I hit Send again, then scoped out an outlet where I could charge my phone later. It was my only lifeline home. I didn't want to think of how abandoned and cut off I would feel if it died.

Quickly, I dialed Ronnie's number, rehearsing in my head what I would say to him. *I know you think you can't care for me right now, Ronnie, but I can help care for you. I can help you keep Marin and Mom alive in memory. I can cook and clean for you. I won't even complain if you want to remarry.*

But he never picked up his phone, and instead I left him a voice mail. "Hi, Ronnie. I just wanted to let you know that I made it down here." I paused. "I want to come home, though. Please let me come back up. We can get through this together. Please? Call me?" I hung up, then dialed Kolby's number.

"Hey," he said, his voice sympathetic and soft, causing homesickness to rip through me. It felt like I had left years ago, not a few hours ago. It seemed impossible that it had only been a week since Kolby and I had walked home from the bus stop together. I'd borrowed his skateboard and pushed myself lazily along as we talked about how glad we were that school was almost over and the stuff we each planned to do over summer break. Neither of us would have ever dreamed we'd be doing *this.* "Everything okay? You still at the motel?"

"No," I said. "Ronnie sent me to Caster City."

"What the heck is in Caster City?" he asked. I could hear the clicking of computer keys in the background, and I could imagine him sitting back in that aloof way of his, a laptop in his lap, Googling Caster City.

I took a miserable, deep breath and let it out. "My biological father."

There was a pause. Even the keyboard clicking stopped. "I didn't know you had a biological father," he said.

"Me either. Well, I knew I had one, but I was a baby when he left."

"What's he like?"

"I don't know. I haven't seen him yet. But if his daughters are any hint, he's not so whippy."

"Whoa, wait, you have sisters?"

"Half sisters, yeah. Meg and Lexi, the personality twins," I mumbled.

"So I take it you don't like them."

"I don't like any of this," I said, feeling my voice rise, feeling my chest tighten. Why didn't Ronnie answer my call? Didn't he understand what he was doing to my life, what this stupid tornado had done to my life?

"How is Milton?" I asked, switching topics before I burst.

"Fine. Dull. But, hey, at least it's a house, right?"

I closed my eyes and nodded. He had no idea.

"My mom is happy to be with her sisters, and Tracy is happy because we've got, like, a billion girl cousins. But I'm kinda sitting around with nothing to do but play games online. And my arm hurts like hell."

"Why?"

"Remember? I cut it on some glass? Back, you know, the day after."

"Still? It's not healed yet?"

"No, it's gross, you should see it."

"No, thanks," I said, but on the inside I was thinking I would totally want to see it if only it meant I could see him, if only it meant that I could see somebody familiar and friendly. If only I could see something I recognized, something that reminded me I had a place to belong. My chest squeezed again and I feared this time I wouldn't be able to stave off the tears. "Listen, I gotta go," I said. "But call me later, okay?"

"No problem," he said. "And, Jersey?"

"Yeah?"

"Hopefully they'll come around," he said. "Your half sisters, I mean. This could be good, right? Sisters?"

I doubt it, I thought. "Yeah, definitely," I mumbled, then hung up, turned the phone off, and stuffed it back into my pocket. I pulled the blanket over my head and bawled into the dirty couch, the sobs reaching so far down into me, they came out dry.

I lay there crying until the sun set and the sky darkened and the noises coming from inside the house slowly dimmed, dimmed, dimmed until they were shut off. Soon all I could hear was the chirping of crickets and the buzzy noise of frogs out in the distance and the occasional shuffle of what I imagined to be wild animals. I wanted to get up and lock the screen door, sure I was going to be murdered on my couch by some madman or a coyote or both, but there was no lock on that door. I might as well have been sleeping right out in the backyard.

But soon I began to tune out the noises and cuddle up in my blankets so much that I felt somewhat cocooned by them. Eventually, exhaustion took over and I started to drift off.

Before I could get into a deep sleep, though, I was awakened by the crunching of gravel under car tires. I didn't even fully realize that was what I was hearing until the slams of two car doors split the air.

I sat up on the couch, hearing footsteps coming around the house, hushed voices floating over the sudden silence.

The screen door slammed open, knocking my heart practically out of my chest, and then there was a scent of alcohol, and a booming voice. "Well, I'll be a sonofabitch," it said.

I blinked and peered through the darkness, into narrow, brown eyes that matched mine.

Standing in the doorway, swaying crookedly, balanced on a pair of beat-up cowboy boots, was my father, Clay Cameron.

CHAPTER
FIFTEEN

A short woman stood behind Clay, her hands on his back as if to hold him up, a gut hanging over the top of her too-tight jeans.

"Oh, goody," she slurred, sounding as drunk as he looked. "The sperm donation is here." She giggled.

"Shut up, Tonette," he said, his words soggy. He leaned over further, his hands clutching the doorframe tight for balance. He peered at me, his head bobbing up and down and side to side, making me feel seasick. I could smell his breath all the way across the porch. "You Jersey?" he said.

I nodded, even though I wasn't sure if he could see me. "Yes."

"Your mom really did die, then, huh?"

"Yes, sir. My sister, Marin, too."

"I ain't got no daughter Marin," he said confusedly, and the woman smacked him between the shoulder blades. "Your mother lies."

"You better fuckin' not," the woman said.

"She was my half sister."

"'S real shame," he said, then stumbled across the porch, his boots so loud on the boards I wondered how his footsteps weren't waking everyone in the neighborhood. He disappeared into the house. "Real damn shame."

The woman staggered after him, swallowed up in the darkness of the kitchen, her whisper escaping before the screen door could swing all the way shut.

"... always said you wanted the bitch dead," she said, and I heard them both giggle. I sat for a while and stared out into the dark yard, the noises outside no longer even registering with me. I'd seen my father for the first time that I could remember in my entire life, and he'd been drunk. Of course. He hadn't even asked if I was okay or said he was sorry I'd lost everything. He hadn't asked one thing about the tornado, and neither had anyone else in the house. Nobody even seemed to care about it. It had devastated our town, killed our families, and they watched their TV shows and drank their booze like it was any other day.

I considered the nasty woman Tonette, talking about my mom without even knowing her. Coming in drunk on a weeknight. Giggling about someone being dead. Her shirt cut low so that her cleavage, even in the dark, was startling. She couldn't have been any more different from my mom if she'd tried. What could Clay possibly have seen in that woman that he didn't see in my mom?

I was wide awake. Sleep wasn't going to come easily, not

for me, not now. I got up and walked around to the back of the couch, digging out Marin's purse. I grabbed a stick of gum, emptying the first pack, a little startled by how quickly it had gone.

I opened up the foil, feeling guilty that I'd called her my half sister to my dad and Tonette. Mom had never allowed us to call each other anything but sisters.

"She's got a different daddy, but she's your sister. No half about it," Mom had told me when Marin was first born, a red, wrinkly squiggle of a thing wrapped up and grunting in a yellow ducky blanket.

"But Dani said that Marin's not my real sister if we've got two different daddies. She said that's what makes her a half sister."

Mom's face had darkened, a frown crinkling her brow as she bounced Marin up and down lightly in her lap. "You tell Dani what makes someone a sister isn't what's in your blood. It's what's in your heart."

Since then, I'd never called Marin a half sister, not to her face. I wasn't even sure if Marin was fully aware that we had two different fathers, though she did sometimes wonder aloud why I didn't call Ronnie "Daddy" like she did.

I sketched an oval-shaped blanket bundle with a little round head at the top of it. *Marin is my sister*, I wrote. I felt better.

I tucked the foil in with the others and pulled out the card deck. I shuffled the cards, then scootched back on the couch and began laying them out. I played Black Hole long past when my back started to feel creaky and my eyes became heavy, thinking about summer camp and Noaychjon, who taught me a ton of solitaire games so I could play even when he needed a day off.

A part of me wondered if maybe on some level Noaychjon had known that one day I'd need to know those solitaire games, because one day I would be so utterly alone.

The screen door slammed, jarring me awake. I opened my eyes to see morning sun, and Kyle and Nathan racing down the walk with backpacks on, the whole time kicking at each other and stopping to bend over and pick up rocks and sticks and other things to be used as weapons.

"You poopface!"

"You dog's butt!"

"You smelly farthole!"

I sat up, realizing when I found a card stuck to my arm that I'd fallen asleep while playing Black Hole. Some of the cards were on the floor. Others were underneath me, bent. I scooped them up, my fingers fumbling sleepily, and straightened them out as best I could, dropping them back into the box.

I stretched, then carefully opened the door and crept into the kitchen.

"I don't see why she doesn't have to go to school. Her house blew away, boo-hoo. She ain't in Elizabeth no more. She's here and she's got a house," Lexi was saying, her hip propped up against the kitchen counter while she shoved something bready into her mouth with her fingers. She made no attempt to hide that she was talking about me when I walked in.

"She ain't registered here," Grandmother Billie was saying. "And they told me not to even try it this year because school's over in a week anyways, so it's out of my hands."

I walked on through, as if I didn't hear anything, and carried my backpack to the bathroom. What business was it of theirs if I went to school or not?

I took a shower, trying to take as much time as possible, hoping the girls would be gone by the time I got out. It almost worked. They were standing by the front door waiting on my grandfather to take them to school, their things all gathered at their feet.

"It's probably good you're not going with us," Meg said, pulling a red lollipop out of her mouth and waving it at me. Her lips and tongue were candy stained. "You'd probably embarrass us anyway. Hey, Lex, ain't it perfect that her name's a cow's name?" She tapped Lexi on the forearm with her lollipop-wielding hand.

"Ew, gross, don't touch me with that thing," Lexi said, wiping her arm dramatically. "You're such a child."

"That's enough now," Grandfather Harold said, coming into the room, keys jangling in one hand. "Get yourselves to school and never mind this one."

The girls glared at me and then pushed through the front door. While I was grateful that Grandfather Harold had made them leave, I couldn't help noticing he'd called me "this one."

I hurried into the kitchen, where Grandmother Billie was sitting at the table, drinking a cup of coffee and reading a paperback novel with a picture of a half-naked man on the front, wrapped around the torso of a woman in a gauzy white gown.

"There's some dishes," she said, without looking up. And even though my stomach was rumbling and I really didn't think it was fair for me to have to do everyone else's dishes when I hadn't even eaten yet, I was afraid to say anything, so I went to the sink and started the hot water. "You get a chance to talk to my granddaughters yet?" Grandmother Billie said.

"Yes, ma'am," I said. I didn't mention them asking for money or calling me an orphan.

Her granddaughters. Clay was *their* dad. Grandmother Billie was *their* grandmother. And even though I shared the same blood, even though he was my father and she was my grandmother, too, nobody saw it that way. I was a stranger, pawned off on their family. I guessed Mom was right—family had nothing to do with blood. It had everything to do with what was in your heart. And there was nothing for me in any of the hearts in this house. The hearts that beat for me were long gone.

Just as I finished, Terry came into the kitchen and immediately began dirtying more dishes. A house this crammed with people seemed like it would never be free of dirty dishes, and I wondered if I would find myself permanently rooted to the spot in front of the sink, scrubbing and scrubbing until I wasted away to nothing. I wondered if they'd even notice that I was gone, and figured they would when the dirty dishes piled up, but that was about it.

"She don't go to school?" Terry asked on a yawn.

Grandmother Billie grunted a negative, turning the page on her bodice-ripper.

I opened a few cabinets until I found some cereal and a bowl. Ordinarily, I wasn't much of a cereal person, but today I was so ravenous I would have eaten anything, and I was too timid to search for something else. Too afraid that I'd break a rule I didn't know about.

"Mother tells me you need some clothes," Terry said as I sat down across from her at the table.

I nodded, the cereal scraping the walls of my throat as I swallowed it without chewing very well. "I need to do some laundry, too," I said.

"I've got a few things," Terry said. "I can't get into anything but my old maternity clothes, anyway. You might as well take them. After breakfast we'll go through my closet if you want."

"Thank you," I said, setting the empty bowl down.

"Clay and Tonette home yet?" Terry said, turning back to my grandmother.

"Yep, they came in last night."

Terry made a face and leaned toward me. "Never can be sure with those two. Some nights they come home; some nights they don't feel like it. Some nights they land their sorry asses in jail."

"Oh, that's only happened twice, Terry, don't be a ninny about it," my grandmother said, but Terry only raised her eyebrows at me as if to say, *See? It's bad.*

It sounded to me like not much had changed with my

father. Like he'd remained the same old drunk he'd always been. In a way I was glad he'd abandoned me and Mom.

Grandmother Billie pushed away from the table, turning down the top corner of her page. Terry stood at the same time, so I figured it was best for me to get up, too, though I wasn't quite sure what to do with myself. I wanted to watch TV but didn't feel comfortable taking it upon myself to go into the living room and turn it on. Grandmother Billie didn't make any offers or suggestions, either. Apparently when it came to doing the right thing for family, the right thing didn't mean you did anything to make family feel welcome.

"Well, the housework ain't gonna do itself," Billie said. She placed her coffee cup in the sink and I tensed. Hadn't these people ever heard of a dishwasher? She turned to me. "After you get some clothes from Terry here, you can get started on your laundry. Machine's in the basement."

She left the room, and soon after, the baby started to cry and I found myself standing alone behind the table. I took my bowl to the sink, then went back out to my porch to fold up my blankets and gather my laundry.

I decided to check in with Dani again.

Any news yet?

She responded right away. Doesn't look good.

Tell your mom I'm sleeping on a couch on a porch. Please. I'm begging.

I'll keep working on her, Dani promised.

When I dumped the laundry out onto the couch, there was a thump as something hard landed in the middle of it. I rooted through the clothes and found the source of the thump—the little porcelain kitten I'd taken from the rubble. The only thing left of my bedroom. The only remnant of my past life, other than memories. Memories I was terrified I'd forget.

Already, I was having a hard time picturing Mom's face. I sat on the clothes, clutching the kitten in my palm, and closed my eyes, trying to conjure it up. But it was difficult to do; there were so many parts of her face I hadn't studied enough. Her eyebrows—I couldn't remember her eyebrows. I couldn't remember which side of her mouth had the tooth that stuck out slightly, which side of her jaw had the little mole.

How was it that I was raised by someone, spent every day and every night with that someone, and didn't know those details about her face? How could it be going murky and fuzzy already? How long would it be before I forgot what everyone looked like?

And then it dawned on me. My phone. I had pictures on my phone. Why hadn't I thought of it before now? I grabbed it and quickly thumbed to the photo album, nearly crying out when I saw the very first picture—Dani and Jane, arms linked, standing in front of Jane's locker. They had their eyes crossed and tongues sticking out. I'd taken it just a couple days before the tornado. I flipped to the next one—Jane and me, similar pose—and to the one after that and the one after that. My friends, my theater buddies, kids from my classes, Kolby showing off a new skullcap, all of us looking so happy, like life was one big party. I touched the faces on the screen. I stared at them until my eyes blurred. Afraid to blink, afraid they'd disappear. I scrolled and scrolled, surprised by how many pictures I didn't remember taking.

And then a picture that made me freeze.

Marin's birthday dinner at Pizza Pete's. Ronnie had taken it. There was a humongous pepperoni pizza on a wooden picnic table. Mom and I were smiling for the camera, Marin making her signature funny face, her cheeks puffed with air and her fingers stretching her earlobes out.

I was flooded with a memory of the three of us—Mom, Marin, and me—standing in front of her bathroom mirror, studying our reflections. Mom had been getting ready for a date night with Ronnie, and Marin and I had wandered into the room like we always did when they were getting ready to go out, as if the party were leaving the house and we didn't know how to have fun without them.

I had lifted Marin up onto the counter so she could see the mirror, and we watched as Mom put on her makeup, occasionally lifting our chins or pooching out our lips or turning our heads appraisingly from side to side.

"You have your father's eyes," Mom had said to me out of the blue, holding her mascara brush up in the air in front of her own eye.

"I do?"

She nodded, turning back to her reflection and applying the mascara. "Sometimes when I look at you, I can see him so strongly."

I widened my eyes and peered at them. "Is that a bad thing?"

"Absolutely not. He's a very handsome man. His eyes were actually what attracted me to him in the first place." She capped the mascara and dropped it into her makeup bag, then rummaged around for something else.

"But you hate him now," I said, thinking, *How can you look at me without hating me, too?*

Mom stopped rummaging and turned my chin to face her. "I hate what he did to us. But that's not you. It never was," she said. "It's important for you to remember that. You may look like him, but you are your own wonderful person."

"Who do I look like?" Marin had piped up. She pulled her ears out and puffed air into her cheeks, making a monkey face in the mirror. Mom and I both cracked up. Mom squeezed Marin's cheeks, and the air came out with a farting sound, which made Marin laugh, too.

"You, girlfriend," Mom said, playing with the back of Marin's hair, "are the spitting image of your father. Who, by the way, is waiting on me, so I'd better finish up."

The memory was so real. It was almost as if the picture on my phone had come to life. Tears clung to my lashes. My nose had started to run and I sniffed. I didn't want to keep falling apart like this, but it seemed to keep happening without my even knowing it. Mom and Marin and I had fought so many times. That's what happens when you're family. We'd been ugly and called names. I'd stopped talking to Mom more times than I could count. I'd even told her I hated her.

But those weren't the memories that assaulted me. The memories that came to me were worse—they were the ones where we were sweet, understanding, patient, kind. They were the ones that made my heart ache, because I'd never have the chance to build another.

In some ways, those were the cruelest memories of all.

I backed out of the photo album and put my phone away. I couldn't look at those pictures anymore. I wiped my cheeks on the backs of my hands, thinking I would get up and dig out Marin's purse. I would draw a picture of her making the monkey face. I would write *Marin is the spitting image of her father.*

But before I could move, the screen door opened and out came a pair of linty socks, topped with wrinkled blue jeans, the bottom cuffs all muddy, and a bare chest. Clay, clutching a beer can and belching loudly, stepped onto the porch. He let the door slam behind him and made a racket of pulling a folding lawn chair, one-handed, from behind a stack of stuff and clattering it to the floor across from the couch.

"So you're Jersey," he said, as nonchalantly as if he were small-talking some stranger in a bar rather than meeting his daughter for the first time in sixteen years.

I sat up straighter, feeling a desire to protect myself but unsure why or how. I was suddenly embarrassed to have my underwear spilled out all over the couch, and hoped I was sitting on most of it. I was also embarrassed to be caught crying and sniffed once more, hoping it wouldn't show. Or that he'd be too hungover to notice.

"You've changed a lot," he said, and I had to resist shooting back with *Well, go figure. I don't look like an infant anymore!* "You look like your mother."

"She always said I looked like you," I mumbled, my thumb rubbing the kitten's porcelain belly.

He laughed out loud, took a swig of his beer. "Did she now?" he said. "Well, go figure. Maybe you was mine after all. Crazy woman."

"What do you mean?"

He leaned forward with his elbows on his knees. "I wasn't the only well she was drinkin' from at the time, if you know what I mean. Let's just say there have been doubts about your paternity." He overenunciated the word: "pah-ter-nit-tee."

I shifted on the couch, uncertain if I understood exactly what he was trying to say. That I wasn't his daughter? That Mom had been sleeping around? That wasn't the Mom I knew. She'd always said we'd been a family—Mom and Clay and I— that he'd walked out on a promise.

"I don't know what you're talking about," I said. "She never said anything about any of that. She was too busy trying to keep her head above water—until she met Ronnie."

He had been in the middle of taking a drink, then stopped and pointed at me with his can-holding hand, one eye squinting while he swallowed. "Now, that's one bastard I'd like to kick the shit out of," he said. "Sending you down here like you was some lost coat I forgot to bring home with me sixteen years ago. Just decides he's gonna screw with me and mine because he don't want to deal with you. So what's the story there? You a pain in the ass or something?"

Even though on the inside I didn't want to dignify his question with a response, I found my head shaking vehemently.

"No," I said. "He…" But I didn't know how to continue. I didn't have any excuse for why Ronnie had done what he had. I was still so angry at him myself.

"He didn't want you no more," Clay finished for me, and as much as I hated to admit it, that was as close to the truth as he could have gotten. Ronnie didn't want me anymore.

Clay looked out into the backyard, shaking his head ruefully. "So the way I see it," he said, "you gonna be a senior next year. And then you got your own life to get on with. I can live with puttin' you up for a year, I s'pose, as long as there ain't no shit going on. No babies, no drugs, none of that shit. But after you graduate, I reckon it's time for you to go. I ain't lookin' for no long-term reunion here, and neither is anyone else in this house." He took another drink, then crushed the can in his fist, burping under his breath. "And you need to understand, them two girls of mine are number one for me, okay? You ain't never gonna be on the same level as them. And I'm sorry if that's hard to hear, but it's just the way it is. I'm bein' honest with ya, just in case you got some big ideas about fairness. Fairness left the building sixteen years ago. Like Elvis." He chuckled at his own joke. "I feel sorry for ya and everything, because what went down wasn't your fault, but you gotta know there's such a thing as too little too late."

The door swung open and Tonette clomped through it, her toes hanging over a pair of turquoise-colored wedge heels. Her hair was damp, as if she'd showered recently, and her boobs were hanging out of a tight T-shirt with a glittery skull emblazoned across the front.

She looked at Clay and me with amusement in her eyes and handed Clay another beer, then popped one for herself.

"You're chubbier than I pictured you," she said. She gazed at me as I felt my face turn red, and then laughed as if it were the funniest thing she'd ever said, her lips wet with beer and lip gloss.

"I'm not fat," I said, trying not to sound as snippy as I felt. I turned my gaze back down to my hands, rubbing the smooth stomach of the kitten with both thumbs now.

"Don't get all boo-hoo about it," she said. "We can't all be supermodels. Besides, Clay says your mama was kinda beefy, so it makes sense."

I glared at her.

Clay noticed the kitten in my hand. "What you got there?" he asked, and my first inclination was to hide it. I balled it up in my fist, covering it, which was dumb, since he obviously knew it was there.

He held out his hand. Slowly, I leaned over and handed it to him, waiting for recognition to register on his face.

He turned the kitten over and looked at it. "Six?" he said. "What's that mean?"

"Six years old," I said, not understanding how he could not know.

He snorted again and placed the kitten in Tonette's outstretched hand. "You six years old now?" he asked.

"It's the only one I could find. The others were all shattered," I said.

"Other what?"

"Cats, stupid," Tonette said, thumping his biceps with the hand that was still holding my kitten. "She musta had a collection." She handed the kitten back to me.

"I did," I said. Confusion etched itself across my heart. "You sent them to me on my birthday every year."

Clay raised one eyebrow. "I did?"

Tonette looked from him to me and back again, frowning like if he had been sending me gifts for my birthday, it had been a personal betrayal against her. "You did?" she echoed.

"No, I didn't," he said, to her rather than to me.

For a moment, I thought maybe he was putting on an act to keep Tonette from getting mad. Maybe he'd had to send them on the sly so Tonette wouldn't know about them, and to admit to it now would mean admitting to sixteen years' worth of betrayal. I sat there uncomfortably, afraid to say any more.

"I didn't send you those," he said, pointing at the kitten. "Your mama probably gave them to you and just said I did."

"But I got them in the mail," I said. "I opened them up myself. In front of Mom."

"Maybe they come from a secret admirer," he said, "'cause they sure as hell didn't come from me. Hell, maybe they came from your real dad."

"You are my real dad," I muttered, but doubt began to needle at me. Could Clay have been right about my mom? Did she have... others? Did I belong to one of them?

Of course not, I told myself. Why would I believe anything that came out of this liar's mouth, especially when it came to Mom? He didn't know her.

Or at least one of us didn't.

"Well, whoever give it to you, you better put it away tight. If Terry's boys get hold of it, they'll use it for batting practice," Tonette said.

Again, I tucked the kitten into my palm, which was sweaty now. "Yes, ma'am," I said.

The screen door opened again and Terry poked her head out. She had the baby on one hip, his T-shirt adhered to his chest with drool, a Cheerio stuck to his chin.

"You comin' or what?" she asked me.

I stood up and started cramming my things into my backpack, zipping the kitten into a small pocket in the front, hoping it would be safe there.

"Back off, Terry, can't you see I'm bonding with my long-lost daughter here?" Clay shot at her, and then he and Tonette both cracked up, Tonette's belly bouncing against the fabric of her shirt, both of them swigging beer.

I swung my backpack full of clothes over one shoulder and headed toward my aunt, leaving Tonette and Clay on the porch, glad to be taking my valuables with me.

I had a feeling Terry's boys were the least of my worries here.

CHAPTER SIXTEEN

"I feel for your mama," Terry said, holding a pair of jean shorts—mom shorts—up for inspection. She was standing in front of her open closet and tossing shirts and shorts to where I sat on the bed. I definitely wasn't going to be in style, but at least I'd be able to change my clothes. Finally. "Taking care of kids by yourself is no picnic. The idea of something happening to me and leaving the boys alone with no mama is one of my biggest fears."

I tilted my face down. I wondered if that was one of Mom's fears, too. Had she ever been able to guess that, if something were to happen to her, Ronnie wouldn't be there for me?

"I guess at least you got Clay, for whatever that's worth," Terry said, shrugging.

"Clay says he's not my real father," I blurted.

She waved her hand at me. "Don't listen to him. That's what he says when he tries to make himself feel better about how everything went down. It's the party line around here. Your grandfather is fond of reminding Clay that it's possible he's not. But that's just who Harold is. Never believes anything for sure until he sees it himself. He's the skeptical type. Of course Clay's your father."

"And if he isn't?" I asked, taking a tank top that Terry was holding up against my torso.

"Well, at least you got a place to stay," she said.

But would that be enough? Because at the moment it felt like it could never be enough. People needed more than a place to stay, more than a porch to sleep on. They needed a home, right? They needed love.

"I miss my mom," I said, barely able to croak out the words. I missed her so much, and saying it aloud only made it feel like a piece of me had fallen away. "I didn't get to say good-bye."

She gave me a sympathetic look. "We got to be pretty good friends when she was married to Clay," she said. "You know that?" I shook my head and she nodded, tossing a T-shirt at me. "I never understood how someone like her got mixed up with someone like him in the first place. She was sweet. And real smart."

She tossed a few more items across the bed and told me to try them on in the bathroom, to bring back the things that didn't fit. But I didn't want to leave. For the first time since Kolby went to Milton, I felt like I had an ally, someone who cared.

"Will you take me to her funeral?" I asked before my brain could catch up with my mouth.

She looked surprised. "They didn't have the funerals yet?" she asked.

I shook my head. "I tried to call my stepdad last night to find out when they are, though. When I know for sure, will you take me?"

She chewed on her lip and looked over at Jimmy's crib, as if the thought of driving three hours north to Elizabeth was frightening for her. As if it would somehow be bad for Jimmy. But after a few seconds, she nodded.

"I'll have to make sure Mother will watch Nathan and Kyle," she said, almost to herself. "But, yeah. I will. You should get a chance to say good-bye at least. It's not right that he sent you here without that much."

I had to restrain myself from throwing my arms around her. I practically floated out of the room. I tried on everything, not even caring that most of her clothes looked so out of style I would have been mortified to wear them in front of my friends.

I gathered all my new clothes and headed down to the basement, where the rickety washer and dryer gathered cobwebs in the far corner.

I'd never been fond of basements, and being stuck in one by myself when the deadliest tornado in forty years ripped through my house didn't help matters much at all. But I was still on a high from my conversation with Terry, and besides, the basement was preferable to the rest of the house, where I might run across Grandmother Billie, who mostly sat in front of the TV all day eating popcorn from a green plastic bowl, or

Clay and Tonette, who alternately clanked around under the hood of an old car in the driveway and fought in the kitchen.

I was almost done folding my small load of laundry when I heard Nathan and Kyle burst into the house on a wave of fighting, followed by the whiny, animated voices of my half sisters. I listened for a while, trying to make out conversations, folding more and more slowly as I neared the bottom of the dryer. I stacked everything in the laundry basket and was about to carry it upstairs when suddenly the single lightbulb flickered out.

At first I froze, the basket pressed against my hip. Almost immediately, I felt panic rise in me, the sound of tornado sirens echoing against the walls of my brain. I could hear wind batting against the smudged, filthy windows and flinched, expecting the next gust, or the one after that, to be the one that sent glass flying or sent the roof flying or sent me flying.

I took a deep breath and swallowed, trying not to let my imagination get away with me, trying not to let my heart jump into my throat, trying not to panic. After all, it's not like a light going out in the basement is a big deal. Happens all the time. Not every dim basement means a tornado is coming.

I set the basket down and headed for the stairs, my hands out in front of me. I'd go upstairs and ask Grandmother Billie where she kept the lightbulbs. I'd replace it myself, so next time I had to do laundry I'd know it was fresh. She'd probably be thrilled to give me an extra chore.

But when I got to the top of the stairs, the door wouldn't open.

"Hello?" I said. I tried the handle again. It turned, but the door didn't budge. "Hello?" I repeated, louder, and then knocked on the door. I thought I heard movement on the other side. Or was that the muffled chug of a storm coming?

I groped around on the walls for the light switch but couldn't find it, then remembered that the switch was on the kitchen wall outside the basement door. The lightbulb hadn't gone out; someone had turned it out.

"Hello?" I said again, this time my voice close to a yell. I felt electricity in the air, and a cottony feeling in my ears, as if they were going to pop. I couldn't tell if it was my imagination, but I didn't care—in my mind, I was right back in the eye of a storm that would surely destroy me. I pounded on the door. "Is someone there?"

This time, I was sure I heard someone on the other side. Giggling. I turned the handle and pushed again, then pushed harder. The door started to open, then squeezed shut, as if someone was putting their weight against it.

"Lexi? Meg? Come on, let me out!" I yelled. My heart raced as my eyes refused to adjust to the darkness. What if it wasn't one of them, but was a chair or something wedged under the doorknob? "Let me out!" I yelled again.

I turned the knob and pushed harder. The door popped open about an inch and then slammed shut again. Sirens blared in my head, swooping up and down, up and down, making me dizzy and nauseous. "Let me out!"

The sun ducked behind a cloud and the basement darkened, even as my eyes tried to adjust. Panic made my skin tingle. I put my shoulder against the door and shoved with all my might, and it finally gave, kitchen light bathing my face. The door swung open with such force the doorknob embedded itself in the wall, the crash reverberating through the house.

Lexi stood by the stove, her hand over her mouth. She looked like she'd been laughing but was now staring at me as I stood at the top of the basement stairs, breathless, my arms stretched out at my sides. Meg, standing nearby, looked incredulous, her mouth hanging open and her eyes wide.

Lexi and I stared at each other for a moment. And then everyone in the house, it seemed, dropped what they were doing and came running. Tonette got there first, with Clay right behind her.

"What the hell happened?" he demanded of Lexi, but Lexi simply pointed at me, one hand still hovering over her mouth. He turned to me, his face red with anger. "What's going on here?"

"They wouldn't let me out," I said, my voice sounding shrill and whiny. "They turned out the light."

Grandmother Billie rushed in and stood between us, looking back and forth as if ready to punish but unsure who to dole out the punishment to, followed by Harold, who immediately went to the door. He pulled it away from the wall.

"Hole in the damn wall," he said, and Billie hurried over to see the damage. "Right through the damn wallpaper."

"I didn't mean to," I said. "I was scared. It was dark down there."

Tonette rolled her eyes. "You're scared of the dark? What are you, five?"

"No," I said. "The tornado…"

"Oh, here we go with the tornado stuff. Fan-freakin-tastic, Clay," Tonette said, "your kid's got baggage."

"Why are you yelling at me?" he said, his voice high, his shoulders shrugged, and his hands spread out.

"I'm sorry," I said to my father, who was glaring at me. "It was their fault for shutting me down there."

"We were playing a trick is all," Lexi said, and her innocent act made me sick to my stomach.

Clay looked from Lexi to me and back again, his hands balled at his sides. He breathed slowly through flared nostrils.

"You gonna hafta fix this wall now, Clay," Grandfather Harold said, and I withered under the glare I could feel coming from him and Grandmother Billie. Grandfather Harold surveyed the kitchen. "Gonna have to replace the wallpaper in the whole damn room, I guess."

"Always something in this place," my grandmother said, and scurried off, as if the tension in the room was too much for her.

Finally, Clay pursed his lips so tight they became white. He turned his face up to the ceiling and cursed. "Sonofabitch!" He seemed to struggle against indecision for a few seconds, his body twitching to go one way and then another, and then he let loose and stomped away.

I hated that Lexi and Meg were watching me cower under Clay's rage. But when I turned my eyes to them, they almost looked frightened, too. I wondered if they'd had to endure moments like this themselves. I wondered if that was why they were so relentlessly trying to draw me into some sort of fight. Did they really hate me, or did they want to use me to deflect Clay's attention off them?

"Nice going, orphan," Meg said with a smirk.

I didn't bother to answer, just left, forgetting about my laundry, which was still down in the basement. Forgetting about Meg and Lexi and the hole in the wall and my grandfather, who still stood, pressing his dry, blunt fingertips against it. Forgetting about everything but getting away.

CHAPTER SEVENTEEN

I stormed onto the porch and pulled my backpack from behind the couch. My hands were shaking, and I still could hear the faintest ring of a siren in the back of my mind. I hated myself for letting them get to me. I hated myself for being scared. But mostly I hated being here. I wanted out.

I dug out my cell phone and called Ronnie's number. He didn't answer. I waited for voice mail.

"Ronnie," I said, and as if someone had punched me in the gut, suddenly I couldn't breathe. It was like when Marin was a baby and she'd fall down and hurt herself. You knew it was bad by how she cried. If she cried right away, it was nothing and you could probably ignore that it ever happened and she'd get up and toddle along on her merry way. But if there was a pause—especially a long pause—you knew it was bad because the tears had plugged up her throat. When she breathed again, you had to cover your ears. You knew she was going to let out a wallop of a cry. My throat felt plugged up like that, and I had to wait until my lungs would move again before I could finish my message. "Ronnie," I begged. "Please. Please let me come back. They hate me here. They're mean and they want me gone and I'm scared. Please, Ronnie. Mom wouldn't want me here. She would want me with you. Please at least let me come up for the funerals. Tell me when they are. I've got a ride. You don't even have to come get me."

The voice mail beeped that I had exceeded my time limit. I thought about calling again. And again and again, leaving the same message over and over, begging until he relented, the way Marin used to do sometimes. Ronnie always gave in to her. Maybe he would give in to me, too. Maybe he would find it in his heart to let me have my way, even if only just this once.

But instead of calling Ronnie again, I decided to call Dani.

"Hey, Jers, what's up?"

I sniffled, wanting to sound happy and excited to be talking to her, too, but hearing her voice only made the tears keep coming. She sounded normal, like her life was normal. It was unfair, and I missed her, and I wanted my life to be normal, too. "Hi," I said.

"You okay? You don't sound good."

"I'm not good."

"What's wrong?"

"I hate it here. I want to come home." I knew how ridiculous that sounded—there was no home to come to.

"Is it really bad?" she asked.

I told her about Meg and Lexi, about Clay's claims that he wasn't really my father, about Tonette saying I was fat, and about the girls shutting me in the basement. "I keep trying to call Ronnie, but he won't answer his phone," I said. "Did you ask your mom about letting me stay with you?"

Dani paused, and I knew her well enough to know that she was probably twisting the end of her auburn hair around two fingers nervously, her brow furrowed, her top two teeth sunk into her bottom lip while she tried to figure out how best to break bad news to me. "She talked to Ronnie," she said. "Jers, he's in bad shape. Mom said he's a total mess and that the whole thing is really sad but she can't get involved because she's not related to you and she doesn't want to get into some sort of custody issue. She said it would probably take some time and you would be homesick, but that you would get over it, and that living with your real dad is probably the best place for you to be right now."

"She doesn't know him," I said angrily. "He's a disgusting alcoholic. And he's mean. He yells at me and his face gets really red when he's mad and I'm scared of him. I'm scared of what he'll do next. Tell her that. Tell her I'm sleeping outside and that I hear coyotes out here all night long and that nobody is going to fight for custody, because nobody wants me. Especially not here."

"Maybe it's not as bad as you think it is," she said. She sounded uncomfortable, as if she were reaching for excuses. "I mean, I know it hurts to be called names, but it's not like you're in any sort of danger."

"You don't understand," I said bitterly. "You don't have to live on a porch. You..." I didn't finish. *You have a mom.*

"I know. You're right. I'm sorry, Jers, I really am. Maybe she'll change her mind. I'll keep asking."

"Thanks," I said. "Do you have power back?"

"We got ours back last night. Which was good, because our phones were dead. But a lot of people still don't have service. Who knows how long it'll be before they get all the towers working? We've got air-conditioning again, thank God, because it felt like it was about ninety today. But they're saying it'll be another week, probably, before they get everyone else's power on. Not that it really matters on the south side of town. Electricity is kind of useless when you don't have a house to put it in, you know?"

I thought about our house. About Ronnie building it up again. And living in it alone.

"Have you heard from Jane yet?"

"Uh-uh. But I heard from Josie Maitlin that Jane's house was totally destroyed, like yours. Josie didn't know for sure, but she thought maybe Jane went up to Kansas City to stay with family."

I sagged with relief. Generally speaking, Josie Maitlin was an endless source of toxic gossip, but for once her report passed on good news. Jane had made it through the tornado alive. "And she's okay?" I asked.

"Josie said she thought she heard that Jane got hurt, but she didn't know for sure. Nobody really knows anything about anybody right now. We're all going on what we hear. Some people have been meeting up at the library, because it's got power and computers and stuff. I saw a couple kids from theater club there yesterday. It was a real cry-fest."

I felt a pang in my chest. I wanted to be there so badly. Dani's mom was wrong—those were the people I needed most right now, not mean, drunk Clay Cameron.

We talked a little more, the mosquitoes coming out and pestering me as it got closer to evening. I was hungry, and I wondered if I'd be welcome inside for dinner with everyone else, or if they were all still pissed at me.

Finally, Dani had to go, but before we hung up, she said, "One more thing."

"Yeah?"

She paused, and then said, "You're not gonna like this."

"Just tell me."

"Okay. So...my mom said Ronnie told her it would be too hard on you to come to the funerals. He said he doesn't want to cause you any more pain."

Anger hissed through me. "Like he hasn't already caused enough? Does he really think I'm not going to feel any pain if I don't go to the funerals? Like, what? I'll forget they're dead?"

"I don't know," she said. "My mom tried to tell him how messed up it would be for you not to be there, but he said you've been through enough already and he wasn't going to change his mind about it."

"Well, too bad for him," I said. "I've got a ride and he can't keep me from showing up. When are they?"

There was such a long pause, I didn't even need Dani to answer. I knew, deep down, what she was going to say. But when she did speak again, her words still punched me in the chest, gutted me. "They were this afternoon."

She kept talking—saying something about the flowers and

157

the crowd and who knew what else, but I had tuned her out completely. Mom and Marin were gone, buried, and I hadn't been there to say good-bye.

"You there? Jers? I'm really sorry. I wanted to tell you, but my mom wouldn't let me. She said it wasn't our place."

I pressed my fingers against my temple. "I should probably go," I mumbled, trying to understand how my best friend could keep this from me, regardless of "place." What was "place" when it came to dead mothers, anyway? Nothing. "Place" was being there for your friend.

"So I'll call you if anything changes with Mom?" Dani said.

"Yeah," I said through numb lips. "But I don't know how long it will be before my phone's shut off. Nobody here is going to pay the bill, that's for sure."

"Don't worry, Jers, it will all work out somehow. It has to, right?"

I wasn't sure if she was talking about the phone bill or the missed funerals or my mom or what, so I just agreed and hung up, feeling myself shut down bit by broken bit.

Before I put the phone away, I called Jane, but, as usual, she didn't answer.

"Hey, Janie, it's Jersey," I said to her voice mail. "I thought you should know that I'm okay, but I'm living down in Caster City with my father. My mom and Marin died in the tornado and my stepdad is a real mess. I heard you're in Kansas City. I also heard that you might have gotten hurt. I hope you're okay. Give me a call as soon as you can. I don't know how much longer I'll have a phone. I miss you."

I hung up, hoping she would call me back before it was too late. Suddenly it seemed as if this would be the fate of every connection I'd ever had—that I wouldn't get a chance to say good-bye. They'd wonder how I was doing at first, but after a while they'd stop thinking about me as much. They'd move on. And eventually they'd forget me altogether. Out of sight, out of mind. It was one thing to lose the people you love. That happens to everybody.

But it was another thing to lose them because you just... faded away.

I didn't want to fade away.

I started to put my phone in my backpack but decided that if I was going to drop off the radar, I wanted to talk to Kolby once more. To thank him for being there when I had nothing. Or maybe simply to hear his voice. I missed him.

I dialed.

"Hello?"

I blinked. I had been expecting Kolby's voice but was greeted instead by his little sister.

"Tracy?"

"Yeah? Who is this?"

"It's Jersey. Is Kolby there?"

"No."

"Oh. You know when he'll be back?"

There was some clicking, and muffled noises of movement. I thought I could hear her mother's voice getting softer and fading into the background, and then I could hear Tracy breathing into the phone. Finally, she said, "No, he's in the hospital right now."

That was not at all what I'd been expecting to hear. "What? Why? What happened?"

"It's not really a big deal or anything, I don't think, but he's got some kind of infection on his arm. Where he got cut. The doctors said something about it being a fungus and they're just wanting to be safe. It's really gross-looking."

I remembered how I'd tried to wrap his arm with that bandanna, to keep the wound clean, and immediately I felt guilty. I'd been calling to thank him for taking care of me those first couple days, and here he was in the hospital because I hadn't taken good enough care of him.

"Is he going to be okay?" I asked.

"Yeah, you know Kolby," she said. "I'm sure he'll be fine."

"Okay," I said. "I'll call back. Tell him I said I hope he gets better soon."

"Okay, Jersey."

I hung up, thinking about how randomly we'd all been affected by the tornado. I'd lost everything. Jane was missing. Kolby was in the hospital. Dani was totally fine. It didn't make sense.

I dropped the phone into Marin's purse and pulled out a piece of gum. I chewed it, the flash of flavor making my mouth water, and thought about all the times I'd called Marin a nuisance, had made her feel unwelcome and unwanted, the same way I was feeling now. Not being wanted was the loneliest feeling in the world, it seemed, and if I could have had one more moment with Marin, I would have been sure to tell her I didn't mean it. She wasn't a pest. I loved her. She was wanted. More than she could ever know.

I didn't have a picture to draw on this piece of foil. Only a message, so I wrote it in careful bubble letters: *Marin is not a nuisance.*

I folded the foil and stashed it in the zippered compartment, liking the way the pieces bounced against one another in the open pocket, glinting at me happily.

Unsure of what to do next, I pulled out Mom's lipstick, rolled it all the way to the top, and smelled it. The waxy scent reminded me of Mom, who had given the lipstick to Marin one night out of the blue.

"Marin," she'd said, holding out the little tube in the palm of her hand. "I don't think this color really works for me. Would you like it?"

I didn't wear lipstick and my mother knew that. But Marin lived to squish makeup onto her face. Anything to make her feel more grown up, more like Mom.

Marin, who had been sitting on the other end of the sofa, sat up, her thumb popping wetly out of her mouth as her eyes grew wide.

"Yes!" she gasped, and stampeded over me with her hand outstretched. Mom had placed the lipstick gently in her hand and admonished her, "Only around the house, okay?"

"Okay, Mama," Marin had responded, pulling the lid off the lipstick and peering down into the tube earnestly. "It's for special only."

She'd run off and put it in her purse. She'd never worn it. Not one time. Marin, who loved lipstick like nothing else. She'd kept it special, like she'd promised.

Once I asked her why she didn't ever wear it.

"It's for special," she'd replied. "I like it sharp."

I knew what she'd meant. She liked the way the lipstick angled up into a tip. She liked how new it was.

I spread some on my lips and pushed them together, smearing it around. Then I capped it quickly, afraid that if I left it open too long I would lose the scent of my mom forever. With her face already receding from my memory, I couldn't afford to lose any more pieces of her. I licked my lips, liking the way the wax felt smooth against my tongue, liking the way it tasted.

'I dug around a bit more, then picked up the playing cards, spreading them out to play a quick couple games of Chameleon.

I played until the house was dark, except for the blue of the constantly running television flickering onto the porch from the living room. I stashed Marin's purse and went inside.

As quietly as I could, I tiptoed to the bathroom, hoping to go unnoticed. But as I passed the living room on my way back, Grandmother Billie's voice cut through the recorded laugh track of whatever sitcom she was watching.

"I don't know if you think you're gettin' outta doin' those dishes tonight because of that scene with the door, but you're not," she said.

With a sigh, I went into the kitchen and bellied up to the sink, which was positively overflowing with dishes. They must have had a feast. I filled the sink with water and started scrubbing, hearing Marin's little voice in my head, singing the song she always sang in the bath. *"B is for bubble. Bubble, bubble, bubble..."*

I made a mental note to draw that on gum foil later. I didn't want to forget the bubble song.

When I was done, I opened the fridge and took inventory. I had no idea what dinner had been, but whatever it was, there were no leftovers. Instead, I made myself a sandwich and cut up a few slices of cucumber. I didn't know if the ingredients were spoken for, but I figured they couldn't starve me. If nobody was going to take care of me, I would have to take care of myself and live with the consequences.

As I sat down with my food, I heard the sound of footsteps on the wooden basement stairs. Aunt Terry appeared at the top of the steps, holding the laundry basket I'd left behind earlier in the day. She extended her arms toward me.

"I brought your laundry up," she said, setting the basket on the table next to me.

I swallowed. "Thank you."

"I heard what happened this afternoon." She pulled out a chair and sat down. "Clay's all upset because he's got to do a little work. It'll be good for him."

I wiped my mouth on the back of my hand and set the sandwich on my plate. "I just wanted out of the basement. I kind of freaked. It's stupid, I know."

Terry waved her hand. "It's not stupid. I get it. Listen, don't take what they say to heart." She ran her fingernail along the side of the basket, tracing the squares. "Lexi and Meg. They're just jealous of you."

"Jealous? Of me?" What did I have that they could possibly be jealous of? They were prettier, they had a mom and dad, and from what I could tell, they had everyone in the house—except for maybe Terry—eating out of the palms of their pretty little hands.

"Maybe I should've said they're threatened by you. They think you're gonna steal their daddy."

I took a breath. "I feel like nobody wants me here."

"They don't," she said. "But maybe they'll come around. You never know. Weirder things have happened."

But something told me that wasn't going to happen. Even if Lexi and Meg found a way to completely ignore that I existed, they would never "come around." Not really. If I was looking for friendship, I was in the wrong place.

"I should probably get myself to bed," Terry said, pushing up from the table with a grunt. "Hey, did you ever find out about the funerals? Are they sometime soon?"

I shook my head. "I missed them."

She froze, and I nearly melted under her sad gaze. "Oh," she said. "I'm so sorry." And then, seemingly struggling with what else to say, she gave up and disappeared down the hall toward her bedroom.

I ate my sandwich in silence, hating how it seemed like everything in my life suddenly could be summed up by that one sentence: "Oh, I'm so sorry."

After I finished eating, I washed my plate and changed into a pair of Terry's pajamas, then went back outside, staying on the porch like the family dog. The air felt crisp and cool, summer night air, and I rolled all of my new clean clothes into tight rolls and slipped them, one by one, into the backpack, which I shoved into its spot behind the couch with Marin's purse.

I curled up in my blanket and listened to the night sounds around me—crickets and frogs and cicadas and barking dogs—and tried not to think about this being my new reality, even while I knew it was.

Nobody was coming to rescue me. Nobody was going to keep me safe. It was all up to me now.

CHAPTER EIGHTEEN

Over the next few weeks, I slipped into a routine at my grandparents' house. Get up, sneak to the shower, get dressed, wash the morning dishes, eat. Go outside, fold my bedding, play cards, think about Mom and Marin, and lie as low as possible until night fell, hoping nobody would bother me once I was asleep.

Ignore my half sisters.

Ignore my father and stepmother.

Ignore the grunts and orders of my grandparents.

Ignore, ignore, ignore.

I wrote a bunch of new foils.

Marin's hair bounces when she runs.

I call Marin "Tippy" because she walks on her tiptoes.

Marin knows everything there is to know about dolphins.

Marin's eyes sparkle when she dances.

Marin is a princess in orange-and-black velvet.

Marin sings in the bath.

Marin likes red Popsicles the best.
Marin can roller-skate.
Marin's eyelashes are so long.

For every foil, there was a memory, so sweet and so clear I thought my heart might break in two. Not saying good-bye to them messed with me, made me mentally curl in on myself, made me pull away. I stopped checking my phone for texts. I stopped calling Dani. I stopped caring what happened to Ronnie or to anyone who wasn't me. In my mind, even Ronnie wasn't grieving as hard as I was, because he at least got to go to the funerals and I hadn't even gotten that much.

Instead, I owned my grief. Turned it into something physical and ugly and carried it around in my gut.

"Hey," I heard one morning while I sat on my couch, staring at the world sullenly through the wet ends of my hair. I picked at the dry skin on my heels, softened by the shower, and zoned out, the tiny squares of the porch screen getting bigger and bigger under my gaze. Aunt Terry stepped out onto the porch, sat in the lawn chair Clay had pulled out that first night and nobody had bothered to put back. "I haven't talked to you in days. You okay?"

I tore my gaze away from the yard and blinked, her face shaded in purple where the light had been in my eyes a few moments before. "Not really," I said.

"You seen your dad lately?"

I shook my head. I'd been avoiding him, and especially Tonette, ever since she'd screamed at me for "taking the last burger" the one night I tried to eat dinner with the family.

"You didn't even think other people might want to eat, did you?" she'd yelled.

Why would I? I wanted to respond. *Who is thinking about me? Who is making sure I get anything?*

"Has he checked on you at all?" Terry asked, referring to Clay.

"No, but I kind of like it that way," I said. "When he's checking on me, he's yelling at me. Tonette, too."

I half expected Terry to argue about it, to tell me that yelling was Tonette's way or that Clay was the kind of guy who didn't show his feelings, or maybe worst of all, to say the same thing Dani's mom had said, that this would take time. But she didn't say any of those things. Because she knew I was right.

"You need a mama," she finally said, very quietly.

I shrugged, numb, and pulled a hunk of dead skin off my heel, letting it drop to the peeling wood floor. Yes, I did need a mama. But my mama was gone. And nobody else could stand in. The end. "Whatever," I said. "Doesn't matter."

"I can't be your mama, you understand. I can't even take care of my own kids most of the time," Terry added.

"I know."

"And Billie ain't a good mama, take my word for that."

I didn't need to take her word for it. I'd already seen what kind of mom Billie was. "I know."

"And Tonette spoils those girls. She don't even know what they're really like, she's so blind."

I shrugged again. It didn't matter what Tonette saw or didn't see in those girls. It only mattered what she saw and didn't see in me.

"Listen, I don't got a ton of money, but how about we go into town and get haircuts or something?" Terry asked.

"Haircuts?"

She shrugged, a sheepish smile crossing her face. "I got boys. Haircuts is the best I can do with a girl."

It occurred to me that nobody was going to say one way or another whether I needed or didn't need a haircut. Or a visit to the dentist. Or to study or to learn to drive or to eat regularly or do any of the things I was used to being reminded to do. It was all up to me now, a thought that was both empowering and frightening as hell.

"Okay," I said, my hands searching the back of my hair involuntarily. "I could use a haircut."

Terry left the boys with Grandmother Billie and we scooted into the car Grandfather Harold had picked me up from the motel in. It was the first time I'd left the house since I'd arrived there. I sat in the front seat, holding Marin's purse in my lap, more out of habit than because I needed it for anything, and marveled at how close the main strip of town was. Out on my porch, I'd felt so very far away from the rest of the world. Five or ten minutes on foot would have had me at the first gas station, another five would have gotten me to the teeny movie theater. Another five would have gotten me to pretty much anywhere else I wanted to be. How odd to feel so isolated when civilization was literally all around you.

Terry pulled up to a strip mall and swung into a parking space outside a shop called Karrie's Kut 'N Kolor.

Inside, I was immediately swept away by the smell. Taken to so many different places in my past that I almost felt pulled apart. Times I'd been with Mom, nervously waiting for a color to set or for a new cut to be revealed. Times we'd taken Marin so she could get her tiny nails painted. Times I'd gone with Dani and her mom for pedicures or waited for Jane to get highlights done.

The last time I'd been in a beauty salon had been the weekend before the tornado, getting my hair fixed for prom.

Dani and Jane and I had decided to go as each other's dates, even though Dani had been asked by three different guys and Jane had sort of started seeing a boy she'd met at an orchestra competition in April, and I probably could have talked Kolby into going with me.

But we'd made the decision that senior prom was for dates and romantic dinners and swanky nights out; junior prom was for fun. This was our "fun" year.

We'd gone all out. Big, floor-length poufy formals filled with tulle that ate us up when we sat down. Expensive mani-pedis and updos, sparkly shoes that we kicked off the second we hit the dance floor and ignored for the rest of the night, dinner at Froggy's, where we played video games while we waited for our food.

It had been so much fun.

And I had completely forgotten about it until I smelled the astringent odors of permanents and hair dyes and nail polish and remover and glue. My old life was that far away. Gone. As if the tornado's damage would never be complete. It had destroyed my present, laid waste to my future, and was now busy eating up my history, too, as I forgot what life was like before.

"May I help you?" a pink-haired woman said, peering up at us over a massive marble countertop.

"We'd like to get our hair done," Terry said. "Whoever's available is fine."

The woman ran her sparkly black-tipped fingernail down a schedule book, then called over her shoulder, "Jonas? You got time for two walk-ins?"

"Yep," a voice called, and she motioned for Terry to head back to wherever the voice had come from.

"Come on," Terry said, grabbing the sleeve of my shirt between her two fingers. "You can help me decide what to do. I haven't had my hair done in a shop in prolly ten years. Always just have Billie cut it."

We made our way back to the salon chair, where a man wearing all black and practically dripping in pomade assessed us over a pair of round-rimmed spectacles.

"Ladies," he said. "Who's first?"

I pointed at Terry, and she sat down in the chair, bashfully taking in her image in the mirror. Her hair was long and limp, hanging halfway down her back in split-ended clumps. Jonas ran his fingers through it appraisingly.

"What are we doing?" he asked, and Terry looked over at me, questioningly, almost panicky.

I shrugged. "What do you want? Short?"

She giggled. "I don't know. I never did this before." She turned back to the mirror and studied her reflection, twisting her head to one side, then the other. "Yeah. Okay. Short will work." She glanced at me again. "Something fun, right? A change. A new me." She reached over and squeezed my hand, the feeling so foreign I almost yanked it away, but caught myself. "We both need reinvention, don't we?"

I nodded. Why not? She was totally right. It hadn't been my choice to reinvent myself. It had been thrust upon me and it sucked. But here I was in my crappy circumstances. This was my life now. Why not make a whole new Jersey? Start over. Who was going to notice, anyway? "Let's get color, too," I said, squeezing back.

She bit her lip and then nodded. "Why not? Let's splurge a little."

Three hours later, we walked out of Karrie's Kut 'N Kolor, our hair cut in sharp punk strips around our faces. Terry's was dyed a solid hot pink. Mine was brilliant purple. We giggled as we got into the car.

"You like it?" Terry asked, pulling down the visor so she could look in the mirror. She played with the ends of her hair.

"It's definitely different," I said. "Mom would hate it." I pressed my lips together. Up until this point, I'd only mentioned my mom when explaining to someone that she was gone, had kept her alive only inside myself. Did it make her more gone if I started talking about her in casual conversation? Did it make her more gone if I did things like dye my hair a color she would have hated?

All of a sudden I felt ashamed. Mom was barely gone. The dirt was probably still fresh on her grave. How dare I make a decision like this without her? How could I be so selfish? I had an urge to run back inside and have Jonas do it all back the way it was. Cut it blunt across the bottom, dye it brown.

"Your grandmother is definitely going to hate it," Terry said. "Which makes me like it all the more." She grinned at me wickedly, then reached over and felt my hair with her fingers. "You look dark and mysterious," she said.

Just what I needed—to look as dark as I felt on the inside.

Terry was right—Grandmother Billie hated our color choices. She called us tramps and ranted and raved that next thing we'd be getting tattoos and having our faces pierced, and she asked Terry if she thought hanging around with me was going to make her young and beautiful, because it wasn't.

The yelling created the kind of scene the family loved to flock to, and before I knew it, Lexi and Meg were standing in the living room doorway, taking it all in with matching smirks on their faces, staring at my hair as if it were so stupid and childish it made them want to laugh.

But the second Tonette came home from work, they started howling about how they wanted colored hair too.

"It's not fair!" Lexi cried, actually squeezing out a few dumb tears. "Terry never got *us* hairdos. Why should *she* get one? Just because she's new."

"You said she wouldn't get any special treatment," Meg added. "This looks pretty special to me."

On and on it went, and I could see Tonette's body grow more and more rigid with anger as they begged. Could see her start to formulate in her head how out of line I was for coming into the house with colored hair.

I knew better than to stick around and wait to see what would happen. I scurried into the kitchen, grabbed a piece of cheese and a banana, and went outside, sneaking right through the porch and around the house with my food.

I kept walking when I reached the end of the driveway, heading back downtown without even realizing that was where I'd decided to go.

I peered in the windows of the shops as I walked from one strip mall to the next, barely recognizing the girl with the purple hair walking opposite me every time I caught my reflection. I fantasized about the things I saw displayed in the windows, remembering how I'd always complained to Mom about how poor we were.

"I have nothing compared to what Jane and Dani have," I used to tell her.

"Well, Jane's and Dani's dads are attorneys," Mom always answered. "But they look so miserable, don't you think?"

"No. They look happy. Because they have flat-screen TVs and video-game systems and nice jeans. I have crappy jeans. And Dani's dad is an accountant, by the way."

"Well, he's got a lawyer air about him," she'd say, waving her hand dismissively. "Whatever he is, he makes more money than we do and that's just part of life."

"But I'm sick of always being the poor one."

"You can get a job if you hate it so much," Mom had said. I'd turned sixteen last July. I was planning to get a job this summer. Hopefully at the community pool. But it, too, had been destroyed by the tornado. *Whoosh*. There went something else—my plans—cycloning into the summer sky.

I'd hated how Mom could never afford to spoil me the way my friends were spoiled by their parents. But we were nowhere near as poor as the people living in my grandparents' house. And now I had nothing. Not even the jeans I used to think were so crappy. Funny how "crappy" turns into something better when you compare it to "nothing at all."

I wandered into a bookstore—one of those cushy ones with the soft armchairs and ambient lighting. The kind of store where people come to kick back, eat a cinnamon roll, and read half a book before buying it. There was a little coffee shop inside the store, and my mouth watered at the smell of the strong coffee, the sound of the cappuccino machine whirring and grinding. People sat at the tables with their laptops open, nibbling on brownies and bagels and sipping out of paper cups while tapping away on their keyboards. This was the life that was familiar to me, and I wanted to cry, I was so happy to have found it.

Someone had left a newspaper at one of the tables and I sat down to read it. Not that I was all that interested in the Caster City news, but it felt good to do something normal and mundane again.

I read every word of every story in the paper. I looked at all the photos, read the captions underneath them. I read the classifieds. Then, not ready to give up the feeling, I rambled through the aisles and ran my fingers along the book spines. Touching the titles, remembering good books I'd read, picking up new ones I hadn't heard of and studying their covers.

I sat back in an armchair and read through most of a book.

I didn't have the money to buy it, so I forced myself to stop reading, feeling a little like I was stealing, even though I knew I only meant to steal the moment of sanity. When I got up and placed the book back on the shelf, I noticed that the café had closed and it was dark outside. Someone had pulled a safety gate about a quarter of the way down in front of the doors, and a voice over the intercom was telling us the store was about to close.

Reluctantly, I left, making a promise to myself to come back and visit again soon. Maybe scrape together some money and buy the book I'd been reading. Something, anything to make me feel normal again.

I was walking along the sidewalk, taking in the neon lights of business signs and the stars above that, when my phone rang. It was Jane.

"Omigod, Janie!" I squealed. "You're okay!"

"Yeah, I'm fine," she said. "I finally got a new cell phone yesterday. My old one got lost in the tornado. I've been dying to talk to everyone."

"Dani said you're in Kansas City?"

"Yeah. Staying with my uncle. Our house got wiped out. Afterward, we were climbing around trying to find stuff, and this big bunch of bricks fell on me and broke my leg in three places. I'm on stupid crutches for the whole summer. Can you believe that?"

At this point, I could believe almost anything. People think a tornado drops down on a cow pasture or a trailer park and everything is fine. They never think about things like infected cuts and broken legs and old ladies crushed by air conditioners in their bathtubs. They never think about orphans.

"Were you in the school when it happened?"

She chuckled. "Yeah. We didn't even know anything was going on. We were practicing and never heard the sirens. We didn't figure it out until the power went off, and then we heard all kinds of horrible noise, crashing and banging, like everything was falling down around us. But everyone was fine. Nobody got hurt or anything. And, thank God, my parents had gone to my brother's soccer game over in Milton, so nobody was home. Our house is completely gone."

"Mine, too. I have, like, nothing left."

"I have my violin, and that's pretty much it," she said. "But the funny thing is, I don't want to play it. At all. The only thing I've got left, and it's still in my dad's trunk."

"It'll come back."

"I guess. Maybe. It just seems kind of pointless now, is all."

So many things do, I wanted to say. "So are you going back to Elizabeth?" I asked instead.

"Yeah. My dad's been down there all week clearing off our lot. I guess right now everybody's just trying to get the debris moved out of the way. There was a minivan on top of my bed." She laughed, then sobered. "Oh, hey, I'm really sorry about your mom and sister."

"Thanks. It's been pretty hard."

"Yeah." She took a breath. "Dani told me you're staying with your dad in Caster City? I didn't even know you had a dad. You never talked about one."

"I didn't have one. He's just a jerk who shares my DNA. And he would argue that we don't even share that much. I'm trying to get Dani to let me stay with her in Elizabeth. I can't live here."

"When everyone gets settled, you should come up to KC for a visit," Jane said, and at last my heart lightened. My friends were coming through. "My cousin Lindy is a trip. You'd like her. I'll ask my aunt."

"Yeah," I said. "I'll call when I get out of here, and then I'll come by."

We talked for a few more minutes about things like where our friends had ended up, what would happen with graduation, given that we didn't have a school and nobody really knew how many seniors were still in Elizabeth, and whether or not the movie theater was standing. It seemed like so long since I'd talked about anything other than the tornado, I hardly knew how to talk about other things. The conversation ended too quickly, as we both seemed to run out of things to say. When had that happened? When did I stop knowing how to talk to Jane?

I hung up the phone and continued walking but only got a few steps when a blast of a horn a few feet away made me jump.

"Where the hell you been?" Clay yelled, hanging out the car window. "Get in the damn car."

At first I stood rooted in my spot. I had that "stranger danger" feeling that we were always warned about when we were kids. Don't ever get into a car with a stranger, we'd been told. Trust your instincts. If your instincts tell you the situation is bad, stay away from it. Never get in the car with a dangerous person; never let him take you to another location.

But nobody ever told you what to do if you got those gut feelings about the man who was supposedly your father.

"What you starin' at? Get in the car, I said!"

Swallowing nervously, I pulled open the passenger door and slid into the front seat, the ripped vinyl making dull tearing noises on the backs of Terry's jeans.

He had the car in drive and was squealing away from the curb before I even got the door all the way closed.

"Been looking everywhere for you. My sister must have lost her damn mind," he muttered, looking more at my hair than at the road in front of him. His tires bumped a curb and he quickly corrected, then overcorrected, the car swerving into the other lane and back again. "Lettin' you color your hair, paying for it with money she ain't even got. The two of you look ridiculous. And now my girls are feelin' left out and Tonette ain't gonna have 'em goin' around lookin' like that, that's for sure. You keep tellin' me I'm your dad, but you don't even ask before you go and color your hair somethin' stupid."

I gritted my teeth, willing my mouth not to open, willing my ears not to hear him.

"You just gonna sit there like a loaf a bread?" he pressed.

But I continued to stare straight ahead, ramrod stiff on the torn passenger seat, watching him sway and swerve and knock into things like a pinball, clenching my teeth and my fists and my heart, feeling my resolve to stay silent crumble. If I didn't speak up for me, who would?

"If you're gonna leave the house, you need to tell someone you're goin'," he ranted.

"Why?" I said, turning on him.

He pulled up to a stop sign, glanced at me. "What do you mean why?"

"I mean why do I need to tell someone?"

He looked at me, incredulous. "So people don't go worryin', that's why."

I coughed out a laugh. "Who is worried? Tonette? Billie? Harold, who never even speaks to me? You? Give me a break. Nobody here cares about me."

"That don't give you the right to disobey the rules."

I hadn't wanted to get into it with my father, but I'd opened my mouth, and now there would be no shutting it again. "Lexi and Meg told me you didn't want me here. Why did you agree to let Ronnie send me?"

He turned hard into a parking lot and screeched into a space. For a second, I got scared that he was going to do something dangerous. "I ask myself that every day," he said, his nostrils flared. "Maybe 'cause Tonette's right and I'm some sorta sap. Guess I figured after all these years of your mom keepin' you from me, I deserved somethin' outta you."

We were staring at each other now, each of us with hate in our eyes. "What are you talking about?" I said. "She never kept me from you. You walked out on us. You never came back."

A slow grin spread across his face and he began nodding as if it all made sense to him now. "Is that what she told you? That I walked out?" He tipped his head back against the seat and laughed, then turned to me again. "I got tossed out. Christine 'wanted somethin' better.'" He made air quotes with his fingers when he said the last three words, then jammed a stubby thumb at his chest. "I told her I could be somethin' better, I'd get a job and stop drinkin' and would take care of you. But she said she deserved more and I'd see you again over her dead body and that was that. And look. She's dead and now here you are."

"You lie," I said through my teeth, but a part of me could tell that he wasn't lying. A part of me could see it in the slight tremor of his thumb, could see it etched into the lines around his eyes. "You never wanted anything to do with me."

His eyes hardened and he paused, sizing me up, the muscles of his jaw working. "Damn shame that's the story she gave you. 'Cause it ain't the truth."

"It's not a story. It is the truth," I said, but my voice was wavering, getting softer.

He put the car into reverse and began backing out of the parking spot. "When I threatened to get the law involved, she started sayin' you weren't even mine." He put the car into drive and glanced at me one more time. "I believed her at the time. She was some kinda messed up and I wouldn't a put nothin' past her at that point. But anyone with eyes can see we got the same DNA." He pulled out onto the road and started heading toward the house again. "And then she was gone. Moved. Wasn't the first time she'd disappeared on someone. I gave up. Met Tonette, started over. Forgot I even had a daughter named Jersey. Didn't seem like there was anything else I could do."

We drove along for a few minutes in silence, the town giving way to squat cookie-cutter homes. I wanted to get back to the house, to retreat to my couch and pull the blanket over my head, try to disappear from the lies, try to ignore the sinking suspicion that the liar was Mom, not Clay. Just thinking it made me feel like a traitor.

If what he said was true, the story of my life was a lie. I'd spent so many hours wondering about him, imagining him, wishing he'd come to my birthday party or to Christmas mornings or would stop by or call to see how I was doing. He never did, and I'd spent so much time hating him for abandoning me.

But according to him, he hadn't. She'd kept him away.

She let me think it was about me. She let me pine for him. She told me he was a monster, worthless, dangerous. She made me afraid of him. She encouraged me to hate him. I refused to believe it. I couldn't.

"So why, then?" I croaked. "If what you say is true, if you tried so hard to stay connected with me, why don't you want me here now?"

"Because I don't need no paternity test to tell me whether or not you belong to me. At this point, I already know you don't. You were Christine's from day one. You ain't my kid. You're a stranger. And you're messin' with my real family."

"I never had a chance to be your real family," I said.

He shrugged. "That ain't my fault."

He pulled into the driveway roughly, and I leapt out. I swung the door shut and tromped around the back of the house while he laid on the horn. I heard the front door open and Tonette's nasal voice squawking, "I'm coming! I'm coming! Jesus, keep your wad in your pants, Clayton!"

I was so busy thinking about my mom as I flung open the door to my porch, I didn't even notice Lexi and Meg until I was practically on top of them.

CHAPTER NINETEEN

My half sisters were sitting on my couch, laughing.

"You look like an old lady," I heard one of them say, but my mind was unable to make sense out of what exactly I was seeing.

They had Marin's purse. It was open on Lexi's lap, the contents bared to the world. Marin's things. My things.

"What...?" I started, but then I noticed that both of them were chewing gum, the foils wadded up and tossed onto the couch, and they both had pink, lipstick-smeared mouths. Lexi was clutching Mom's lipstick in her hand, rolled all the way to the top, the pretty slanted point ruined. Across the front of the purse they had written "COW" in Mom's lipstick.

"You got some seriously messed-up taste in lipstick, Granny," Lexi said, but she looked nervous as she said it, as if she knew they had crossed the line this time.

I reached out and snatched the lipstick out of her hand.

"That was my mother's," I said, feeling a rage swelling so big inside me, I wasn't sure how to contain it. I'd unclenched my teeth, and everything I'd been feeling in that car ride home— hell, everything I'd been feeling since the tornado—strained to get out of me. I felt bare and taut, an exposed nerve, a caged animal, a spring.

I'd lost everything at this point. I had nothing left but my memories—the ones that came from me, the ones I could trust—and they were trying to steal those, too. They couldn't. I wouldn't let them. If I let go of my memories, I might never recognize me again.

"Well, your mom has gross taste, then," Meg said.

I reached down and picked up the purse, grabbed the foils they'd discarded on the couch, dropped everything inside, then hurriedly zipped the purse shut and hugged it to my shoulder, the lipstick they'd drawn on the outside smearing up against my skin.

"Hey," Meg said, standing up, her nose a couple inches away from my chin. Lexi followed half a beat later but took a small step to the side, hanging back a little. Meg grabbed for the purse, but I clamped my elbow down on it. "Nobody said you could have that back."

"It's not yours to take," I said.

"Anything in my house is mine to take," she said. "And if I want to take your ugly-ass lipstick and your little gum stash, I will. And that goes for anything else you might have, Jersey Cow. Because you don't get to say what goes on in this house. You don't belong here and everyone knows it."

"Meg," Lexi said. I glanced over. Lexi was looking worriedly between her sister and me. "Come on, let's go to Jeff's party now."

"What?" Meg said defensively. "It's the truth. The only reason she's here is nobody wants her."

She had turned toward her sister, but my eyes were firmly planted on Meg. On her delicate little ear with the earrings snaking up the side. On her sharp, freckled cheekbone. On the corner of her hateful little mouth, where lipstick collected in a pink pool.

My mother's face swam before my eyes, coming out of the bedroom, the pink lipstick making her skin look creamy and smooth. Marin's voice echoed in my ears: *It's for special. I like it sharp.*

And now the tip was blunt and ragged, ugly. It had been stretched across the lips of two horrid girls who had only worn it to be cruel, had been dragged across the face of Marin's purse, no longer special, no longer new. That lipstick had probably been Marin's most prized possession, and these two bitches had no right.

Before I knew what was happening, my hand reached out and grabbed Meg's face, slapping up against her mouth as I dug my fingers in and clawed, trying to wipe the lipstick from her lips. She didn't deserve it; she wasn't special enough. These were *my* memories. *Mine.* And I would die before I would let anyone take them from me.

Meg gave a surprised little yelp, stumbling backward. Her heels caught the edge of the couch and she sprawled back onto the floor, her head knocking against the boards loudly. I followed her down, clawing and scratching at her face, mashing her lips against her teeth with my palms, dragging my hands across her mouth over and over again.

I was so intent on getting my sister's lipstick back, I was only vaguely aware of the racket we were making. I was grunting, crying, repeating that she didn't deserve to use my sister's lipstick, that she wasn't special enough, to give it back. Meg was screaming as much as she could through my fingers, her eyes wide and frightened, her hands flailing at my hair, my face, my chest. And in the background, I heard Lexi's voice as she cried for help.

There was blood. I could see there was blood. Meg's pink mouth had been replaced by a much larger red one. I didn't care. I didn't care about anything anymore. What did it matter? What did anything matter now? I was alone. I had no home, no family, nowhere that I belonged. In that moment, I finally and truly understood what it meant to have nothing to lose.

I kept after her until I was yanked to my feet roughly by two hands under my armpits. As soon as I was pulled off her, Meg curled up on one side, her arms flung over her mouth, her cries more like muffled shrieks.

I turned wildly, half ready to fight whoever had pulled me from her, but was surprised to see that it was Grandfather Harold. His fingers dug into my shoulders, his face a deep, wrinkled scowl. Lexi gaped at me over his shoulder, trembling, tears running down her cheeks.

"Let me go!" I shrieked, twisting violently out of his grasp.

"What the hell is going on?" Grandmother Billie said, bursting through the screen door, her nightgown swishing and swinging above her hairy ankles. She looked from Meg to Lexi to my grandfather to me, her head whipping around almost comically.

"She attacked Meg," Lexi said. "She scratched her up bad."

I turned my hands over and gazed at the blood on my fingers. I was still out of breath, so angry I could hear my pulse in my ears, but in a way what had just happened seemed impossible, like it had happened to someone else. Had my hands not been all bloody, I might even have tried to deny it.

Grandmother Billie hurried over to Meg and knelt next to her, trying to pry her arms away from her mouth so she could see the damage.

"They..." I said, then paused. How could I continue? *They stole my sister's lipstick. They stole my memories.*

Grandfather Harold took a heavy step toward me. "These girls ain't never been in a lick of trouble until you got here. Now I understand why Ronnie wanted to be rid of you."

"I've never been in trouble, either!" I cried out. "You don't have any idea what I'm like."

"I shouldn't have agreed to this, family or not," Grandmother Billie said.

By this time, Terry had joined the crowd, staring out through the screen door, Jimmy perched on one hip, rubbing his eyes. She pushed Jimmy's head against her shoulder with one palm and shushed him but didn't say anything.

I gazed at her, feeling ashamed.

Grandfather Harold motioned to Lexi. "Help your grandmother clean up your sister. We'll deal with you tomorrow," he said to me. "I s'pose we should call Tonette and get her home."

They all shuffled back into the house, Meg's cries turning to wet snuffles, Lexi glaring at me over her shoulder through slitted eyes. Aunt Terry watched me for a second longer; then I heard the sound of the screen door lock clicking into place.

At first I stayed rooted to my spot near the couch, the covered barbecue grill behind me, a stack of broken plastic lawn chairs close by. I blinked in the darkness, wondering how I had gotten here. How I'd gone from reading in a cozy armchair in a real bookstore to scrabbling open the skin of my half sister's mouth in the space of half an hour. Or how I'd gone from cooking dinner for my family to sleeping alone on a porch in little more than a month. It all seemed so surreal. My life no longer felt like mine.

We'll deal with you tomorrow, Grandfather Harold had said, and though I didn't know exactly what he'd meant by that, I knew it wasn't going to be good. Worse, he'd planned to call Tonette, interrupt her night of barhopping to let her know that I'd beat up her precious little girl. I would be in huge trouble, because as angry as my grandparents had been, it wouldn't be anything compared to how angry Clay and Tonette would be when they found out.

"Well, I'm not going to give you the chance," I said aloud. I needed to get out of this place where truth and lies swirled and bled together and stole all that I had left of me. I dropped to my knees and felt around until my hands landed on my backpack, which had been stuffed far behind the sofa, probably when Lexi and Meg were looking for something to steal. I pulled it out. It had been unzipped, but it didn't look like anything was gone. I quickly grabbed the blanket that lay folded up at the end of the couch, stuffed it inside, zipped it, and pounded through the screen door into the night.

I wasn't sure where to go. I hadn't wandered around enough to have more than a vague idea of what was beyond the cookie-cutter houses and the strip malls. I could see pastures behind the house, and a thicket of trees on one side. I could maybe find an old barn to sleep in, or a clearing under a tree. But what if a storm came? I hated that I now got panicky over something so silly, but I couldn't help it. Every day that the tornado sank deeper into my soul, I became more and more afraid of it.

In the end I decided to go with what was familiar, and headed into town.

CHAPTER
TWENTY

Morning took a long time to come. I hadn't slept at all, and I was exhausted from constantly looking over my shoulder, waiting for Clay or Harold or a cop to jump out at me.

I'd spent the night wandering around the main strip of Caster City. At first I'd hung around the back door of a boutique, sitting on smashed shipping boxes, playing cards until the stench from the Dumpster behind the Chinese restaurant next door overpowered me. I'd moved to a tiny grove of evergreens behind a fast-food place and stretched out on my back, studying Mom's face in the photo on my phone and softly singing Marin's bubble song until the mosquitoes drove me away.

I spent some time texting Jane, who was up watching movies with her cousin.

How's life in Hickville? she'd asked.

I'm running away, I'd responded.

To where?

I don't know yet.

I'd waited around, half-hoping she would extend an invitation to run to her, but she never did. Instead, she replied, I'll keep you company.

While Jane and I texted, the passing cars got sparser and sparser, and soon there were none, and the stoplights began blinking yellow and even the gas station closed for the night. I felt alone, stranded, and somehow that felt right. I moved around to the front of the strip mall and window-shopped, as if this were something I often did at three o'clock in the morning.

But it was a long time before the sun came up, and I'd found myself wedged into the back doorway of a furniture store, using my backpack for a pillow, my eyes heavy and grainy from lack of sleep, my butt numb from the concrete.

I turned my hands over in my lap and studied them in the daylight. Somehow, the blood had been rubbed away from the skin, but there was still a ruddy brown color under my fingernails. I wanted to wash them—wash Meg off me forever—and ended up tucking my fingers under my thighs so I wouldn't have to look at them.

In time, I heard the sounds of the world waking up. Truck brakes hissing and car doors slamming and the occasional horn or voice. I packed up my things and started walking again, pulling my cell phone out of my pocket. I dialed Kolby's number first. I could confide in him. I could tell him how terrible it was down here. I could tell him I was running away and he would help me.

"Hello?" a hushed voice asked.

I paused. This was the second time Kolby wasn't answering his own phone. "Um, hi? Is Kolby there?"

"Who is this?"

"This is Jersey. I was...I was hoping he could give me a ride somewhere?"

There was a sigh on the other end of the phone. "Oh, Jersey. This is his mom. How are you? I heard you're living down south with your dad now."

"Um, I was, but I'm not anymore. That's kind of why I need a ride up to Elizabeth. Can Kolby come get me?"

"Honey, Kolby's in the hospital."

"Still? For the cut on his arm?"

A pause. Then, "Well, yes and no. The cut got infected. He's got to...he's going to be here awhile. I'm afraid he won't be up to driving for a bit."

I stopped walking, trying to make sense of it all. I'd never had a cut get infected but figured it was just a matter of getting some antibiotics and going home. Why was this taking so long? "Oh. Okay," I said. "Just tell him I called."

"I will, honey. It will mean a lot to him to hear from you."

"I'll come see him when I get back to Elizabeth."

"Honey, maybe you should stay down there. Stay with your dad. I hate to see you get in a bad situation."

"My dad's house was a bad situation," I said sourly. "I've got to go. I'll see Kolby later, okay?"

I hung up before she could say any more. I understood why she would think it was best for me not to run away. But she had no idea what I was running away from. I resumed walking, scrolling through my address book and selecting Dani's name.

"Hey," she answered, sounding groggy, like she'd been asleep. "How's it going?"

"Terrible. I ran away. Can you ask your mom to come get me?" I already knew the answer, but it was worth a shot to try again. Maybe when her mom saw how desperate I was, she would change her mind. She was the only hope I had at this point.

"Whoa. Wait. Slow down. You ran away?"

I proceeded to dump everything on Dani—what Clay had said about my mom keeping him away from me and how he'd given up on me long ago. I told her about finding Meg and Lexi with Marin's purse, and about the fight that had ensued, all the way up to me gouging Meg's face last night.

"I need someone to come get me," I said. "I need to get home. Please ask your mom."

"I already did. She said no."

"Tell her I'll get Ronnie to take me back. She can drop me off at the motel. Just...anything. Come on, Dani, please? I need to get out of here."

"But you're, like, three hours away."

"I'll wait."

"Yeah, but my mom isn't going to want to drive six hours today, especially since she's already said she didn't want to get involved. She's going to say you need to give it more time. She's going to say this is between you and Ronnie. Maybe you should go to the police or something."

"Oh, right, the police. Since I'm a runaway and all." I leaned against the scratchy wall. Suddenly the Chinese restaurant smelled really delicious. My stomach growled, and I was thirsty. "Please? Just ask. Please, Dani?"

Dani sighed, then said, "Hang on." I could hear her cover the mouthpiece of her phone, and then some hushed mumbling as she talked to her mom. Their conversation seemed to go on forever and I prayed she was going to come back with good news. "My mom wants to know where you're going to be waiting," she said at last. Her voice sounded funny, monotone and flat.

I tipped my head back into the sun and smiled. "Thank you. Thank you thank you thank you. There's a bench outside the bookstore in the strip mall on Water Street. I'll be waiting for you there. I love you, Dani, you know that?"

"I love you, too, Jers," she said, and again her voice sounded dull. "See you soon."

I had to keep myself from running to the bookstore. I didn't want to get too tired or thirsty and I definitely didn't want to wait outside in the open for too long, just in case Clay and Tonette were looking for me. It would be hours before Dani and her mom got here. Long enough for me to figure out what I was going to do once I got back to Elizabeth. I recognized that if Dani's mom didn't want me there, and Ronnie didn't want me with him, I was going to be just as homeless up there as I was down here, but at least I'd be homeless in a familiar place. I had far more options in Elizabeth.

I was pretty thirsty by the time I got to the bookstore, so I made a beeline for the water fountain. When Dani's mom arrived, I hoped she'd get me something cold to drink. Maybe stop by a gas station for a slushy. And something to eat. And maybe I'd ask her to let me use her washer and dryer, take a shower, maybe take a nap on a real bed.

But as I straightened up, swallowing the cold water, I heard a deep voice behind me.

"Jersey."

I froze. It was a voice I recognized.

I turned around.

"Ronnie? What are you doing here?"

"Come on," he said, turning and stalking off toward the door, not even bothering to wait to see if I was following him.

We walked to the parking lot, where his truck sat filthy and ragtag right up front. I wondered if I had walked past it going into the bookstore, my mind so far away I hadn't even noticed that the truck that had been parked in my driveway for six years was sitting right there in the parking lot.

We climbed in, and I pushed my backpack and purse onto the floorboard between my feet.

"What are you doing here?" I repeated as he pointed his truck toward the highway. I watched the lane turn into two lanes, and then four, my spirit soaring higher with each growing lane, with every mile between me and that awful house.

"Harold called me last night," he said. "Told me you beat up one of their girls and I needed to come get you. Then your friend Dani's mom called, said you'd run away and would be at the bookstore, in case I wanted to call the police to pick you up and send you back to the Camerons' house."

I was stunned into silence. All that low mumbling and the

funny tone in Dani's voice...her mom had told me yes just so I would be sitting somewhere long enough to let the cops come get me.

"I sent you down here to stay with Clay," Ronnie grumbled, looking straight ahead, his dashboard rattling on the road. "But I know how headstrong you can be, and your mother would not want you being a runaway." His mouth straightened into a tight line at the mention of my mom.

"Thank you," I practically whispered. Something about being with Ronnie didn't feel right, but it felt so much better than being with my father. I didn't mention the things I'd wanted to say to him all this time. *Why didn't you ever call me back? Why didn't you let me come home for the funerals? Why did you make me leave in the first place?* I wanted to ask him if he had himself under control now, if his grief was still consuming him. *Have you brushed your teeth?* I wanted to ask him. *Have you changed your clothes? Is the motel room a rotting mess of empty food containers and filthy sheets?*

But instead I asked, "Can I get a Coke?"

He pulled over at the next fast-food restaurant we saw and bought me one, handing it across the seat, our fingers brushing. His fingernails were dirty. His hands were dry. Meg's blood was still under my nails, but I didn't care.

"Have you cleared out the house?" I asked when we got back on the road.

"Some," he said, and I could tell he didn't want to talk about it, but I pressed. It was my house, too, and I had a right to know.

"Did you find any of our stuff?"

"Some," he said again.

"Anything worth keeping?"

He shook his head, took a deep breath. "Total loss."

"You didn't keep anything?"

Annoyance crept into his voice. "No, Jersey, it's trash."

I pondered that. Our whole lives, the lives of four people, tossed in a landfill with all the other garbage. Why do we spend so much time collecting stuff, anyway, if that's what it comes down to in the end?

"So are you still living at the motel?" I asked.

"If you call it living, sure," he answered.

"Is there power in Elizabeth yet?"

"Yes."

I sipped my soda, feeling the cold sink down into my fingers and toes, the sugar and carbonation rushing to my head. I kicked off my shoes and held my feet under the floor vent, letting the air-conditioning dry my sweaty toes. I'd run out of things to ask him. He wasn't going to give me answers—not real ones, anyway—so what was the point? We both slipped into silence. I leaned my head against the window and watched the lines being eaten up by the front of the truck, until my eyes were too heavy from watching and I fell asleep.

I awoke when my body sensed that we had stopped moving. I sat up straight, stretching my stiff neck, and looked around. We were in a parking lot, but not one I recognized. I peered out the window. We weren't in Elizabeth, I could see that much. Ronnie had put the truck into park and was staring straight ahead through the windshield, his hands resting on the bottom loop of the steering wheel.

"Where are we?" I asked on a yawn. I grabbed my soda and took another sip. It had gotten warm and watery, but it still tasted like heaven. A sign on the side of a nearby building said WAVERLY PUBLIC LIBRARY.

"Waverly," he said, as I made the connection. His voice was rough and scratchy. *He was born in Waverly*, Grandfather Harold had said of Clay. *About an hour thataway.*

"Waverly? Why?"

Waverly was about an hour southeast of Elizabeth. We'd driven through it once or twice on road trips, and Mom had always pointed out that she'd grown up there.

"Godforsaken hellhole," she'd always say. "Hold your breath. You don't want to breathe in judgment. Oppression is contagious." And even though we had no idea what she was talking about, we'd always make a game of it—see who could hold their breath the longest. See if we could make it all the way through the town without taking a breath.

Ronnie picked at the steering wheel with his dirty thumbnails. "At the funeral…" he said, and then he paused so long, I wasn't sure he'd ever finish. He reached up and wiped his jaw with his hand a few times, then went back to picking. "Some people showed up, Jersey."

"I wanted to be there. I should have been."

"I was trying to keep you from being hurt."

"My mother died. It's too late to keep me from being hurt. I should have been there."

"Your mom's parents came," he said, leveling his eyes at me at last.

I sat back, stunned. I had never met my mom's parents. Mom hadn't seen or talked to her parents since before I was born. They'd told her that if she wanted to run off with that drunk troublemaker Clay Cameron, she no longer had a family to come home to, and Mom had taken them at their word. She had been glad to do so. She always talked about how they judged her, how she was never good enough for them, how they never understood her and forced her to be a perfect little princess when all she wanted was to be normal. When they disowned her, she was glad to be done with them. To hear her tell it, she had no idea where they lived, much less if they were alive or dead. I think in our hearts we all assumed they were dead.

But they were alive.

And she was the dead one.

Ronnie went back to picking, I think because it kept him from having to look at me. "They didn't even know about Marin," he said. "They knew about you because your mom was pregnant when she ran away. But they didn't even know Marin existed."

"She didn't run away. They disowned her," I said, not caring a bit. "That's their own fault."

"They live here in Waverly," he said, as if I hadn't spoken at all, and my insides started to turn cold as all the pieces fell into place. Mom growing up here, telling us to hold our breaths so we didn't catch the oppression and judgment alive and well in

Waverly. Ronnie was driving me to the very town where my grandparents lived. "They've always been right here. They still live in the same house your mom grew up in."

"But they didn't bother to come by until now?" I wanted to keep him talking, to turn the conversation around. Maybe I could stop what I knew was coming. Maybe if I made him understand how much Mom hated them, he wouldn't do what he was about to do. Again. "They didn't care enough to try to see us until after she was dead?"

Ronnie shrugged. "They said they tried. When you were a baby. But according to them, your mom called the police to have them escorted off her property. She told them she never wanted to see them or speak to them again. Of course, this was when she was still with Clay. They ... gave up."

"You don't do that," I said, and I realized that I wasn't sure if I was talking about my grandparents or about Mom or about Ronnie himself. "You don't give up on your family. You don't just ... leave ... when your child ... needs you." My breath hitched every few words as tears and dread fell over me.

"I'm sorry, Jersey," Ronnie said, letting his hands rest limply in his lap. "I called them this morning. They're willing to take you in."

"No," I said. My nose dripped and soaked into my jeans. I clutched at his elbow. "Please, Ronnie. I want to go home. I'll be good, I promise. I won't cause any problems. Ever. I don't know them, and Mom hated them. This isn't fair. Why do you hate me so much? Why do you think it's so bad to have me around?"

He shook his head and put the truck into drive. My hand slipped off his arm and landed in my lap in defeat. "I don't hate you," he said. "But I can't take care of you. Every time I look at you, I see her. Every time I hear you talk, I think about how I let everyone down. I think about how I couldn't save any of you. Not one." He glanced at me as he turned down a side road, the street sign reading FLORA. The houses were tidy, landscaped, painted. Not big, but bigger than our old house. "What good am I to anyone if I can't be there when it most matters?"

"But I'm still alive. You can still save me. It matters now."

He pulled into a driveway. My tears slowed as I took in the white-and-brown Tudor-style house, flowers blooming in orderly raised beds surrounding the swept sidewalk. More flowers blooming in quaint window boxes. A saintly-looking statue on the front porch. The door opened slowly. I wiped my face with my palms.

"I know you don't understand," Ronnie said. "But you've got to make this work, Jersey. I'm selling the property, anyway. Going back east. I've already got the transfer okayed at work. You can't come home. There's not going to be one."

I tore my eyes away from the pale hand that still clutched the door. The hand must have belonged to one of my grandparents, but the shadows kept me from seeing who.

"You're not going to stay where they're buried?"

"Every time I look at that neighborhood, at the house, at every business and building I pass, I'm reminded of how I failed them. I can't live a life that way. I've got to go."

"So you're abandoning all of us," I said, not a question, but a statement.

"I'm saving myself," he said very quietly.

It dawned on me that on some level I had expected Ronnie to change his mind. To get a little distance, heal, see his mistake, want me back. In some ways, I was more aghast at the realization that he would never change his mind than I was at seeing Mom's lipstick smeared across Meg's and Lexi's faces. I was more insulted by this than I'd been by Clay and Tonette insulting me and saying I didn't belong. I was more shocked by Ronnie's selfishness than I had been by the tornado itself. This wasn't how it was supposed to be. Life wasn't supposed to work this way. He wasn't supposed to choose himself over us.

"You're a coward." But before I could say any more, a gray-haired man wearing a plaid shirt and a baseball cap knocked on Ronnie's window. My mouth snapped shut. The man had a large, bulbous nose and huge eyebrows. But he also had wet, pouty lips that sort of reminded me of Marin's, and out from his cap, several curly strands of hair snaked around his ears.

Ronnie rolled down the window.

"Thank you for this," he said to the old man, and the anger returned. I wanted to punch Ronnie. For casting me out, for abandoning Mom and Marin, for being so dry-eyed and cavalier about the whole thing.

The old man nodded. "Not a problem. She got any bags?"

"Not really. Just a couple up here she can carry. We lost everything, as you saw."

My jaw tensed. Ronnie had taken them to my house? To

Mom's house? How could he? Mom would have been furious. She'd kept them away on purpose.

"You get any word from FEMA yet?" the old man asked, and as Ronnie answered, I tuned him out, turning my gaze to the woman standing in the front doorway, wringing her hands, a melon-colored sweater hanging over a lighter melon-colored tunic. Even from the truck, I could see that she shared my knock knees, my rounded shoulders, my thick waist. All this time I'd been wondering who exactly I looked like, when the person I resembled most was right here in Waverly.

"Ready?" the old man said, and I realized he had been peering past Ronnie over to where I sat.

"Huh?"

"You ready?" Ronnie said.

I glared at him. "No. But I guess I don't have a choice," I said.

"No," he said, "you don't. You've got to make it work this time."

He went back to his picking on the steering wheel, and the old man slowly maneuvered his way around to my side of the truck. I clutched the top handle of my backpack and pushed Marin's purse tightly up my shoulder. My grandfather opened my door and I slid out.

"Have a nice life," I said to my stepdad.

I knew I would never see him again.

CHAPTER TWENTY-ONE

My grandmother said my name in pretty much every sentence. "Jersey," she kept repeating. "Jersey, would you like some coffee cake? Jersey, let's put your things away. What time do you like to wake up in the morning, Jersey?" It was like she couldn't get enough of it. It was driving me crazy already.

I followed behind her in my burr-covered socks, my shoes left by the front door next to theirs. She showed me to my room, a lavender-and-white monstrosity of ruffles and gingham and scented soaps and fabric flowers, so different from the porch at my other grandparents' house it made my brain ache. A plate of cookies sat on the nightstand. I could smell them from the doorway. My stomach rumbled.

"This used to be Christine's room," she said, stepping aside to let me pass. I shuffled in, trying to imagine my mom in such a space. Trying to see her stretched out across the cloud of bedding, her feet kicked up in the air behind her as she talked on the phone. Trying to imagine her pushing out the window screen and shimmying through to meet Clay, kissing him on his boozy mouth.

It was getting harder and harder to call up mental images of Mom. Especially any version of Mom that might have lived here—this was so different from the Mom I'd known.

There was a framed photo on the dresser. A little girl on a man's shoulders, his hair a mess, the little girl holding a baseball cap proudly in the air.

"That's Christine and Barry," the woman said, and when I continued to stare at her blankly, she added, "Barry's your grandpa. I'm Patty. Did you know that already? I don't know what Christine shared with you."

I said nothing. She didn't want to know what Mom had shared with us about them. And even if she did, I wasn't in the mood to tell her. The eight-year-old inside me was afraid to breathe in this house, afraid of catching the oppression Mom had always talked about. Afraid of being judged. How did I know who this woman really was? How did I know she wouldn't turn on me the way Dani's mom had, or give up on me the way Clay had, or lie to me the way Mom had, or cast me out the way Ronnie had? If I'd learned anything from the tornado, it was that I couldn't trust anyone but myself. My new grandmother might want to pretend that we were all one big happy family, but I knew the truth. One framed photo of a little girl mugging on her dad's shoulders a decade before being kicked out of the family does not make up for a lifetime of being cast out.

In that regard, Mom was the same as me, I realized. We were both motherless. The realization flooded my heart, made me feel closer to her somehow.

My grandmother interrupted my thoughts. "You can call me Grandma, though," she said. "I'm so happy to finally meet you, Jersey. We both are." I stared at her, unmoving, until she finally withered back from the doorway. "I'll let you get settled. The bathroom's right across the hall here. Feel free to take a nap or explore or do whatever it is you want to do. We'll have dinner at six, but if you get hungry before, you can have those cookies there." She pointed at the plate. I refused to look at it. "Or we can get you something else. Just holler, Jersey."

She shuffled out and closed the door.

The moment she left, I devoured the cookies, greedily, guiltily.

Once they were gone, I stood by the night table, not sure what I was feeling anymore. The room was nice. It smelled good and it was bright and cozy. My mom had a history here, so in a way it felt comforting. But she'd hated that history. I was torn. If I decided to be happy here, wouldn't I be betraying Mom's memory?

I finally shrugged my backpack down onto the floor and dug through it for some clean clothes. I pulled out a shirt and shorts from Terry. The shirt had a CCHS Captains logo on it, and for some reason, my old Elizabeth Barking Bulldogs sweatshirt popped into my mind.

I wasn't ever the biggest on team spirit. My friends and I were hardly athletes. In fact, we theater geeks never understood why anyone would want to run around in a field or in circles on a track, and the athletes never understood why we performing-arts-center groupies wanted to sweat under a spotlight reciting Shakespeare sonnets in language that didn't make sense. It was a mutual misunderstanding that neither of us had any desire to rectify.

But everyone owned spirit wear. We wore it on football Fridays, mostly. Even if we never exactly bothered to go to the game.

Marin was obsessed with my Elizabeth Barking Bulldogs sweatshirt. She loved its cartoon bulldog and bright orange lettering. She'd drag it off my bed or out of the clean laundry basket and would dance around the living room in it, on her tiptoes, total Marin-style, the sweatshirt hanging to her ankles, the sleeves flapping in the air.

I told her once that when I graduated she could have my sweatshirt. You'd have thought I'd bequeathed her a diamond mine, the way she whooped and hollered and jumped around the room. I didn't have the heart to tell her that by the time she got into high school, the sweatshirt would be way out of style and ugly and old and she wouldn't want it.

Sitting on my mother's old bedroom floor, with Ronnie gone and me having no choice but to breathe in Waverly, I was glad I hadn't told her those things. I was glad she was still looking forward to things on the day she died.

I sank to the floor and picked up Marin's purse. Most of the lipstick had wiped off, but it was still rubbed into the cracks, the stitching. I grabbed a tissue from a box that sat on the dresser and scrubbed at the face of the purse. The lipstick was mostly gone, but if I looked hard enough, I could still see traces of pink.

I pulled the lipstick out of the purse, then rubbed across the top of it with the tissue, too. The stick was no longer sharp, the way Marin liked it, but at least it didn't have Meg's and Lexi's germs on it anymore.

I dropped it back inside the purse and found a piece of gum. I drew a sweatshirt on the foil.

Marin is a Barking Bulldog.

I hid it with the others, noticing that the collection was getting pretty big now. Which meant that the gum supply was getting low. I didn't want to chew the last pieces. To run out of Marin's gum would seem like an end that I hadn't fully realized yet, and didn't want to.

I smoothed the foils from Meg's and Lexi's gum.

Marin loves Minnie Mouse the most because she has a bow.

Marin has tiny toenails.

I changed into clean clothes and lay back on the bed, staring at the ceiling, thinking about all the things I could write on foils for Marin. All the ways I wanted to remember her. I could probably start writing and never stop.

But eventually there was a light tapping on my door and I sat up guiltily, as if I'd been doing something wrong. My grandmother poked her head in.

"Would you like a snack?" she asked.

I thought dinner was at six, I almost answered sarcastically, but then I remembered that I wasn't speaking to these people—at least not yet—so I just stared at her. I held my breath.

"I've got some strawberries," she said hopefully.

I let the air out through my nose, then took another silent breath in and held it again.

"Would you like a soda, Jersey?" she tried.

Nothing. I let my mom's hatred fill my eyes.

My grandmother chewed her lip. "We want to help you, Jersey," she said. "We know this is hard for you."

I turned my gaze away from her then, pointed it straight at the photo of my mom. Did they? Did they really know how hard this was for me? To lose everything? To be bounced around to see who wanted me the least? To know that I would never have my life back again and that I was totally alone? It was like the tornado had ripped through my house and torn me away. It was impossible that they could understand the rage inside me. The confusion and guilt and surrender. The hard edges that had begun to rub open, raw sores onto my heart. Because even I didn't understand it, and I was the one living it. And besides, if they really understood what it felt like to be inside my head, my heart, right now, they would run in fear. They would leave me alone.

She stayed, propped up by the door, for what seemed far too long, then finally sighed.

"Well, here, will this help, anyway?"

Curiosity kicked in and despite myself, I turned to see what "this" was. She reached around the doorframe and held out a phone.

"I thought you might want to call your friends. I'm sure you're wondering what's happening back at home." She waggled the phone in the air. "You can talk as long as you need to. We don't mind."

I did want to call my friends, actually. Even though I had already talked to everyone that morning—everyone except Kolby, that was—and even though Dani's mom had sold me out to Ronnie, I still wanted to talk to someone familiar. But if I took that phone from my grandmother, if I made that concession, she would think I wanted to be here. So I went back to staring at the photo silently and refused to look again until she had backed out of the doorway and shut the door behind her.

I'd purposely missed dinner. Had even crawled into bed and closed my eyes when she knocked, knowing she'd leave me alone if she thought I was asleep.

But I was starving, so when I stopped hearing the voices of the TV and the strip of living room light blinked out under my doorway, I crept to the kitchen. I froze when I found my grandfather sitting at the kitchen table, with only the light fixture above the table illuminating him. I noticed a traditional solitaire game laid out in front of him. He was missing an obvious black seven, red six.

"Patty left you a plate in the refrigerator," he said when I walked in. "Pot roast. She makes the best in the world."

I didn't answer. I contemplated going back to my room. But I was so hungry, and pot roast sounded too good to be true.

I padded over to the refrigerator and found the plate, ripped off the plastic wrap, and heated the food in the microwave.

"We ask that you don't eat outside of the kitchen," he said, still not looking up from his game. He'd found the red six but had gotten stuck again.

The microwave beeped and I sheepishly took my plate to the table, after first pulling open every drawer in the kitchen to find silverware. He didn't try to help me find it, and I was oddly grateful for his lack of effort. I sat on the end opposite my grandfather, keeping my eyes straight down on the plate.

He softly cursed and I heard him gather up the cards and shuffle them.

"She's grieving, too," he said, breaking the silence between us. I paused, then resumed chewing, still facing the pot roast, which was so tender it melted in my mouth. I hadn't had anything this good to eat since the tornado. "Even though we hadn't heard from Chrissy in sixteen years, your grandmother still hoped every day your mom would come around. So she's grieving. She feels like it's been sixteen years wasted." He paused, the slapping sound of cards on the Formica telling me he was laying out a new hand of solitaire for himself. "We both do," he added. "We didn't even know about your half sister."

"Sister," I said, before I could stop myself. I felt my face flush with heat over having spoken.

"I stand corrected," he said in a very matter-of-fact voice. *Slap. Slap.* "Your sister."

I scraped the last bit of mashed potatoes onto my fork and licked it off, wishing I had another plateful. I got up and took my plate to the sink, rinsed it, placed it in the dishwasher, and poked through cabinets until I found one with drinking glasses. I filled a glass with tap water and took a big swallow. Everything felt too normal, too much like home. But this house wasn't home for me. I wouldn't let it be. Maybe this was what Mom meant by the oppression being contagious here. Maybe I'd already caught it.

"Anyway," my grandfather said, as if he'd never stopped talking, though it had been several minutes since he'd last spoken, "you might find that you can help each other out, your grandma and you."

I blinked at him, trying to convey my doubt with silence. He got stuck again and started flipping through the deck. He hadn't moved the ace of hearts up to the top, which would have freed up a whole slot of cards. But I didn't tell him that.

I walked to my bedroom and crawled back into bed, my stomach full, my eyes heavy.

I was asleep seconds after my head hit the pillow.

CHAPTER TWENTY-TWO

When I got back to the bedroom after my shower the next morning, I found that my cell service had been turned off. I held the phone in my hand for a long moment and stared at it. I had expected it would be shut off at some point, but there was something so depressing and final about it. Like my last grasp on my old life had let go.

My grandmother had left a plate of Pop-Tarts on the dresser, along with a glass of apple juice. I wolfed it all down and sat on my bed, wondering what to do next.

I was well rested and my stomach was full. I didn't want to watch TV, mostly because there was no TV in my bedroom, and I didn't want to risk running into my grandparents in the living room. But I was getting bored and lonely with no entertainment, and though I wanted to make the statement that these people were to be loathed by me, I knew eventually I would have to come out and talk. I had nowhere else to go.

Even I could admit, it wasn't reasonable to believe I could live with my grandparents for the next year or more and not ever talk to them.

I grabbed the phone my grandmother had left on the dresser the day before and headed outside, where a striped patio swing looked out over an eager garden. I sat down, sinking my bare toes into the thick grass. I called Dani first.

"Do you hate me?" she asked.

"No. I wish you would have warned me, but I don't hate you."

She whispered into the phone. "It's my mom. She thinks you're going to have a mental breakdown or something, and she doesn't want to have to be the one to handle it. Are you?"

"Am I what?"

"Are you going to have a mental breakdown? I mean, your mom *died*."

"I know she died, Dani," I said, trying to shake the irritation. Why on earth would her mom pull away from me if she thought I needed help? My mom had been right—Dani's parents thought like lawyers. "And I don't think so. I mean, I'm not sure. What does a mental breakdown feel like?"

"I don't know. Like you're going to lose it? I think I would be losing it if I were you."

I pinched the bridge of my nose between my thumb and forefinger. I was feeling a too-familiar anger welling up inside me. I'd never been an angry kind of person, and it didn't make sense why it kept coming back. I was sad, not angry. I was scared and lonely, but I didn't understand why I felt so mad. Being mad all the time did sort of make me feel like I was losing it. "I guess," I said. "It doesn't matter."

"Of course it matters."

"Not to your mom."

"Come on, Jersey. That's not fair. My mom's got a lot going on right now, too."

Really? I wanted to scream into the phone. *Like what? Did some shingles get damaged? Did she have to go without her blow-dryer for a whole week? Did the poor baby break a nail picking up a board in her driveway? How on earth did she possibly manage?* Instead, I concentrated on my breathing, trying to will away the fury.

"Hello?" Dani said.

"I'm here."

"Hey, um, not to change the subject, but I heard something about Kolby."

I let go of the bridge of my nose and sat up straighter. "What?"

"It's probably just a rumor, but someone said he got this weird infection in his arm."

"Yeah. He did. I tried to call him a couple times. He was in the hospital over in Milton."

There was a pause. "I heard it was pretty serious is all."

"How serious?"

"I don't know."

But something in her voice told me she did know; she just didn't want to say. I needed to talk to Kolby myself.

"Listen, I've got to go. I'll call you back," I said.

"Okay, but about my mom? Don't be mad."

Just let it go, my brain seethed. *Let it go.* "Yeah, it's all right. I'm not," I said. "I'm going to try to call Kolby again."

"Call me back when you know what's up," she said. "Everybody's wondering."

"Okay," I said.

I hung up and immediately dialed Kolby's cell, pacing back and forth through the grass, kicking up swarms of tiny flying bugs.

"Hello?" Still not Kolby.

"Tracy? It's Jersey. Is Kolby there?"

"Um. Jersey? Yeah, he's here, but um . . . hang on."

It seemed like it took a long time, but when the phone was finally picked up again, it was Kolby on the other end.

"Hey," he said. He sounded bleary. "Are you back in Elizabeth?"

"No. I'm in Waverly with my grandparents. But what's going on with you? Is it serious?"

"It's fine. I got an infection in the cut on my arm. It's some fungus spelled with about a thousand letters. The doctor said something about it being common after natural disasters."

"Are you going to be okay?"

He cleared his throat, his voice craggy and clotted. "I guess it damaged a lot of tissue. Real gross-out stuff. Looked like something out of a comic book. I half expected a bionic arm to pop out." He laughed weakly.

"But it's healed now, right?"

"Sort of. They had to do a skin graft." He chuckled. "They took skin off my butt and put it on my arm."

I stopped pacing. "Wait. You had surgery?"

"Yeah. But I'm getting out of here soon. I have to relax for a while, make sure it heals up and stuff. Not a big deal."

"Sounds like a pretty big deal," I said. Kolby, who played baseball in the street all summer long, who skateboarded and pushed his sister on swings and pulled his mother out through their basement window on the day of the tornado, had to have surgery? Because of a cut? How was this possible?

He yawned loudly. "So I should probably go. The pain meds are kicking in, and you never know what I'm gonna say on those. I might profess my deep abiding love for your toe lint, no joke." I could hear the smile in his voice, but I couldn't match it. It seemed like the hurt would never stop coming. I felt shaken, frail.

"Okay," I said. "Let me know when you get out of the hospital. Take care of yourself. I mean it."

"You keep being bossy like that, and I'll be forced to touch you with my butt-arm." He yawned again.

"I'm being serious, Kolby," I said, though I couldn't help smiling a little. "I don't want anything to happen to you."

"Aw, Jers, if I didn't know any better, I'd think you miss me a little."

I closed my eyes. "More than you could ever know," I said.

After hanging up, I stood in the middle of my grandparents' backyard, barefoot and shivering. The phone dropped from my hand and landed in the grass, but I made no move to pick it up. I was shaking so hard my fingers couldn't hold the telephone. Maybe Dani's mom was right—maybe I was losing it and I was too far gone to even know. Maybe this was what losing it felt like.

"Jersey?" my grandmother's voice sounded from the sliding glass door.

I turned slowly. "Huh?" Speaking, without even meaning to.

"We're headed to the grocery store. Why don't you come along?"

I nodded. Despite myself, I freaking nodded. *Sure, the grocery store, why not? My whole stupid world is falling apart, so why not the freaking grocery store, right? Because grocery stores, those are normal and those are sane and those might make me normal and sane.*

Half an hour later, I found myself trudging down the cereal aisle, the bread aisle, passing the canned goods and the pasta. My grandparents chattered as if this were the most exciting day of their lives, reading labels and pointing at sale tags and asking, asking, asking me so many questions, until I felt like my brain might explode.

"Jersey, do you eat biscuits and gravy? Your grandfather makes wonderful biscuits and gravy, Jersey."

"Yeah, I guess."

"Jersey, what kind of deodorant do you wear, honey? What kind of shampoo, Jersey? Do you need a razor, Jersey, a hairbrush, Jersey, do you like these protein bars, do you drink a lot of milk, do you like oranges, Jersey, Jersey, Jersey?"

"Yeah. Okay. That's fine. No. I don't know."

My grandmother stopped and talked to no less than ten other people, gave them all the same spiel: *This is our grand-daughter, Jersey. I'm sure you heard about the tornado up in Elizabeth. Such a sad, sad thing. Yes, we lost our only daughter. It's very traumatic for all of us, but we're muddling through, aren't we, Jersey?*

And then would come the introductions, as if we were at some stupid cocktail party: *Jersey, this is Anna, this is Mary, this is Mrs. Donohue. Her son is a marine, her daughter teaches English at the community college, she used to babysit your mother, can you believe it?*

To all observers, we were a reunited family on the mend. My grandparents, the saints, had taken in a sullen, sunken-eyed, purple-haired granddaughter they didn't even know and were helping her rebuild her life. We shopped together. It was so cute.

I wanted to vomit.

I wanted to scream and run out into the parking lot and hurl cans of green beans through the windows. I wanted to bash the headlights out of Anna the marine-mother's car. I wanted to lie down on the cool tile and press my cheek against it, fall asleep, cry, rage, rampage, hurt things, hurt myself.

But instead, I nodded. I answered questions.

Because I had no other choice.

CHAPTER
TWENTY-THREE

The Waverly mall could hardly be called a mall. It was mostly two department stores, with a couple food stands placed here and there, and almost no people. My grandmother led me around the clothing racks, asking questions about sizes and taste, herding me into fitting rooms with armloads of shirts and shorts and bras. I tried them all on dutifully, but within moments of leaving the fitting room I couldn't even be sure if I'd been in there at all. I didn't remember what anything looked like on me, and I didn't care.

I stuffed my feet into shoes and picked up shiny, glinting earrings and carried around shopping bags, while my grand-mother ran a never-ending monologue about clothes and the changing nature of fashion. She asked me questions, so many questions it made my ears throb. *Do you like to wear shorts, Jersey? Oh, Jersey, what do you think of this shirt, aren't the hearts cute? Jersey, try this one on. I think that'll look great on you, Jersey. What kinds of things did you wear at home, Jersey?* I wanted to plug my ears, to slap my palms over them and start chanting *la-la-la* to drown her out.

At my other grandparents' house, I'd been able to shut myself down, bit by solitary bit. But here it was impossible. I felt under a microscope, heated by a spotlight, poked and prodded and analyzed. Day after mind-numbingly normal day, my grandparents dragged me places, talked to me, showed me things, introduced me to people, made me participate, even though doing so meant I felt like an open sore, too roughed over to ever develop a protective scab. I began to feel like an exposed nerve.

"You hungry for lunch, Jersey?" she asked.

"Okay," I said, that same mechanical response I'd been giving her all day long.

"You like nachos?"

"Okay."

I sat at a food court table, surrounded by shopping bags full of things I couldn't remember choosing, much less caring about, while my grandmother ordered a plate of nachos to share. She came back and we ate mostly in silence.

Finally, as I picked up the last nacho, she said, "How would you like to go to church with me on Sunday, Jersey?"

I paused, the nacho dripping most of its ingredients back onto the tray. "No."

She tipped her head sideways. "But there are so many kids there your age. I thought you might like to get to know some of them before school starts in the fall."

I felt a headache begin to pang on the side of my head. I didn't even want to think about school—about starting senior year as a new kid.

"No," I said, dropping the nacho and wiping my hands on a napkin.

"Why not?"

"Because..." *Because I'm tired of everything being new. Because I just want something familiar. Because making new friends might mean getting rid of old ones. Because I can't think when you keep saying my name like that.* "Because I've never been to church."

She frowned. "You mean Christine didn't ever take you?"

I shook my head, trying to look self-righteous about it, as if my mom had a great reason not to take me to church and how dare she, my grandmother, the woman who hadn't even known my mom for over a decade, question it.

She pressed her lips into a tight line. "Well, that surprises me. She loved church. She came to church every Sunday before she got mixed up with that Clay Cameron. I'd have thought once he left her, she'd go back to her church home."

"Her home was with me," I said. "She didn't need church."

We ate in silence for a few moments, me trying to picture Mom in a church. It was getting so hard to remember her with all these new versions coming at me every time I turned around. Clay's version, my grandparents' version, my version—they were getting muddy, competing, blurring her memory. It felt like trying to recall someone I'd never met.

"Would you be willing to try it once?" my grandmother

asked. "If you hate it, you'll never have to go back. But it was very important to your mother at one time. You can see where she grew up."

I rolled my eyes, but my resolve was weakening. I imagined walking into a stuffy church and hating it, feeling looked down upon by everyone inside. I imagined myself tipping my head back and railing at God—*How could you? How could you do this to me?*

But I could also see me walking in there and feeling enveloped by Mom, by Mom's past, a past I didn't know about. I could see me learning about her there.

"Will I be going to the same high school she did?" I asked, trying to buy myself time to think.

"Yes." My grandmother wiped her mouth, letting me change the subject. "Waverly Senior. You guys are the Tigers."

"We used to be the Bulldogs," I said, as if that mattered. *Barking Bulldogs*, I heard Marin's voice sing out in my head. *Barking Bulldogs, Barking Bulldogs.*

"Yes, I heard you had quite the football team. Did you know any of the kids on the team?"

Of course I did. I knew them all. We'd grown up together. I wondered how many of them would be playing next season. How many of them wouldn't be playing at all? "I was in theater," I said.

"Oh! Fun! What plays were you in, Jersey?"

I couldn't blame her for asking. I actually got asked that a lot. People never assumed someone who loved the theater would love being behind the lights the most. But still, her asking irritated me. It wasn't the fact that she didn't know, it was the fact that... *she was my grandmother and she didn't know.* I gritted my teeth against the irritation, but it was useless. This was all too much. Too fast, and too much. I pushed my chair away from the table, and it made a loud squeak that echoed through the food court and made people turn and look.

"I need a new cell phone," I said, abruptly changing the subject. "Mine got cut off."

"Oh." She thought it over. "Okay. But we can just pay the bill on your old one, get it transferred over to our names. That way your number won't change."

"That's fine. Then I'm ready to go home," I said, suddenly too pissed at all the changes in my life to feel the relief I wanted to feel over not having to get rid of my old phone and the precious photos on it.

My grandmother didn't say anything. She followed as I huffed it to the parking lot, my legs fueled by the weird anger that had begun following me around like a ghost.

CHAPTER
TWENTY-FOUR

Two weeks had passed since my grandmother's church invitation, and I'd been hoping she'd forgotten. But on the third Sunday after our trip to the mall, she stood in my doorway, having swapped her trademark khakis and pastel sweater-and-tunic combo for a dress and stockings, the lined toes peeking out through a pair of rattan sandals. Her knees were knobby and her calves were covered in varicose veins that the hose did nothing to hide.

I sat cross-legged on my bed, playing cards, and pretended I didn't notice my grandmother standing there. They seemed to have introduced me to everyone and taken me everywhere and were finally, blissfully, leaving me alone. I'd become an expert at being invisible; now if I could just become an expert at making them invisible.

She knocked lightly on my doorframe. "Jersey?" I squinched my eyes shut to keep from yelling at her for once again saying my name in a question. "Are you sure you don't want to go to church?"

I didn't look up. "Nope."

But instead of getting her to go away, my short answer only seemed to move her to try again. She stepped into the room and sat gingerly on the edge of my bed, making the cards slide. I scooted back and scooped them up into a deck again.

"It could help," she said, and if I hadn't hated her so much, I might have been touched by the soothing tone of her voice. She acted as if she really cared. The same as when she left plates of home-baked cookies on my dresser or bought me a new set of headbands or a shirt or a little trinket to help me build my life back up again.

I felt sorry for her in those moments, because she didn't know that Mom had raised us to see her as the enemy, that it would be a betrayal for me to love her. She didn't know how broken I was on the inside, that I couldn't have let her in even if I'd wanted to, because the part of me that had once loved was now gone. She didn't know that while I found her house a somewhat acceptable place to hang for the time being, I was only waiting for the time to come when I could leave it. And that when I left her house, I would also leave her forever.

"I don't need help," I mumbled. I shuffled the cards, bridging them expertly.

"Jersey, eventually you're going to need help. You know that, don't you? You've lost a lot, Jersey, and this could be your first step."

Two cards slipped out and I pounded my fist—the one

holding the deck—against my leg. "Please," I said, closing my eyes and trying to sound civil but knowing I was skating on the edge of not sounding civil at all. "Please stop saying my name so much. It's driving me up the wall. It sounds stupid."

She opened her mouth like she wanted to say something but seemed to think better of it and closed it with a curt nod. She got up and left my room, not another word about church, and not another utterance of my name. Thank God.

I stayed right where I was until I heard the front door close and saw through the curtains my grandmother's car backing down the driveway.

I got up and headed for the living room, hoping to get some TV in before they came back.

But my grandfather hadn't gone with her. Instead, he sat, baseball cap and plaid shirt in place, at the kitchen table, with a deck of cards.

I walked past like I didn't see him and got a soda out of the refrigerator, planning to drink it out in the living room while I watched something mindless.

But when I headed for the living room, I couldn't help noticing he was once again neglecting to move the ace.

"You do know you can move that to the top, right?" I asked, pointing to the ace.

He looked up, like he hadn't noticed me, and I had a moment of wondering which one of us was the better actor. Probably neither of us. "Huh?"

I moved around to his side and picked up the ace, making a new row above his cards. "You can move this up and start building that pile. Same suit, the ace is a one. That way you can flip here." I flipped over the card that the ace had been on. It was a ten of spades that he could play.

"Well, I'll be," he said. "I've been playing it wrong my whole life?"

"If you've been playing it this way, then yeah, it looks like it," I said. I popped the lid on my soda.

He moved around a few more cards, then got stuck again. I helped him by placing a queen on a king, but then we were both stuck and he had to sweep the cards back into a pile. He glanced up at me.

"You play cards?" he asked.

I shrugged, taking a sip of my soda. He might have thought he was being all TV-shrink-clever, but I wasn't about to let him trick me into opening up for some Tell-Me-About-Yourself-Jersey boo-hoo-fest. "Your mother played cards," he continued, as if he hadn't even noticed that I had ignored him. "She was smart as a whip with a game of Go Fish. Did you know that?"

I stared at him over my soda. My mom hardly ever played cards, even when we begged. She said she hated it. Something else I didn't know about her.

"Of course, she got the gene from me." He shuffled, bridged, smirked. "I'm unbeatable."

I couldn't help myself. I made a *tch* noise and rolled my eyes.

"You don't believe me? It's true. You couldn't beat me if you tried."

"Doubtful," I murmured, and he tilted his head, cupping one hand around his ear.

"Huh? Gotta speak up. I'm an old man."

I lowered my soda. "I said it's doubtful that you could beat me."

Slowly his mouth turned up into a smile. "Think so, eh?"

"I know so. It's sort of my thing," I said. "I learned at camp. I can play pretty much anything."

He shuffled the deck. "Oh, really? Have you ever played Humbug?"

"I told you. Cards are my thing. Deal."

He dealt all of the cards, flipping the last one face-up, and we started playing, my TV plans on hold for the moment. I'd forgotten how good it felt to play cards with an opponent.

The best thing about playing cards is that you can play them with anyone. Friends, enemies, even perfect strangers. In some ways, I liked playing with strangers the best, because there were fewer distractions, less posturing.

"Learned at camp, huh?" my grandfather asked.

"My counselor had a book full of them. I always won." I took the trick as if to prove the point.

He made an approving noise. "My mother—she was your great-grandma Elora; you never met her—was something else with a deck of cards," he said. We laid down our cards and he took the trick, surprising me. "She always had a deck in her purse." I thought about the deck I had stashed in Marin's purse. "She taught me a lot of games, but I learned this one in the service."

We played along silently for a few minutes. I won the game and gathered up the cards to start a new one.

"Rummy?"

He wiggled his eyebrows in you're-making-a-mistake style and nodded. I shuffled and dealt.

"Patty's a hell of a gal," he said at last, pulling his cards together and fanning them out. "She tries too hard sometimes, but she doesn't mean any harm by it."

"I'm not going to church," I mumbled, knowing where this was heading. I slapped my discard down pointedly, and he drew without missing a beat.

"No, no, me either," he said. "It's her church, not mine."

I glanced up, but he wasn't looking at me. "I didn't know my mom ever went," I said.

He nodded. "Oh, yeah. It was a big deal to her for a while there. Your grandma and I are pretty surprised she never took you. That's why your grandma thinks it'll help you to go. Might make you feel closer to your mom somehow. Might help you to pray for her a little. Or, hell, pray for yourself. Lord knows I've done my fair share of that in my lifetime. You don't have to go to church to pray."

"I don't know how to pray," I said, and once I'd admitted it, I realized that this was what had been keeping me from going all along. Not that I'd never gone to church or that I hated my grandmother or any other excuse. I'd been so freaked out when they died, and then I'd missed the funerals, and had gotten immersed in my problems in Caster City. I'd learned about the lies, about how I didn't really know Mom at all, and I'd gotten angry. And I don't know if the real problem was any of those things or all of them, but the truth was I didn't know how to talk to my mom now that she was gone. I didn't know what to say. And I felt so guilty about not saying anything. My mom and sister had died more than a month ago and I had never talked to them since. Had never told them how much I missed them or how I was feeling about everything or that I was fine and that I wasn't mad that they weren't home when the tornado hit or that I didn't hate Ronnie. I had never even tried.

I laid my cards facedown, suddenly too tired to concentrate. My grandfather still held his, rooted through them with his forefinger, choosing one and laying it on the discard pile.

"Well, I'm nobody's man of the cloth, but I believe you just pray by saying what's in your heart," he said. "I don't think there's any special formula for it. But your grandma'd know a lot more about that than I do. You should ask her."

But that was the problem. I had so much going on in my heart, and it didn't often go together or make sense or even stay the same from moment to moment. How did I speak from a heart that didn't understand itself? What did I say?

When the garage door rattled open, I was surprised that an hour had gone by so quickly.

My grandmother came in and for a moment just stood and watched our game, her light-brown old-lady purse dangling from her wrist, a pair of giant sunglasses on her face.

"Lunch?" she finally asked, peeling the glasses from her face and setting the purse on the counter.

232

"You betcha!" my grandfather cried, laying down his cards to win the game. I slapped down my remaining cards in frustration. "My belly button's rubbing my backbone."

"No, thank you," I said. "I need some fresh air."

I could see it, the bewilderment, as it crossed her face. Surely she had come in and seen me playing with him and thought I'd turned some big corner. Maybe she even thought this was the mark of a great beginning for us. A breakthrough.

But it was too much. All of it was too much. I didn't know what I was feeling, but I knew I needed some time alone, some space to think about everything.

CHAPTER
TWENTY-FIVE

The day had turned sort of cloudy but was still warm. Someone nearby was mowing a lawn and I breathed in deep as the scent of lawn mower, gasoline, and cut grass reached me. The smell made me nearly double over with memories.

Marin, outside with her plastic lawn mower, following Kolby around as he worked the real lawn mower in lines across his front yard. Her feet were bare in my memory, her toes painted pale pink and glittery. She was wearing a leotard—the one with the ladybug appliquéd to the front from a spring preschool recital— and was singing, though her song was drowned out by the noise.

Mom was kneeling in the flower bed, her hands in a pair of blue-and-gray-striped gardening gloves too big for her fingers. She gripped weeds in her left hand, using a trowel with her right to dig up stubborn roots, while at the same time asking me questions about school.

"How is Jane doing?"

"Fine. She got some award at the Model UN thing last weekend."

"Oh, wonderful! Tell her congratulations from me. What about you? What do you have coming up?"

"Not much. Drama club is doing monologues. Dani's performing a scene from *Alice in Wonderland*. You should hear it. It's really good. She made Mrs. Robb cry."

"What play is yours from?"

"I'm just doing the lighting. I don't have to do a monologue if I don't want to."

"Oh, but why don't you?"

I was drinking lemonade Mom had made that day because she'd gotten off work early. She'd even bought fresh raspberries—something we couldn't often afford—to sink in the bottom of the glass. The front door was open, the house dark behind the screen. Everyone was outside, playing or working, soaking up the cool early-evening air.

It was the best. It was a random day and could have been swapped with so many other days that were similar to it, yet it was the best.

And now I was walking through a strange neighborhood, alone, knowing I would never be outside with Mom, Marin, and Kolby again. I passed several neighbors, who all seemed to be eyeing me funny, and wondered how many of them knew my story. In a small town like Waverly, probably most of them did. Stories tended to be the favorite pastime in places like this. Stories about scandal or death or destruction even more so. And my story had all of the above.

Is that Patty and Barry's granddaughter?

Oh, yes, I'm sure it is. That ungrateful Christine's daughter, I suppose.

So-and-so told me she lost everything in that awful tornado up in Elizabeth. Can you imagine?

Poor thing. If her mama had stayed here . . .

I felt icky under their stares, but I also wasn't sure if I was imagining them, so I pointed my face down and kept walking.

I'd gone a good ways, and had a good ways to get back to my grandparents' house. Not that I was eager to get there, but I'd noticed that the sky had continued to darken, and now the faint rumbling of thunder sounded off in the distance, hastening my heartbeat. A storm was coming. How could I have not noticed when I left?

The wind began to pick up, the hair of the little girls playing ball whipping around their faces. They yelled louder to be heard over the wind as they played.

I checked the sky. The clouds seemed to be tumbling and roiling, blocking out the sun and making me feel cold inside. There hadn't been a storm since the rain stopped two days after the tornado. I had never been afraid of storms before, but I found my pace quickening, my breathing getting deeper as I lunged down the sidewalk, hoping to get back to the house before the storm really rolled through.

This wasn't me. I kept thinking that as I felt my limbs shaking, my brain filling up with panicky thoughts. I didn't even know who I was anymore, and it hurt to feel myself changing. I wanted my life back. I wanted so much that I couldn't ever have, and everything felt so horrifically unfair and frightening and sad, it took all I had to keep control. I felt like I was slipping away.

The thunder got louder and more frequent. I could see them. I could see my sister and mother, backing away from the windows at Janice's studio. I could hear the little girls crying, could feel the phone buzzing in my mother's pocket as I called her. I could see my mom, holding the phone to her ear, shouting, telling everyone to get back, unable to hear me on the other end of the line.

I could see them, hand in hand, sprinting across the street to the grocery store, ushering the little girls along in their sparkly leotards and their tightly bound updos. I could hear the girls' frightened voices, could smell the electricity in the air, could feel the sirens bleating through their bodies.

I could see them, eyes going wide as the tornado became visible, and then squinching down tight as debris and cars and streetlights and entire roofs looked like dots of litter in the sky, before crashing down onto the streets.

I could feel them, fear sinking in—fear and the instinct for self-preservation—as they thrust themselves down the aisles at the grocery store, hoping to get far enough....

I reached the end of the street and turned the corner to get back to Flora Lane, picking up to a jog, and then a run as raindrops—pregnant and insistent—began to beat down on me. Out of the corner of my eye, I saw the ball the kids had been throwing earlier, bouncing in the wind down the center of the street.

It had gotten so dark. So very dark.

I pushed myself harder. My stomach hurt from exertion and panic. My grandparents' house still seemed so far away.

And then I skidded to a stop, gasping and pressing my palms hard over my ears as the tornado alarm started sounding.

CHAPTER TWENTY-SIX

My grandmother was standing on the front porch, one hand holding the top of her head as if she were afraid her hair was going to fly off. Her face was deeply lined with worry as she glanced at the sky and then moved her eyes up and down the street. She called my name twice before she saw me, half-jogging, half-staggering along the sidewalk, hands over ears, ragged breath tearing dry tears out of me.

I didn't want her to be a beacon of safety for me. I didn't want to feel like I was running home while running to her. But my heart leapt around in my chest when I saw her.

"Jersey! There you are," she said, and I could barely hear her over the siren. "I was worried."

The rain began to splatter around me as I cut through the front yard, my legs feeling exhausted and jelly-like as I pounded one foot in front of the other. For a terrifying, almost dizzying moment I was afraid I'd be unable to make it those last few steps. I was sure my legs would give out and crumple beneath me, that I would sprawl facedown in the grass, my grandmother unable to pull me up. I imagined the sky splitting open and an angry tornado reaching down to scoop me up and toss me into its eye with flying debris and swirling dead people; people like my mom and sister.

But somehow I made it, and even though my grandmother was reaching out to me, I lunged right past her and into the house. I raced through the hall and down the basement steps without even pausing to search for the light switch, my brain briefly flashing back to the day Meg and Lexi had shut off the basement light and I'd gotten so spooked. The memory only served to agitate me further, and I could feel fury rushing through me.

Down in the basement, it was quieter. The sirens were muted and the wind was no longer beating in my ears and the rain sounded far away up on the roof. Still, I was buzzing. My head was making a siren noise of its own. My ears were ringing and my breath panted out of me as I paced, moaning and crying and growling. I didn't know what was wrong with me. I'd never felt or acted this way in a storm before. But I couldn't stop it. I couldn't stop the fiery, tossed feeling in my chest, and I couldn't stop my body from acting on it.

"Jersey?" my grandmother called, and seconds later the basement was bathed in light. I saw her feet pad down the carpeted stairs. "Jersey? Can you hear me?"

And maybe it was the way she kept saying my name—always, constantly, saying my name—or maybe it was the fear or the siren, which had gotten into my head. Or maybe it was those words—"Can you hear me?" Those words that I had said to my mother a few weeks before. Those words, which had gone unanswered.

Maybe it was all of the above, but I panicked. My chest squeezed tight and I dropped to my knees on the floor, surprised by the sensation. My hands, which were shaking, clutched at my chest and I gasped and gasped. I could feel my eyes bugging out, but I couldn't see my grandmother or the carpeted basement steps anymore.

All I could see was the bottom of Ronnie's pool table, the papers as they blew around me, a rolling ashtray. All I could hear was the collapse of my kitchen down into the basement, the roar of a wind mightier than anyone had seen in forty years, death and destruction balled up inside its nasty, painful grip. I could hear the sound of glass breaking, of bricks thudding to concrete, the squeak of wood splintering. Myself screaming.

Screaming and screaming and screaming, my eyes squeezed shut so tightly I was no longer sure where I was. Only that I felt paralyzed by fear—the fear that began on the day my mom took Marin to dance and never came home again. The fear I'd been holding at bay, had been pushing down inside myself, all through the days after the tornado, through the time at the motel with Ronnie, through those frightening nights of wondering what Lexi and Meg would do to me. The fear washed over me, held me down, made me feel like I was going to die—just lie down and join my mother and sister.

I don't know how long I remained that way. But eventually, as if coming up from the deep end of a pool and taking my first breath, I began to sense things. My grandmother's voice, saying my name over and over again, her hands gripping my shoulders, and a movement that sharpened into shaking.

"Jersey!" she was barking. "Jersey, dammit! Stop screaming. It's going to be okay. Jersey!"

She shook harder and harder and I felt my head moving back and forth on my shoulders, and finally the shrieking just... died out. I blinked through the tears and the swollen eyelids and saw my grandmother kneeling before me, looking stern.

"Stop it," she said. "Stop screaming. They've turned off the sirens."

My mouth clopped shut, my lips slippery with snot, and I tried to catch my breath.

"It's all clear," she said, her voice still barking, but softer now. She'd given me a soft shake on the words "all" and "clear" but then must have seen some recognition that I was back to reality, because she nodded curtly and let go, then stood up. My grandmother crossed her arms and gazed down at me unyieldingly.

"You can't go disappearing like that," she said, and I wondered if this sharp-featured woman was the Patty my mom had hated so much. "We were worried sick with the storm coming in. You could have been anywhere. Grandpa Barry is out there right now, driving around looking for you."

"I didn't tell him to come find me," I said, my numb lips barely opening to let the words out.

"You could have gotten hurt. Or worse."

"Worse," I repeated, then coughed a dull, mirthless laugh. I felt like I was dying. Or maybe like I would never finish dying. Like I would be stuck in this pain forever. I turned my eyes up to look at her, furious and scared and swinging wildly with my words. "You mean I could have lost everything I ever cared about? Bad news, that's already happened. Or do you mean worse like I could have died? Because that would actually have been better. I should have died with them. I wish I had died with them." Somehow, despite my fatigue, I managed to pull myself to standing. "Death would be a blessing," I said, though I knew I didn't mean it, and I knew that the words hurt her and scared her. I didn't care. I was beyond caring. I was so confused and so overwrought and so tired of all of this. What did it matter if someone else got hurt? She could join us—the walking-wounded club.

She softened, tried to reach out to me, but I shrugged away. "Oh, Jersey, you don't mean that. I know you were close to your mom, but—"

"Don't talk about my mom," I snarled, my voice ratcheting up again. "She hated you. She ran away from you before I was born, and she never wanted anything to do with you again. It's actually a good thing she's dead, because she would rather die than see me be raised by you."

My grandmother stiffened, and I was almost certain I saw her eyes go soft and watery, but she kept herself together. "Unfortunately, we're your only choice," she said.

"You can't call it a choice when there's only one option," I said. "I didn't choose. I don't know anything about you.

Because my mom didn't tell us anything. Marin lived and died with no grandparents, don't you understand that? Marin never even asked about you, because you didn't exist to her. So thanks for the 'choice,' but no, thanks."

This time I did see a tear roll down my grandmother's softly wrinkled cheek, and I was sick enough to feel satisfaction. I even smiled, though inside I knew it was wrong to hurt another person this way. I wasn't the only one hurting, and my pain wasn't her fault, wasn't anyone's fault. She was just the one getting the blame.

"Jersey, we want to help you," she said softly. She reached toward me again, and this time I skirted her and headed for the stairs. "We can get you some grief counseling," she called to my back. "We can get you whatever you need. We love you."

I stomped up the stairs. Grief counseling. Like that was going to work. Like some New Age bullshit-spouting therapist with "coping techniques" was going to bring my mom and sister back.

"Well, I don't love you," I said coldly over my shoulder, not bothering to break my stride. "None of us ever did."

I slapped the light switch as I reached the top of the stairs, leaving my grandmother in darkness, the same way Meg and Lexi had left me.

CHAPTER
TWENTY-SEVEN

It rained off and on for the rest of the day and into the evening. I could hear my grandparents puttering around the house, doors opening and shutting softly, words spoken too low to make out.

I curled up in my blankets and stared through the window at the gray sky, the raindrops on the glass making funny shadows on my comforter.

I felt awful. I couldn't help myself. Now that I'd dumped everything on my grandmother, I was consumed with guilt. Partly for hurting her, but also partly because I'd begun to doubt my mother. What if my grandparents weren't the only ones to blame? What if she'd been hardheaded and hard-hearted, too? I knew it was possible, because I'd barely recognized myself down in that basement.

And what did it matter, anyway? Mom's fight with them was most definitely over now. Had it been worth it to her? Did she know her parents had come to her funeral? Did she know I was with them now? Did she approve?

I wished so badly I could talk to her, that I could ask her these things.

Under the covers, I shut my eyes and pressed my palms together, waiting for words, but it was like something inside me was afraid to approach my mom, even in prayer. Every time I got close to thinking a direct thought to her, my brain backed away, my heart closed down, my words failed me. Talking to her this way meant she was dead, and I couldn't go there.

My door opened and the light switched on, making me wince and blink. My grandfather stood in the doorway, which surprised me. Usually it was my grandmother who came to my room. He'd never once come in.

"Grandma went to bed for the night," he said evenly. "She was upset and had a headache. So if you want dinner, you're gonna have to make it yourself. Unless you want peanut butter and jelly. I can make that much."

"No, thanks, I'm not hungry," I told the streaks of rain on the window. But after he left, leaving the door open behind him, I found that I was actually starving.

It took me a few minutes to work up the nerve to enter the kitchen, where I knew he would be. But there was something about my grandfather that I didn't mind so much. Maybe it was the cards, but I almost felt a sort of connection with him, even if I didn't want to admit it. There was something about him that seemed trustworthy. It felt like it had been so long since I'd had someone to trust.

I wasn't surprised to see him at the kitchen table, playing solitaire. And losing, as usual.

"Three of clubs on two up top," I muttered as I walked by. Out of the corner of my eye, I could see him pick up the card and move it, while I searched through the cabinets until I found a box of macaroni and cheese. I flipped it over to look at the directions, even though I pretty much had them memorized. It had been so long since I'd gotten to do something as mundane as make myself macaroni and cheese. It felt good, like a routine revisited. I put a pan of water on the stove and turned it on, then leaned against the kitchen counter, unsure of what else to do. "There's a jack there," I said.

My grandfather stared at his cards, his hands hovering above them. I stepped forward and pointed.

"Right there."

He moved the cards.

"Why do you keep playing that game?" I asked. "You always miss the cards."

"Oh," he said, pulling three cards out of the deck in his hand and flipping over the last one, "I suppose I think it's keeping me mentally agile." He glanced up, winked at me. "Imagine how many I'd miss if I didn't play."

I couldn't help giggling. "You'd miss none. Because you wouldn't be playing."

"Huh," he said, acting as if he were pondering. "I guess I wouldn't, would I? Or maybe I'd miss them all. Care to join me? We can play Spit."

I grinned. Spit was all about speed. No one had ever beaten

me at Spit. Once, I'd even made Marin cry during a game of Spit, it was such a slaughter. "Deal me in."

The water began to boil behind me and I poured in the pasta and gave it a quick stir, then slid into the chair across from my grandfather as he counted out twenty-six cards for each of us.

"Quite a storm we had this afternoon, wasn't it?" he said absently as he dealt.

I bit my lip. I didn't want to talk about it. I wasn't ready yet to confess to him that I felt guilty for how I'd lost it down there. For how I'd attacked my grandmother.

"You know, we get pretty intense storms around here all summer long. Break off our tomato plants, blow the barbecue grill to the other side of the porch. One time we had hail so big it busted out the skylights."

I picked up my cards. What was he getting at?

He gathered his cards and leveled his gaze at me. He didn't look angry, but he did look serious. "We've never once had a tornado here. In all my sixty-two years, not one."

I understood what he was getting at—that I needed to let go of my fears because the chances of ever being in another tornado were so slim. The devastation in Elizabeth was unexpected for a reason—because tornadoes as huge as ours almost never happen. It was a freak accident, losing my family. That fact didn't make it suck any less, but the chances that it would happen again were almost zero. And I couldn't keep living my life expecting tragedy around every corner.

"You said you learned how to play in the service," I said, trying to change the subject. "Were you ever in a war?"

"It's a long story," he said. "But yes."

And maybe it was because playing cards relaxed me. Or maybe it was because I felt guilty for what I'd done to my grandmother. Or maybe I had finally gotten so lonely, so sick of my thoughts being my only company. I suddenly wanted to talk.

"I've got time," I said.

So he proceeded to tell me about the Vietnam War, where he was a young private, barely out of high school, scared for his life. He told me how he'd felt insanely homesick and how every cross word he'd ever uttered to anyone he loved plagued him as he watched young men dying around him every day. He said he'd lie awake at night and replay all the good times and bad that he'd had with his family, hoping that if he died, they'd only remember the good. He'd never had a girlfriend before he got enlisted, and he worried that he'd die over there and never know what it was like to fall in love.

"That was the worst," he said. "I would rather have had someone to love and left her too soon than die never knowing love at all." He let that sink in while we flipped cards over. "But," he said with renewed vigor, "turned out I wasn't supposed to find Patty before I went. I met her the day after I got home, can you believe that? The day after."

I rooted through my cards, then drew a nine that I needed and laid it down. "Why didn't you talk to my mom again? I mean...after she split up with Clay."

My grandfather drew a card and studied it. "I wish we had" was all he said.

*   *   *

There was a sizzling sound as the pot of water boiled over. I jumped up to stir it and turn the flame down, absently setting my cards on the edge of the table. They fell off with a whisper, spreading themselves across the linoleum floor. I calmed the overflowing pot, then went down to my knees to pick up the cards, which had fanned underneath a side table.

That's when I noticed it for the first time—a porcelain kitten tucked away on a low shelf. I picked it up and turned it over in my hands, forgetting about the cards as I stood up.

It was a glossy orange-and-white tabby with a number three on its chest, pawing at a purple butterfly.

I held it out to my grandfather, feeling like someone had stolen my breath. "Where did you get this?" I asked.

He frowned at it over his glasses in the same maddeningly nonchalant way he did everything. "That? Oh, I think it belonged to Christine. Her mother bought her one for her birthday every year. Christine loved cats. She treasured that collection. She left the whole thing behind." He took the kitten out of my hand and looked it over. "Your grandma packed them all up and put them away. All except this one. She keeps it out because it was Chrissy's favorite." He set the statue on the table between us. My eyes felt riveted to it as pieces of my life snapped into place. "You'd better tend to that pot," he said. "It's fixing to boil over again."

I walked over and took the pot off the stove, then searched until I found a colander and drained the pasta, stirred in the cheese and butter and milk. But I did these things on autopilot. In my mind, all I could see was a padded manila envelope, one each year, sitting on our old kitchen table back in Elizabeth.

"It's another kitten, I'll bet!" I could hear myself say excitedly, a birthday girl waiting for cake and presents.

I could see the sour look on my mother's face as she watched me tear open the envelope year after year. I'd always assumed she'd looked so sour because they had come from Clay. I'd always assumed that was why Marin never got one.

But how could Mom tell me? How could she tell me they were from the grandparents she'd raised me to believe were so mean? How could she admit that they weren't absent after all, but were reaching out to me in the only way they knew how?

On second thought...how *couldn't* she tell me these things? How could she be so stubborn? How could *she* be the cruel one?

Because she'd never in a million years thought I'd find out, that was how. She'd never have guessed that one day I would be playing Spit with her father at the kitchen table she'd grown up eating on. Whatever grudge match had occurred between them, she'd never thought I'd learn about it.

I took a bowl out of the cabinet and spooned in some macaroni.

"You got any extra? I'm not really in the mood for peanut butter and jelly," my grandfather said.

I glanced over to find that he had picked up my spilled cards and dealt.

"Cheater. I didn't see you deal those," I said, reaching up to pull down a second bowl.

He spread his palms over his chest, making a show of innocence. "Cheater? I'm an innocent old man," he said.

"Uh-huh," I said, carrying the bowls to the table and setting one in front of him. "Redeal, old man."

He swept the cards together and shuffled, chuckling, as I blew into my bowl to cool it off, keeping one eye on the kitten the whole time. I'd treated these people horribly. I'd refused to speak to them, refused to be pleasant. I'd said awful things to my grandmother, and her only response had been to tell me she loved me. My grandfather had invited me to play with him. They understood, even when I was being unfair and selfish and ugly.

They'd acted like…family. Like they were offering a place to belong. I just had to take it.

My grandfather started laying cards out on the table again. "As if I need to cheat," he blustered, "against a girl with purple hair."

CHAPTER
TWENTY-EIGHT

As dire as the sky had looked the day before, it looked that much brighter the next morning, as if the sun were trying to make up for lost opportunity. For the first time since arriving at my grandparents' house, I awoke without one of them waking me, a shaft of sunlight warm across my face, like a caress.

The night before, after Grandpa Barry and I had played Spit and then three hands of rummy, I'd made brownies from a box I found in the back of the pantry. I'd placed the plate of brownies on the table between us and poured two glasses of milk. I taught him how to play Seven Bridge, and he won the first game, which included a lot of crowing and laughter on his part. I blamed the loss on distraction. How was I supposed to concentrate on the cards with the kitten in the center of the table?

Grandpa Barry was good at keeping me from brooding. We chatted about places that had the best ice cream, whether or not soccer was a boring sport, books we'd read, and the Waverly theater company, which he thought had a summer program that I could get involved with if I wanted.

Not one word about storms or tornadoes or my freakout or the way I'd been acting or the lifelong grudge my mother had held against them. Just brownies and milk and cards.

And for a few minutes, none of that reminded me of Mom or Marin.

When I realized that I had spent time not thinking about them, I instantly felt guilty. I tried to call up their faces in my mind. They were fuzzy, but they were still there. I imagined their voices as they spoke to me. I was pretty sure I could remember those. I told myself that eating brownies and playing cards wasn't going to make them deader. It wasn't like a bowl of macaroni and cheese with my grandfather meant I was forgetting they ever existed.

I pulled myself out of bed, showered and dressed, then padded into the kitchen, where my grandmother sat over a newspaper, a pen in her hand. She looked surprised to see me but didn't say a word as I passed by. I tried to act as if everything was totally normal between us, going to the fridge to grab a cup of yogurt I'd seen in there the night before.

I sat across from her and ripped off the top of my yogurt. "Where's Grandpa Barry?"

"He went into town to pick up a few yard supplies. Got some fertilizing to do this weekend," she said. She leaned over and wrote something into a crossword.

"He going to be gone long?" I spooned yogurt into my mouth, my heart beating, knowing what I was about to ask.

"Oh, a little while," she said. "You never know with him. He runs into people and gets talking. How come?"

I swallowed. "I thought maybe we could go to Elizabeth today. I've never seen my mom's grave." I let the words fall between us, my stomach sinking further the longer she took to respond.

She lifted her chin, tapped her pen to it a few times, looked out the window. "Well, I don't know if he'll be back in time to go."

"Just the two of us," I said. "Me and you."

Almost instantly, the end of my grandmother's nose bloomed red. I only noticed it because that was something that always happened to my mom, too. The moment she even thought about crying, her nose would redden, starting with the tip.

"I need to put on some decent clothes," she said. "I can do that right now." I could tell she was making an effort to not look as hopeful and eager as she felt.

I let out a breath I hadn't realized I was holding. "Okay."

She pushed away from the table, leaving the crossword right where it was, then hurried out of the kitchen. From the living room, she called, "We can have lunch at Orrie's. It was one of Chrissy's favorites."

"Sure," I said after a pause, and even though I still felt all kinds of uncertain, something about the day ahead felt right, too.

She left a note on the kitchen table for Grandpa Barry, and we got in the car. I watched out the window as we pulled through town.

"Is that the high school?" I asked, pointing to a brick building about half the size of my school.

"Yes, ma'am," she said, "but your grandfather and I have been talking. If you'd like to stay at your school for senior year, we'd certainly understand. We've got a little money put aside and are willing to use it to rent a place in Elizabeth for the school year. It won't be home, and we probably will need to come back to Waverly on the weekends to tend to the house, but we want you to be happy."

"Really?"

"Of course. Chrissy wouldn't have wanted you to be uprooted your senior year. They're saying your school will be rebuilt by August, can you believe it?"

I shook my head. I almost couldn't believe anything at this point. The thought of getting to spend senior year with my friends, at our favorite places to hang out, in the lighting booth and on the stage, made me feel somehow whole again.

"Thank you," I breathed. "Thank you so much. We can come back every weekend, I won't mind."

"Well, some weekends you might want to stay, if you have things to do with your friends in Elizabeth," she said. "But we'll work it all out."

It didn't make sense. How could the grandparents Mom had told us were so horrible be the kind of people who'd be willing to move to another city so their grandchild wouldn't have to go to a new school? How could oppressive and judgmental people never say anything less than a kind word to me, even when I hadn't been kind to them? I'd never questioned

Mom. Never. But it didn't add up. The things she'd said about Barry and Patty were...well, they seemed wrong. And did it really matter anymore, anyway? Mom was gone; my grandparents were all I had.

We drove a little while longer, until I couldn't take it anymore. "What happened?" I blurted out as we turned onto the highway.

She glanced at me, then changed lanes. "What do you mean?"

"What happened between you guys and my mom? Why did she hate you so much? She told us you disowned her."

My grandmother's hands wrapped tightly around the steering wheel, her eyes locked straight ahead. She hesitated, and for a moment I worried that nobody would ever tell me what had happened. I would never know the truth.

"We did," she finally said. "She got mixed up with Clay. His whole family was a mess. A bunch of criminals and drunks. We told her that we didn't approve and that she couldn't see him, but Chrissy was so strong-willed. Always had been, ever since she was a toddler."

I thought about my mom. I'd hated arguing with her, because there was no winning. When Mom got her mind set on something, it was going to happen, whether you liked it or not, no matter how much begging and pleading you did. It was good to be reminded that some of the things I knew about her were absolute truths.

"Anyway," my grandmother continued, "she started dating him, and next thing we knew she was getting in trouble, too. Ending up in jail. Once she got arrested for taking off her bikini top and throwing it up onstage at a concert. She was so drunk she didn't even care that she was topless. We tried putting our foot down, but she pushed back harder. Found ways to be with him no matter what we did. He had a hold on her like we'd never seen before."

"So you disowned her because she wouldn't listen to you?"

"No," she said. "She got pregnant, but she was still doing all the same old destructive things. We got worried. About you, Jersey. We were afraid she was going to hurt you. So we tried to get her some counseling, but she said if we insisted, she would run away and marry Clay. We told her if she did, she might as well never come back. And she ran away. And she never came back."

"But you told her she couldn't."

My grandmother glanced at me. "If there was one thing we wished we'd never said, that would be it. We immediately began searching for her, but she'd moved out of Waverly and we had no idea where she'd gone. When we finally found her in Elizabeth, she'd already had you. We were so excited and ready to put everything behind us. But he still had such a hold over her. She wouldn't come home, and she called the police. So we left. And we worried so much about you, but Chrissy wouldn't budge. She loved him, and the way she saw it, we were the enemy."

These things didn't sound like Mom, and I had a hard time imagining her turning her own parents away in favor of that disgusting man I'd met in Caster City.

"But they split up, eventually," I said. "Why didn't she come back after he left?"

"I don't know," my grandmother said. "I really don't. We sent some...letters...some packages over the years, but we never heard anything back. We worry that we gave up too easily. Like I said, if only we could do it all over again."

"The kittens came from you."

She paused, then nodded. "Yes. You got them?"

I opened Marin's purse and pulled the black-and-white kitten out and held it up. She glanced at it several times, trying to keep her eye on traffic. "This is the only one that survived the tornado. I thought they came from Clay."

"They were from us. Chrissy had a set. She loved them, and they were the best way we could reach out to you and let her know that we still loved her, too. They were our way of saying we were thinking about you both the whole time," she said. "And praying that you were okay."

All those years, Mom and I were alone. I'd grown up believing that our aloneness was something that had happened to us—something we had to prevail over—but really it was only something that had happened to me. Mom had wanted it, and she had not given me a choice in the matter.

And all the time there was this family out there wondering about me. Caring about me. Wishing me safe and imagining what my life was like and giving me a place to belong in their hearts, even if I never showed up there.

But now here I was, and it was up to me whether I wanted to claim my spot.

"What was my mom like when she was my age?" I asked. "Before she met Clay, I mean?"

My grandmother smiled wistfully. "She was a ball of fire. Independent, outgoing. She was a cheerleader in junior high, you know."

I blinked. Mom, a cheerleader? I tried to picture her hopping around in a short dress waving pom-poms. I couldn't do it.

"She always thought she was going to be a hairstylist," my grandmother continued. "One time, in elementary school, she cut her own bangs. Chopped them so short the other kids teased her mercilessly. They called her T-square for months. But Chrissy didn't care. She was the kind of person who was going to do what she wanted, the whole world be damned."

"She pretty much stayed that way," I said. And then, thinking about Marin's relentless begging for me to dance with her, added, "My sister was like that, too."

My grandmother glanced at me, her mouth turned down at the corners. "I wish I'd met her," she said.

And I couldn't help thinking that Marin would have liked our grandparents. "Yeah," I said softly. We drove along for a while longer. I held the kitten in my lap, stroking its side with my thumb. "Are there other relatives?" I asked, breaking the silence. "Like, cousins and stuff?"

"Yes," she said. "I have a sister and a brother. Barry has two brothers. But they're all in St. Louis, where we both grew up. Maybe we'll take a ride out there someday," she said, then amended, almost shyly, "if you want."

I didn't know if I wanted to do that or not. I was curious, but this felt like it was all happening so fast. I shrugged. "Someday," I said. "If you grew up in St. Louis, why are you here?" To me, St. Louis seemed so much more exciting than Waverly.

And as we drove along the highway toward Elizabeth, my grandmother told me stories about my family. She talked about how she met my grandfather and their move from St. Louis to Waverly and everything that led up to having my mom.

She told me more things about my mom—that she hated being an only child and asked Santa for a baby sister every year, that she could swim like a fish and do splits in both directions and that, before she started smoking, she could outrun every girl in her class, and most of the boys, too.

And then she talked about Clay's family, how they were notorious throughout Waverly as being a nuisance. How they always had so many babies around you wondered where they all came from, but there was never any mistaking a Cameron baby because they all looked alike. *We* all looked alike.

Before I knew it, we were driving up the exit into Elizabeth, all at once the surroundings looking familiar and unfamiliar to me, as if I'd been gone forever. This part of town had been untouched by the tornado, and other than a few downed trees, you would never have guessed that anything unusual had happened here. We stopped at a grocery store and bought flowers to put on the graves. I picked out pink carnations for Marin's, because the florist had sprinkled glitter across them. I knew how much Marin had loved pink and sparkles. My grandmother bought red roses, because those represented love.

We shared memories, and picked out the perfect flowers, and by the time we reached the cemetery, my mom and sister were in some ways more alive to me than they'd ever been.

CHAPTER TWENTY-NINE

We both stopped talking as we drove through the cemetery. There was a very somber feeling about being there, so somber I almost felt a buzzing in my ears. Someone was being buried near the entrance; the mourners' dresses fluttered in the breeze as they stood with their heads bowed.

Everywhere I looked, it seemed, there were mounds of new dirt. New graves. My grandmother had told me that the final death count from the tornado was one hundred twenty-nine. One hundred twenty-nine lives stolen, only two of them from me. It seemed so weird to think of so many families grappling with the same sadness I'd been wrestling. This was the only cemetery in Elizabeth, so most of them were likely buried here.

"Let me see..." my grandmother said as she turned right down one of the little side roads that snaked deeper into the cemetery. "I think it's over by that fence back there."

I gazed out the window, trying to find two fresh mounds

near the fence, swallowing against the lump in my throat. This was where they were—my mom and my sister. This was where they would be forever. The finality of their deaths hit me on a whole different level. This wasn't temporary. They were really gone. They were never coming back. At the end of this nightmare there would be no happy reunion.

Finally, my grandmother put the car in park and turned it off. She let her hands rest in her lap, gazing down at them for a few minutes. The only sound in the car was the crinkle of the plastic around the flowers as I squeezed them tighter.

"You ready?" she asked.

I turned back toward the window. The two graves were obvious now that we were near them. "As ready as I'll ever be," I said.

We got out and traipsed toward the fence line. I read some of the names on the headstones, not recognizing a single one, and idly wishing that there were at least one person nearby that Mom would have known. Someone to keep her company. But I guessed she had Marin for that. I clutched the flowers so tight my fingers ached. Marin's purse bumped along my side.

"They don't have headstones yet," my grandmother said as we got closer, but it was as if she wasn't really talking to me so much as she was talking to herself. "I hope he bought her one, at least."

I couldn't imagine Ronnie not buying them headstones. But who knew what Ronnie would do and not do these days? After all, I'd never have guessed he'd abandon me. Boy, did he ever surprise me with that one.

We stopped walking, and even though I suddenly didn't want to, was suddenly terrified to, I had no choice but to look at their final resting place.

I turned my eyes forward, expecting to be hit by an onslaught of sadness. Maybe even weakness, grief pulling me to my knees.

But it was just dirt.

Two splotches of dirt in an otherwise grassy field. One splotch of dirt much longer than the other. My mom and Marin were under there somewhere, but these splotches of dirt weren't them. Now that I was here, I wasn't even sure why I expected them to be.

My grandmother sniffed lightly, and I caught movement out of the corner of my eye, which might have been her wiping her eyes, but I was too riveted to the dirt mounds to pay her much attention.

"They're gone," I said. The obvious. "Ronnie sent me away before the funerals. I didn't get to say good-bye, and now it's too late because they're gone."

"I didn't get to, either." She paused for a really long time. Then finally, "But I like to think they knew I loved them, even if Marin didn't know me."

"But I never got to say it. I never told them."

She sniffed again, and then said, her voice louder with resolve, "You can tell them now."

I turned to her. "But I can't. I don't know how."

My grandmother looked like she was slowly melting. She tried to keep it in, but her face jiggled and wobbled and soon crumpled in completely. She nodded, letting out a sob. "I know," she said. "And I don't know how to help you. I feel like the only thing I can offer my daughter after all these years is to help you let her go, and I can't do it. How can I, when I'm not ready to let her go myself?"

I stood awkwardly in front of her. I hated that she was crying, but this whole grandmother-and-granddaughter thing was so new to me, and I was such a volcano of conflicting feelings myself, always feeling so near eruption I barely wanted to move.

I bent my knees and dropped the flowers on the ground, then stood up again. Slowly, I opened Marin's purse, then unzipped the small compartment inside. The foils shone at me, as if they were lit from within rather than reflecting sunlight. I scooped them out and held them in my palm, offering them to my grandmother.

She sniffled some more, blinking and calming down as she tried to understand what I was giving her.

"What's this?" she said, pulling a crumpled tissue out of her pants pocket and wiping her cheeks with it.

I licked my lips. "This is Marin," I said.

Slowly, with shaky hands, she reached out and plucked a foil out of my palm. She unfolded it, looking uncertain.

" 'Marin loves scorpions,' " she read. She flicked a curious glance at me, then reached out and took another. " 'Marin is a monkey.' "

And even though my drawings couldn't possibly have made sense to her, she took another and then another, reading each one aloud, sometimes laughing a wet laugh and sometimes unable to finish the sentence for the tears in her voice. She met her other granddaughter that way, one chewed-up memory at a time.

We sat down on the ground together at my mom's feet, the purse open between us so my grandmother could put the foils down without their blowing away. I explained some of them. The same way she told me about my mom's cut bangs and swimming prowess, I told her about Marin's peach-colored leotard and about the East Coast Swing. I picked at the petals of one of Mom's roses as I talked, and my grandmother cried and asked questions and laughed and interjected and cried some more.

Finally, when we were both talked and cried out, I turned onto my knees and placed the bouquets of flowers on each grave, wiping dirt that had gotten stuck on my palms onto the sides of my shirt. I assessed how the flowers looked, and then, struck by a moment of bravery, I decided that if I was on my knees anyway, I might as well give talking to my mom a try.

At last.

CHAPTER
THIRTY

My grandfather had said that to pray was to speak from my heart. So that's exactly what I did. I pressed my palms together and closed my eyes, feeling shaky and nervous and self-conscious. I talked silently, in my head, so my grandmother couldn't hear what I had to say. We had started to get to know each other, but that didn't mean I wanted her to know everything. I still wanted to keep some things to myself.

Hey, God, I said. *I know you're keeping Mom and Marin safe up there and everything, and I'm really glad about that. I'm sure they were scared when they got to you. So thanks for taking care of them.* I took a breath and squeezed my palms together tighter. *I'm, um...not sure how to do this, but I'd really kind of like to talk to my mom, if that's okay. I haven't gotten to say anything to her since she died.*

My knees pressed into the soft ground, and I let my butt sink slowly to rest on the backs of my legs. I squeezed my eyes tight, like I'd done before, and tried to picture Mom's face in my mind.

And just when I thought the image would never come, it did.

She was smiling at me. Laughing, maybe. There was sunlight highlighting the top of her head and she was wearing that ridiculous pair of sunglasses that I'd always made fun of because they were so huge.

I felt such love radiating off her, the words poured out of my heart.

Hi, Mom, I said in my head. *I'm sorry you haven't heard from me until now. I didn't know how to talk to you at first and I was afraid that if I started talking to you it would mean you were really dead. Which is stupid, of course, because you've been really dead all along. I've just had a hard time believing it.*

So I guess you've seen everything that's happened since you died. All the stuff with Ronnie and Clay and Lexi and Meg. I'm not gonna lie, Mom, it's been hard. And scary. And every day I wish I had died with you. Not that I'm suicidal or anything, so you don't need to worry about that. Just that I wish I hadn't been left behind, all alone. That part really sucks.

But I've learned a few things. Like that Ronnie loved you so much he can't live without you. Which, even though it hurt me, is kind of cool in a way.

And that Clay is maybe the worst man on earth and I will never, ever be stuck in the same room with him again. At first I didn't understand why you lied to me about him leaving us, and I felt really betrayed. I thought everything I knew about you might have been a lie, but since meeting him and your parents, I've realized that the parts of you I knew weren't untrue; they were only part-truths. There were lots of things about you that I didn't know, and learning those things has actually been comforting in a way. They make me feel closer to you. And I can see that actually there's one real truth, and that is you loved me enough to do anything it took to protect me. I think that's something I've known my whole life. I'm thankful for it.

Grandma Patty and Grandpa Barry. Well, they're not so bad, Mom. Maybe I just haven't seen the bad side of them yet, and maybe someday I will and I'll totally understand all the things you said about them. But right now I don't feel like I have to hold my breath when I'm around them as much, which is good, because they're my only choice.

I think about you all the time. You and Marin both, but mainly you. I remember all the stuff we did together, and the little moments when you did awesome things like get us out of bed to go get ice cream or buy us snowboards or that time you read the entire Harry Potter series out loud to us. It took you like six months, but you never complained.

Do you remember that time you took me to the water park? Just me, because Marin wasn't born yet and you hadn't even met Ronnie. I think I was in third grade, maybe? You wore your red polka-dotted swimsuit and I had that bikini with the stripes that I hated because it made me feel fat.

Anyway, we went to the water park and we rode that huge slide. I think it was called the Slippery Cyclone. Remember how you had to talk and talk to get me on it? I was so scared. That slide was so tall and the pool at the end looked so deep and I wasn't sure if I could touch the bottom.

I was afraid something would happen to me if I sat down and let myself go. But, worse than that, I was afraid something would happen to you. That you'd fly off into the woods and smash onto the rocks below or that the slide would cave in and crush you or that you'd just never come down and I'd be treading water at the bottom of that slide forever and ever waiting for you. Waiting for those red-and-white polka dots to swoosh around that last corner.

That's how I feel now, Mom. Like I'm treading water and you're not coming down the slide. I can't touch the bottom here, and I'm scared. I want you back.

There are some things I never got to say. I'm sorry, Mom, for all the times I got mad and was mean to you. I'm sorry about the time I told you I hated you because you wouldn't let me go to Jane's house on Ronnie's birthday. I'm sorry I didn't tell you I loved you when you took Marin to dance the night of the tornado. If I had to do it all over again, I would like to say I'd take all those things back, but I don't know if I would. We were close, so close sometimes we screamed at each other, and I've been thinking that maybe those things were just different sides of the same coin. When we were screaming hateful things, it was only because we were feeling loving things. I don't know, maybe that sounds stupid. But I like to think that way, because it makes me feel as if even though I didn't show it sometimes, you still knew how much I loved you.

270

I've been thinking a lot about the word "everything." Whenever something horrible happens, you hear people say they "lost everything." They lost their house, or their car or their stuff or whatever, and to them it feels like "everything." But they have no idea what it's really like to lose everything. I thought I knew, but now I realize even I haven't lost everything, because I still have that polka-dot swimsuit in my memory. I still have those ice cream nights and the snowboards and the scorpion that scared Marin and the Barking Bulldogs sweatshirt and the robin's-egg-blue nail polish. Somehow having those things makes the other stuff matter less.

I'm wondering if it's even possible to lose "everything," or if you just have to keep redefining what "everything" is. Because I didn't know it before, but somehow Grandpa Barry and Grandma Patty fit into my "everything" now, and even if I'm not sure yet how they fit, they're there.

I guess that's just my way of saying you don't need to worry about me giving up. I'm just going to keep redefining "everything" for as long as I need to, because I'm pretty sure that's the best way to keep on going when you feel like you've lost it all.

I've learned a lot of new things about you from a lot of different people, but one thing everyone agrees on is that you were headstrong. You were tough. You taught me how to be tough, too. You taught me how to tread water and how to swim out of the deep end. But I'll probably be looking for that red swimsuit for a while yet.

I love you, Mom, and I miss you so much. Tell Marin I said I love her, too. And I miss the way she hums.

CHAPTER THIRTY-ONE

The first thing I carried into our Elizabeth duplex was a litter box. I'd set it in the laundry room closet and poured litter into it, hoping Swing would get the hang of it in our new place.

She was a gray-and-white ball of trouble, or at least that's what my grandfather called her after the fourth or fifth time he had to pluck her from the top of the drapes, which she was forever climbing, and she still had blue eyes. My grandmother said eventually her eyes would turn gold, like other cats' eyes, but for now the fuzz and the wide blue eyes made her so heart-breakingly cute I could barely stand it.

Marin would have been over the moon with her.

We had gone out and adopted the cat the day my grandparents found the duplex we'd be living in from August to May. She was our celebration.

"What are you going to name her?" my grandmother had asked in the car on the way home, the little kitten mewing loudly in my lap. I stroked her head to calm her.

I'd thought about how much Marin had wanted a cat, how she'd never even gotten one of the porcelain birthday kittens that I had gotten every year. I wanted to name this cat something important to Marin.

"Swing," I said. "E. C. Swing."

"Sounds fancy," my grandfather had said, and I'd grinned. Marin would have loved a fancy name for a fancy cat.

We officially moved in the week before school was supposed to start. Most of Elizabeth was still barely out of cleanup mode, just beginning to rebuild, and we were uncertain who all would be making it back for senior year. The library remained the place where everyone caught up, and as the first day grew nearer, more and more of us showed up there, taking over the parking lot. The librarians didn't appear to mind. They seemed to like being the place where the crippled community felt comfortable gathering again.

I went with Dani a few times, while my grandparents stayed at the duplex and got us settled. Jane was still in Kansas City, and it didn't look like her house would be rebuilt before school started. Which meant she wouldn't be back for senior year. Dani and I would be a duo, and I wasn't sure how we would do without Jane. We made her promise to visit a lot.

Three days before school started, Kolby showed up in the library parking lot, his arm still wrapped in a weeping bandage. His sister, Tracy, who seemed to have grown up so fast, hovered near him every step he took. At first people stared and whispered, but then someone asked him about it, and when he told the story, girls cried and people called him a badass and he smiled, relaxed.

I sidled up to him. "I'm really sorry," I said.

"About what?"

I pointed at his arm. "I didn't clean it good enough."

He held it up and shrugged. "It's not your fault, Jersey," he said. "It's nobody's fault. It is what it is. The whole thing is what it is."

"Did it hurt?"

He shrugged again, shook his head, then grinned and nodded. "Like ten thousand mothers," he said. "Not as bad anymore, though. But at first it was wicked. And I was pissed off."

"Yeah," I said. "I know the feeling." In some ways it was like Kolby and I were both nursing the same infection, only mine was on the inside. We were both healing, but not without the scars to remind us that the cut, deep and painful, had been there.

Some girls came by and told him they were inspired by his story, and Kolby kind of ate it up a little bit, the good old Kolby I'd always known. After they left, his mom pulled up to the curb and honked, ducking and bobbing her head to find him in the crowd. He bumped my shoulder with his. "So admit it. I have a pretty nice ass, don't I?" he joked, holding his arm up and waving it in front of me. I couldn't help laughing.

"You're disgusting," I said, but I was happy to see that what had happened to him hadn't broken his stride any, and hadn't changed things between us.

"Come on, Kolby, we gotta go," Tracy said, heading toward the car. He started after her, then turned back.

"I'm glad you came back to Elizabeth," he said. "'Cause there's something I want to ask you."

"What?"

He held out his arm and pointed to the bandage. "How do you feel about guys with scars? Pretty hot, right?"

I laughed, a little tingling sensation in my chest, and nodded. "Definitely hot." I tugged at my hair. "That is, if you care what purple-haired chicks think."

"I was hoping you'd feel that way." He smirked. "And I like the purple. Makes your eyes stand out." Quickly, he bent and kissed me on the cheek, then strode to his mom's car without missing a beat. "I'll call you," he said as he ducked inside.

Later that night, when Dani's mom dropped me off at the duplex, I found my grandmother pushing the couch out of the way, against the wall in the living room.

"Oh, good, I'm glad you're home," she said when she saw me. She bent and fiddled with the little CD player that had been in their garage back in Waverly.

"What's up?" I asked.

Music started to pour out of the speakers, and my grandmother twisted the volume knob to make it louder. Swing swatted at the power cord, which hung down the back of a little table. My grandmother turned and held her arms out as horns started playing in the background.

"What's...?" I asked again, but then it dawned on me what she was doing. She began to bob, bending her knees up and down to the time of the music.

"May I have this dance?" she asked, and I laughed out loud.

"Sure, why not?" I said. I kicked off my shoes and dropped Marin's purse next to the front door and went to her.

When Marin was born, my mom told me that family had nothing to do with blood, but only had to do with what was in your heart. I felt sad for her, that she'd cut her family, my grandparents, out of her heart.

And I felt sad that she'd left me with a heart so empty of family. Without her, I had been confused and lonely, unsure who I belonged to.

Clay was right. He wasn't my family, because I wasn't in his heart.

But my grandparents' hearts were open. I still didn't know when or how far I could open my own heart, but I knew that if I wanted the family I'd never had, all I needed to do was open up and let them in.

My grandmother enveloped me in her arms, perfecting our form, and then slowly moved her feet for me to follow. "Betcha didn't know your sister's dance genes were inherited," she said.

I stumbled, frowned. "I think I missed that gene."

Suddenly, she whisked me into a twirl and I giggled. When we were face-to-face again, she raised her eyebrows. "That's why you have me," she said.

And she taught me the East Coast Swing, both of us humming along happily.

ACKNOWLEDGMENTS

First and foremost, as always, I want to thank my agent, Cori Deyoe at 3 Seas Literary Agency, for the many hours spent pushing me forward, holding me up, and making me smile.

Thank you to my editors, Pam Garfinkel and Julie Scheina, for discussing and suggesting and making sure what's inside my head matches what's on the paper. Thank you to everyone at Little, Brown, including Barbara Bakowski, Erin McMahon, Victoria Stapleton, and the many others who work tirelessly on my behalf.

Thank you to Daffny Atwell for the name suggestion, and to her sister, Jersey, for letting me borrow. Thank you to Susan Vollenweider for the constant support.

Thank you to Paige, Weston, and Rand for letting summer break be all about the revisions, and thank you, Scott, for... just everything.

A special thank-you to Joplin Public Library, which refused

to cancel my appearance scheduled for just weeks after tornado devastation destroyed much of the city. Thank you to the many community members who came to hear me speak, and especially to librarian Cari Boatright Rerat, who took me on a driving tour of the devastated area after my presentation. The spirit of Joplin inspired me.

AUTHOR'S NOTE

On a late Sunday afternoon in May 2011, the city of Joplin, Missouri, was hit by a deadly EF-5 tornado. The twister was nearly a mile wide and carved a six-mile gash through the city, the 200-mile-per-hour winds destroying everything in their path. Homes were leveled and businesses devastated, causing billions of dollars in damage. More than 150 people died. Many others lost everything.

For months, I had been scheduled to speak at the Joplin Public Library. My appearance was supposed to happen just weeks after the tornado, in late July. Of course, upon seeing the news coverage of the tornado, I was sure my program would be canceled. Who could expect the people of a ravaged town to have time for an author event? I e-mailed the librarian, telling her that my thoughts and prayers were with them and I'd be happy to reschedule whenever they were ready.

How shocked I was when I received a response just days

later, informing me that the show was to go on. *Our community needs this*, she told me.

Joplin is not a long drive from my town of Liberty—only 165 miles or so. As I drove the two and a half hours, I couldn't help thinking what a very short distance those 165 miles would be for a tornado. Had things shifted only slightly, had the tornado raged north for another couple of hours, it could have been my town that was destroyed. I could have been one of the people who lost everything.

A study by the National Oceanic and Atmospheric Administration discovered that many Joplin residents failed to heed the tornado warnings that day, because they'd become desensitized to the sound of tornado warning sirens. I get it. I've lived my whole life in the Midwest. Tornado watches and warnings are a way of life. I don't want to say we don't take them seriously, but when you get so many of them, you can become complacent, and complacency can be deadly.

Just like Jersey, who didn't want her cooking to be interrupted, you sometimes get skeptical or lazy or just too darn busy to be inconvenienced by what you imagine will be yet another false alarm. Sometimes you just assume disaster is never going to happen to you. How could the people of Joplin have foreseen what was going to happen to them on May 22?

After my library visit in Joplin, I took a tour of the devastated area. Even after weeks of cleanup, the destruction was knee-buckling. Whole houses, gone. Street signs and other landmarks, gone. Trees, gone. Everything, just...gone. I was speechless, and my heart ached for the people who had lost so much.

But even more shocking than what I saw in the tornado's path outside was what I saw inside the library that day. It was busy, bustling, and a full crowd turned out for my event. I couldn't believe that in the midst of tragedy, people were still dedicated to living their previously scheduled lives. The librarian was right: The community did need the show to go on, not necessarily to hear me speak, but to do something normal. To do something planned. To be with one another, to laugh and smile, to show that they may have been down but they were definitely not out. Far from it.

After what I saw in Joplin, I began to think about what it means to "lose everything." Everyone has his or her own version of a tornado—fire, earthquake, hurricane, tsunami, war, illness, terror attack. An unexpected disaster rages; someone loses everything.

But is it really possible to lose absolutely "everything"? Can we lose our spirit? Can we lose our drive? Can we lose whatever it is that makes us continue in the face of overwhelming adversity? Can we really lose that uniquely human ability to hope?

Or is it possible to step up to the enormous task of redefining "everything"?

These were the questions I wanted to put to Jersey Cameron. I wanted to strip her of absolutely everything and see what she did with the bare bones that were left. I had a feeling she could answer the call to adversity with strength and integrity. And in the end, I think she did. Her path wasn't easy or straightforward, and she wasn't without her hiccups and undignified moments. But the point was that she kept going, she kept fighting, she kept trying to remember what and where her "everything" was.

Every so often, I think about those people in Joplin who came to hear me speak. I can still picture some of their faces. They were grim but open. They were tired but interested. If ever there was a visible spark of hope, it was in that room. I imagine Jersey sitting among the crowd, her own face grim and weary, her own spark of hope glimmering behind her eyes, her own redefinition of "everything" writing itself on her heart.

This book is for all of those in Joplin who showed me firsthand what survivor spirit looks like, and for the countless others out there who have suffered devastation and tragedy and have managed to build on. It's for all of you who unexpectedly have found yourselves forced to redefine what "everything" means to you. To those of you called to rebuild a life you didn't plan on living. And did it anyway.

Thank you for reading Jersey's story.

Jennifer

THE LIST WAS MY IDEA.
I DIDN'T MEAN FOR ANYONE TO DIE.
WILL YOU EVER FORGIVE ME?

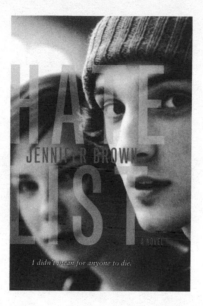

Five months ago, Valerie Leftman's boyfriend, Nick,
opened fire on their school cafeteria. Val was as shocked
as everyone else—but, despite her own serious injury,
she's been implicated in the crime because of the list.
The list she and Nick made of people they hated.
The list Nick used to pick his targets.

Turn the page for a sneak peek at *Hate List*.
AVAILABLE NOW

[*From the Garvin County Sun-Tribune,*
May 3, 2008, Reporter Angela Dash]
The scene in the Garvin High School cafeteria, known
as the Commons, is being described as "grim" by inves-
tigators who are working to identify the victims of a
shooting spree that erupted Friday morning.

"We have teams in there going over every detail,"
says Sgt. Pam Marone. "We're getting a pretty clear picture of what went on yesterday morning. It hasn't been
easy. Even some of our veteran officers got pretty shaken
up when they walked in there. It's such a tragedy."

The shooting, which began just as students were
preparing for their first class, left at least six students
dead and countless others wounded.

Valerie Leftman, 16, was the last victim shot before Nick Levil, the alleged shooter, reportedly turned the gun on himself.

Hit in the thigh at close range, Leftman required extensive surgery to repair her wounds. Representatives at Garvin County General list her in "critical condition."

"There was a lot of blood," an EMT told reporters on the scene. "He must have hit her artery just right."

"She's very lucky," the ER nurse on duty confirmed. "She's got a good chance of surviving, but we're being really careful. Especially since so many people want to talk to her."

Reports by witnesses at the scene of the shooting vary, some claiming Leftman was a victim, others saying she was a hero, still others alleging she was involved in a plan with Levil to shoot and kill students whom they disliked.

According to Jane Keller, a student who witnessed the shooting, the shot to Leftman appeared to be accidental. "It looked like she tripped and fell into him or something, but I couldn't tell for sure," Keller told reporters at the scene. "All I know is it was all over real quick after that. And when she fell on him it gave some people a chance to run away."

But police are questioning whether the shot that took down Leftman was an accident or a double suicide gone awry.

Early reports indicate that Leftman and Levil had discussed suicide in some detail, and some sources close to the couple suggest they talked about homicide as well, leaving police wondering if there is more to the Garvin High shooting than originally thought.

"They talked about death a lot," says Mason Markum, a close friend of both Leftman and Levil. "Nick talked about it more than Valerie, but, yeah, Valerie talked about it too. We all thought they were just playing some game, but I guess it was for real. I can't believe they were serious. I mean, I was just talking to Nick like three hours ago, and he never said anything. Not about this."

Whether Leftman's wounds were intentional or accidental, there is little doubt in the minds of the police that Nick Levil intended to commit suicide after massacring nearly half a dozen Garvin High students.

"Witnesses at the scene tell us that after he shot Leftman he pointed the gun to his own head and pulled the trigger," says Marone. Levil was pronounced dead at the scene.

"It was a relief," says Keller. "Some kids actually cheered, which I think is kind of wrong. But I guess I can understand why they did it. It was really scary."

Leftman's participation in the shooting is under investigation with Garvin County police. Leftman's family could not be reached for comment, and police will only

divulge that they're "very interested" in speaking with
her at this time.

* * *

After I ignored the third snooze alarm, my mom started
pounding on my door, trying to get me out of bed. Just like
any other morning. Only this morning wasn't just any other
morning. This was the morning I was supposed to pick myself up and get on with my life. But I guess with moms,
old habits die hard — if the snooze alarm doesn't do the
trick, you start pounding and yelling, whatever kind of
morning it is.

Instead of just yelling at me, though, she started getting
that scared quavery sound in her voice that she'd had so
often lately. The one that said she wasn't sure if I was just
being difficult or if she should be ready to call 911. "Valerie!"
she kept pleading, "You have to get up now! The school is
being very lenient letting you back in. Don't blow it your
first day back!"

Like I would be happy about going back to school. About
stepping back into those haunted halls. Into the Commons,
where the world as I knew it had crashed to an end last
May. Like I hadn't been having nightmares about that place
every single night and waking up sweaty, crying, totally
relieved to be in my room again where things were safe.

The school couldn't decide if I was hero or villain, and I
guess I couldn't blame them. I was having a hard time de-

ciding that myself. Was I the bad guy who set into motion the plan to mow down half my school, or the hero who sacrificed herself to end the killing? Some days I felt like both. Some days I felt like neither. It was all so complicated.

The school board did try to hold some ceremony for me early in the summer. Which was crazy. I didn't mean to be a hero. I wasn't even thinking when I jumped in between Nick and Jessica. It's certainly not like I thought, "Here's my chance to save the girl who used to laugh at me and call me Sister Death, and get myself shot in the process." By all accounts it was a heroic thing to do, but in my case . . . well, nobody was really sure.

I refused to go to the ceremony. Told Mom my leg was hurting too much and I needed some sleep and besides, it was a stupid idea anyway. It was just like the school, I told her, to do something totally lame like that. I wouldn't go to something so dumb if you paid me, I said.

But the truth was I was scared of going to the ceremony. I was scared of facing all those people. Afraid they'd all believed everything they'd read about me in the newspaper and seen about me on TV, that I'd been a murderer. That I'd see it in their eyes — *You should've committed suicide just like him* — even if they didn't say it out loud. Or worse, that they'd make me out to be someone brave and selfless, which would only make me feel more awful than I already did, given that it was my boyfriend who killed all those kids and apparently I made him think I wanted them dead too. Not to mention I was the idiot who had no idea that the guy I loved was going to shoot up the school, even though he basically told me so, like, every day. But every time I opened my mouth to tell Mom those things, all that came out was *It's so lame. I wouldn't go to something so dumb if you paid me.* Guess old habits die hard for everyone.

Mr. Angerson, the principal, ended up coming to our house that night instead. He sat at my kitchen table and talked to my mom about . . . I don't know — God, destiny, trauma, whatever. Waiting around, I'm sure, for me to come out of my room and smile and tell him how proud I was of my school and how I was more than happy to serve as a human sacrifice for Miss Perfect Jessica Campbell. Maybe he was waiting for me to apologize, too. Which I would do if I could figure out how. But so far I hadn't come up with words big enough for something this hard.

When Mr. Angerson was in the kitchen waiting for me I turned up my music and crawled deeper in my sheets and let him sit there. I never came out, not even when my mom started pounding on the door, begging in "company-voice" for me to be polite and come downstairs.

"Valerie, please!" she hissed, opening the door a crack and poking her head into my room.

I didn't answer. I pulled the sheets over my head instead. It's not that I didn't want to do it; it's that I just couldn't. But Mom would never understand that. The way she saw it, the more people who "forgave" me, the less I had to feel guilty about. The way I saw it . . . it was just the opposite.

After a while I saw headlights reflecting off my bedroom window. I sat up and looked into the driveway. Mr. Angerson was pulling away. A few minutes later, Mom knocked on my door again.

"What?" I said.

She opened the door and came in, looking all tentative like a baby deer or something. Her face was all red and splotchy and her nose was seriously plugged up. She was holding this dorky medal in her hand, along with a letter of "thanks" from the school district.

"They don't blame you," she said. "They want you to know that. They want you to come back. They're very appreciative of what you did." She shoved the medal and letter into my hands. I glanced at the letter and noticed that only about ten teachers had signed it. Noticed that, of course, Mr. Kline wasn't one of them. For about the millionth time since the shooting, I felt an enormous pang of guilt: Kline was exactly the kind of teacher who would've signed that letter, but he couldn't because he was dead.

We stared at each other for a minute. I knew my mom was looking for some sort of gratitude from me. Some sense that if the school was moving on, maybe I could, too. Maybe we all could.

"Um, yeah, Mom," I said. I handed the medal and letter back to her. "That's, um . . . great." I tried to muster up a smile to reassure her, but found that I couldn't do it. What if I didn't want to move on just yet? What if that medal reminded me that the guy I'd trusted most in this world shot people, shot me, shot himself? Why couldn't she see that accepting the school's "thanks," in that light, was painful to me? Like gratitude would be the only possible emotion I could feel now. Gratitude that I'd lived. Gratitude that I'd been forgiven. Gratitude that they recognized that I'd saved the lives of other Garvin students.

The truth was most days I couldn't feel grateful no matter how hard I tried. Most days I couldn't even pinpoint how I felt. Sometimes sad, sometimes relieved, sometimes confused, sometimes misunderstood. And a lot of times angry. And, what's worse, I didn't know who I was angry at the most: myself, Nick, my parents, the school, the whole world. And then there was the anger that felt the worst of all: anger at the students who died.

"Val," she said, her eyes pleading.

"No, really," I said, "It's cool. I'm just really tired is all, Mom. Really. My leg . . ."

I pushed my head deeper into my pillow and folded myself into the blankets again.

Mom bowed her head and left the room, stooped. I knew she would try to get Dr. Hieler all worked up over "my reaction" at our next visit. I could imagine him sitting in his chair: *"So, Val, we probably should talk about that medal . . ."*

I know Mom later put the medal and letter away in a

keepsake box with all the other kid junk she'd collected over the years. Kindergarten artwork, seventh grade report cards, a letter from the school thanking me for stopping a school shooting. To Mom, somehow all those things would fit together.

That's Mom's way of showing her stubborn hope. Her hope that someday I'll be "fine" again, although she probably can't remember the last time I was "fine." Come to think of it, neither can I. Was it before the shooting? Before Jeremy walked into Nick's life? Before Dad and Mom started hating each other and I started searching for someone, something to take me away from the unhappiness? Way back when I had braces and wore pastel-colored sweaters and listened to Top 40 and thought life would be easy?

The snooze alarm sounded again and I pawed at it, accidentally knocking the clock to the floor.

"Valerie, come on!" she yelled. I imagined she had the cordless in her hand by now, her finger poised over the 9. "School starts in an hour. Wake up!"

I curled up around my pillow and stared at the horses printed on my wallpaper. Ever since I was a little kid, every time I got into trouble, I'd lie on my bed and stare at those horses and imagine myself hopping on one of them and riding away. Just riding, riding, riding, my hair swimming out behind me, my horse never getting tired or hungry, never finding another soul on earth. Just open possibility ahead of me into eternity.

Now the horses just looked like crappy kids' wallpaper art. They didn't take me anywhere. They couldn't. Now I knew they never could, which I thought was so sad. Like my whole life was all a big, dumb dream.

I heard clicking against the doorknob and groaned. Of course — the key. At some point, Dr. Hieler, usually totally on my side, gave my mom permission to use a key and come into my room whenever she pleased. *Just in case*, you know. *As a precaution*, you know. *There was that whole suicide issue*, you know. So now anytime I didn't answer her knock she'd just come right in anyway, the cordless in her hand, just in case she walked in and I was lying in a pool of razor blades and blood on my daisy-shaped throw rug.

I watched as the doorknob turned. Nothing I could do about it but watch from my pillow. She crept in. I was right. The cordless was in her hand.

"Good, you're awake," she said. She smiled and bustled over to the window. She reached up and pulled the Venetian blinds open. I squinted against the early morning sunlight.

"You're in a suit," I said, shading my eyes with my forearm.

She reached down with her free hand and smoothed the camel-colored skirt around her thighs. It was tentative, like it was the first time she'd ever dressed up before. For a minute she looked as insecure as I was, which made me feel sad for her.

"Yeah," she said, using the same hand to pat the back of

her hair. "I figured since you were going back to school, I should, you know, start trying to get back full time at the office."

I pulled myself to a sitting position. My head felt sort of flat in the back from lying down so long and my leg twinged a little. I absently rubbed the dent in my thigh under the sheets. "On my first day back?"

She stumbled over to me, high-stepping over a pile of dirty laundry in her camel-colored high heels. "Well . . . yeah. It's been a few months. Dr. Hieler thinks it's fine for me to go back. And I'll be there to pick you up after school." She sat on the side of my bed and stroked my hair. "You'll be fine."

"How can you be so sure?" I asked. "How do you know I'll be all right? You can't know. I wasn't okay last May and you didn't know that." I pulled myself out of bed. My chest felt tight and I wasn't sure I wasn't going to cry.

She sat, gripping the cordless in front of her. "I just know, Valerie. That day won't ever happen again, honey. Nick's . . . he's gone. Now try not to get all upset . . ."

Too late. I was already upset. The longer she sat on the side of my bed and stroked my hair the way she used to do when I was little and I smelled the perfume that I thought of as her "work perfume," the more real it was. I was going back to school.

POWERFUL NOVELS FROM CRITICALLY ACCLAIMED AUTHOR
JENNIFER BROWN

A digital-original story

theNOVL.com NOVL

Lacey Crough

JENNIFER BROWN

writes and lives in the Kansas City, Missouri, area with her husband and three children. Her debut novel, *Hate List*, received three starred reviews and was selected as an ALA Best Book for Young Adults, a *VOYA* Perfect Ten, and a *School Library Journal* Best Book of the Year. Her website is jenniferbrownya.com.